Woman OF HONOR

Woman of Honor

PAT MOSEL

ISBN: 978-1-965679-22-7 (sc)
ISBN: 978-1-965679-23-4 (e)

Rev. date: 10/08/2024

This novel is dedicated to my Grandmother, Ruth and to my father, Denys Shaw Mosel. Some of the descriptions of places and events are historically accurate, while others are purely fictional. The characters, including Ruth, derive from my imagination and resemble no-one I know, either alive or dead. I want to thank those people, including my publishers, who have given me their time, patience and encouragement.

*T*he *murder in the family was seldom talked about after the funeral. It was as if there was some stigma attached to being murdered. Socially, it was akin to an embarrassment. Max's mother talked about his 'tragic death' or sometimes went so far as to refer to 'the death from unnatural causes of my beloved son'. I told people my husband had been killed, which suggested a cataclysmic act but didn't confess outright that he had been murdered. I did this out of deference to my audience and for self-protection. To say the word 'murder' hurt.*

I tried to imagine, as if I still loved him, Max's last day, his last minutes. He got up, as usual, showered, dressed, had breakfast, and brushed his teeth. These things, such ordinary events, are packed with significance if you are aware that it is the last time they will take place. The last time you will ever do them. If you knew that by nightfall you would be dead, would you brush your teeth more carefully? Or, would you think that perfect teeth-brushing no longer mattered? Would you wear your favourite tie or shirt or jacket? He wore casual brown trousers. He never wore jeans. And he chose a pink-striped shirt and his usual brogues. He might have had some presentiment but I doubt it. If he had known, he might have relented in his critical attitude towards me. He might have softened. He might have loved me a little.

A murder is a greedy memory. It eats at the brain and protests starvation when it hasn't been attended to for a while. It wakens me from my sleep with pictures of my dead husband. Of Max lying still and pale on the grass on that summer night. Nothing moved. No bird. No fox. No rabbit. My cousin, Jack, stood beside the body, in shock for that moment. The sound of the shot had rung out, signalling the end, signalling death. Around me the hills of the Scottish Borders faded from view; even the rocks that formed the conical hill were blurred. My senses were in limbo. Only my eyes focused on a particle of the world. Only a man standing. And a man lying inert, cold on the ground. I had frozen in a movement. My legs couldn't walk. I could not undo the action my body had perpetrated. Still pointing the pistol at the place where my dead husband had stood, when one moment before he was alive and walking.

I am fascinated by the memory of his walk because that's what he was doing when he was stilled. Simply walking. He had a strut. No, a swagger. Whatever it was, it said to the world that he was Maximilian Heriot-Ross; he was a successful lawyer and he owned land. His whole bearing proclaimed that he was a man to be reckoned with. The aristocratic nose, the straight back – the very back that was pierced by the bullet. It shot through him, into his back and lodged in his heart. Max was overthrown by one small missile. Max wouldn't live to dominate my life any more.

As he grew older, wrinkles formed on his brow and there were lines around his mouth, turning downwards as if the years of disapproving had stayed and stamped their sign on his face. These lines that so many women ignored in favour of his blue eyes and the late-greying hair. He didn't have time to get old. He was fifty-six when he was murdered. When I see him in my nightmares he is locked into that age; the wrinkles are intensified and his eyes are as cold and calculating as they ever were. His mouth is open in protest and there are thin lines of blood trickling down his chin from the corners of his mouth. He is standing and his hands are menacingly cupped as if he were about to strangle me. I wake up and search for a photograph of the man I married. An earlier time when there was love between us. Yes, I had loved Max. At one time. I was young and easily convinced by his self-assuredness. We met in Edinburgh not long after I'd arrived from what was then Rhodesia, now Zimbabwe. It is strange to think of it now, but I fell in love the moment I set eyes on him. He could be very charming. And I think the feeling was mutual. We met at a bridge game in an elegant flat near the city centre and not long after that he invited me out to dinner at a French restaurant. The meal was great and we talked urgently about our backgrounds, about his public school upbringing, about Rhodesia which he had visited. After our plates had been taken away, I was sitting with my forearms resting on the table, my ringless hands loose and relaxed. He paused in his conversation and placed a hand on one of mine. I felt the warmth and excitement of it. Then he withdrew his hand. 'Just testing,' he said, smiling.

We did a lot of smiling in the years immediately after that, when we were married and particularly when Nicky, our son, was born. Who can say exactly when things turned sour? It's hard to pinpoint when just testing became tested and rejected. I suppose it must have been some years after Nicky was born and I was immersed in being a mother. Max became demanding and critical. Then he turned to a full-blown affair with his secretary. We were never to reclaim the love we had at the beginning. He ended the affair and we decided to carry on with the marriage for Nicky's sake, but the love was gone. That was when I started to have destructive thoughts towards my husband. Briefly, intermittently, I wanted him dead.

I never let these vile thoughts grow to any proportion because Max was the father of my son. I never let myself forget that.

And then he was dead.

My feelings following the murder were turbulent and contradictory. I watched Nicky mourn his dad and felt confused and ashamed. Now that it had happened, I was wracked by both the hate in my heart and the memory of love. Nicky was devastated. He cried and he raged. He stood in front of me, tall enough to be above me and put his hands on my forearms and he said, 'Why, Mum, why? I couldn't answer him because I was crushed by his grief. Then he put his arms around me and hugged me, and I felt what energy I had left drain into his body. My legs became weak and I could have cried out because of the strength of his grip. He was heavy around me and the pain I had lacked became his pain. The suffering of my son was my suffering. It seemed to me that the hug lasted for hours and I came out of it a different person – a person who would mourn the husband she disliked.

Max's mother, Monica was the opposite. She didn't share her grief like Nicky did. She belittled my loss by trying to possess the grief of the whole family, by letting it consume her until she became the prima donna of the tragedy. To give her her due, there can be nothing worse than the death of a child but Max was Walter's son too. Monica became shrill, calling on her husband to comfort her, to wait on her, to sympathize with her. She not only humbled me, she became more than ever critical of me. 'Of course, the way your marriage was going I knew it would be the death of him' Her eyes were like pin-heads and her lips were swollen, cruel, distorted. 'If you can't say something nice about somebody, don't say it,' Walter quietly admonished her but his words fell on deaf ears. To make herself feel better, she then began to focus her undoubted organizational skills on the funeral and it was then that I finally stood up to her.

Since I met her, Monica had been treating me as definitely beneath the family with its background of titles and its aristocratic connections. She had a way of making me feel I was honoured by Max's attention, that I was really only a little girl from Bulawayo in Rhodesia. Which I was, but I was a woman and I had lost my homeland. Nor did Max understand the extent of that loss. He had enough money in the bank to visit Zimbabwe twice a year if he so wished and, he argued, it was the same land that I had left behind, regardless of the change of name from Rhodesia to Zimbabwe. But, as I saw it, I had lost my homeland and my heart was still there. I had long been prepared for Black African majority rule and ready to see Black Africans having a shot at democracy, although events now suggest a different story. With my head I welcomed a change in politics. With my heart I mourned the loss of my childhood and, what's more, it seemed that the familiar 'edifices' of childhood were being demolished behind my retreating back. With the change of name, the country had a new soul and I was excluded from this. It was not just the country that had changed its name when it became independent from Britain in 1980. The street names of my home town of Bulawayo changed too. Grey Street became Robert Mugabe Way. Selborne Avenue became Leopold Takawira Avenue. Wilson Street became Josiah Tongogare Street. There are various new names for various streets in the hot, dry, dusty town. The name of the town itself, Bulawayo, an African name, means 'the place of killing'. That didn't change.

Homesickness is a withering claw. Homesickness is a disease like arthritis. It gets into your joints and causes pain. I suffered from it for many years until, unlike someone with arthritis, I started to get better. The pain became numbness. I had been in pain from the memory of something that no longer existed. It was not just the change; it was the violence of it. A dying. Hundreds, perhaps thousands died in the war between African nationalist forces and the Rhodesian security forces. It was a killing of people who could have been brothers and sisters. Cruelty, carnage and brutality leading to more brutality. Could it all have been avoided? If, for instance, the Rhodesian Prime Minister, Ian Smith, and his supporters had not resisted majority rule for so long? A tragic episode in an ancient African history, in a beautiful country in the heart of Africa.

I felt the withdrawal from my country intensely at first. I longed for the sunshine, the African sky, the exotic plants, the long stretches of open road all to myself and my car, the wide streets of Bulawayo, the easy-going people, the lack of pressure of time, my parents and all that they symbolised. My soul was still with the past. However, after about ten years the pangs eased slightly. I looked back with pleasure as well as pain. Most of this was private. I didn't reveal my longing to many people. Ten years and numbness took over my long-distance relationship with Zimbabwe. More than anything, I did not want to go there. I didn't want to open the wounds by seeing the changes. I wanted my frozen view of Rhodesia to remain intact. I wanted to keep what I had left of a childhood spent in the sun. Part of it was that I was growing older. Also growing, was a love for my adopted country, particularly the Scottish Borders, which I consider one of the most beautiful places in the world. As if by osmosis, I became less obviously a foreigner. I started to feel familiar, to grow a sense of belonging. I'll never be anything but an incomer here but I have grown a skin that passes as living in Scotland, if not born a Scot. It amuses me to think that I have now lived in Scotland longer than I lived in Rhodesia.

My cousin, Jack, will never go through this process. He will never grow the skin that would comfort him in his homesickness because he has shrivelled at the quick. Unlike me, he fought in the 'bush war' and he lived in Zimbabwe after Independence. He loved the land in the way of someone who had fought for it and farmed it. Unlike me, he supported and believed in Ian Smith. He scorned the 'chicken run', the name given to the route departing Rhodesians took when they left the country for good. I took that run. I betrayed Rhodesia by leaving before the end of the war. I travelled in convoy, escorted by Rhodesian soldiers, along the road to the South African border. As far as Jack was concerned, I had indeed betrayed my country, just as my parents did by going to live in South Africa, but Jack in part forgave me out of a familial fondness for me.

The concept of forgiveness has been very much in my mind for several years. Strangely, I forgave Max's murderer almost immediately. I think it is because the deed was really too ghastly to contemplate. I have been working on forgiving myself for wanting Max dead and also on forgiving Max for his cruelty towards me in the later years of our marriage. It is almost as if focusing on the hurt is less painful than dwelling on the times of hope and happiness in our lives together. This is because of regret that setting out lovingly turned to cold attempts to dominate me, on his part, and feelings of resentment, if not hate, on my part. It is so sad that we spent so many years together in a stale relationship when we could have made a clean break. It should not have taken murder to separate us. We told ourselves we were staying together for Nicky's sake. But what a legacy. Looking back, I think that Nicky would have benefited if Max and I had divorced.

The real trial was the pretence. We presented ourselves to the world as a couple when all the while the 'edifices' of our marriage were crumbling and we were at odds, if not at war, with each other. I had schooled myself to be passive, to take whatever Max would throw at me. That numbness crept in again to protect me from loss because I had lost the man I had fallen in love with, even before his death. It was not just his affair with Grace, his secretary, which humiliated me; it was the daily criticism and put-downs. I found myself cowed, unable to be myself. Ruth.

On the Thursday before the party, when the murder took place, Nicky came into the kitchen, uttered an unrepeatable swear word and slid onto his bottom on the wet floor.

I left off cutting circles to make scones and helped him up.

'You should put up a sign saying slippery floor,' he admonished me. At twenty-one, Nicky still didn't know where he wanted to go in life but he did know what he expected of his parents.

'I'm sorry, Nick.' But I couldn't help smiling.

'How many times do I have to tell you not to call me Nick? It sounds like a police station or a prison, or the Devil himself.' He was on his feet and feeling his trousers for damp.

'But you must admit your entrance into the kitchen was a bit funny.'

He wasn't going to be drawn into that. 'How many guests have you got coming?'

'Eight staying and five more for lunch on Sunday.'

'How many times have you cleaned this floor?'

'Millions of times over the past twenty-four years.'

'You exaggerate, but I mean in the last two days.'

'Twice.'

'Do you really think your guests are going to inspect it?' He sauntered off without waiting for an answer.

During teenage, dealing with Nicky was a delicate affair although now he was growing up faster than I realized. It was not so long since I found myself censoring what I would like to say only to discover that what I had censored might have been appropriate after all and what I did say turned out, instead, to be provocative. The one guide I had was that if I wanted him to do something I should suggest the opposite because he would react. Max said I was too cautious with our son, that he needed a strong set of rules to go by. Whenever Max said that, I expected another lecture on the importance of discipline. I have erased from my memory some of Max's standard lecture. It seemed to me it had something to do with getting up at five in the morning and having a cold shower but it could be applied to anything - housework, socializing or making a car journey. It could be brought to bear on anything one didn't want to do. Max would extol the virtues of discipline without ever seeing the need to follow the rules himself. He rarely got up at five, getting up at about six instead, and I had only his testimony that he took cold showers.

* **

It was Friday, mid-July 2004, the day most of the guests were due to arrive. Wearing pink rubber gloves, wrists deep in white foam, I paused and wondered, as I often did, how many people could have such a view from their kitchen window. An expanse of lawn, cared for, rectangular, surrounded on two sides by a beech hedge with copper-bronze leaves catching the light, a boundary for privacy. This side of the hedge the scene stretched in layers. The scalloped flower bed - mainly of roses, lupins, lavender and lady's mantle - ran along the length of the hedge opposite the window. In the middle ground were the four mature apple trees, gnarled and knotted, trunks host to lichen, with their crooked branches now laden with green, tight fruit waiting to ripen. In the foreground, lawn and a partial view of the plum trees around which I had planted fairy rings of crocuses that flowered in the autumn. Our kitchen garden in the Scottish Borders in July contained the possibilities and inevitabilities of all the seasons. I could imagine winter stark trees and few flowers. A snowman, with a carrot for a nose and two pieces of coal for eyes, and Max's uncle's bowler hat. It seemed there was more snow when Nicky was a child. There used to be a swing for him, hanging from one of the apple trees, and a sandpit, now grassed over. In those days, summer and winter, I would watch him from the window; saw him making sandcastles. Patting and brushing, decorating his castles with leaves and stones, building and trampling. As I say, the sandpit had gone; those days were now over.

Every spring I waited at the kitchen window for the blooming of the daffodils under the fruit trees. Hundreds of them, in many different varieties, shot through the green grass. They were well sheltered by the hedges. Like trumpets, they triumphed over the dark days of winter. They and the little heroes, the snowdrops. We were very close to the seasons at Auld Oak Hall.

The house was named after a tree that stood at the bottom of the front garden, at the entrance to the driveway. It was massive and loveable. The place belonged to Max. He had inherited it from his bachelor uncle, along with a lot of antique furniture and silver. I had no say in any decisions that concerned Auld Oak Hall apart from minor household details like what washing machine to buy, or when to clean the silver. I had responsibility but no authority. Fourteen years before, when Max and I nearly split up, he told me that it was he who allowed me to live at the Hall. Presumably, that meant he thought it was he who decided whether I stayed or went.

Yet, from the moment we moved in, I fell in love with Auld Oak Hall, the space in it, the setting, the quietness. I treasured the privilege of living amongst natural beauty; beautiful landscape, beautiful things, but I had to work hard for it. Thank God for my home help, Heather. She would come twice a week and together we could meet the standards Max expected and I had absorbed.

'You fuss too much,' Nicky would say. 'Who cares if there's a speck of dust on the TV or a cobweb in the dining-room? You've got your priorities all wrong.'

I couldn't argue with him. I just carried on doing what I always did. At the same time I kept up my freelance writing business. I nurtured and developed contacts beyond the Scottish Borders which was an essential part of making money for the business. I wrote about house interiors, gardens, stately homes and produced profiles of people and, every now and again, I would write a romantic fiction story. However, when we had guests the housework and cooking took precedence.

When Max's old school friends came to stay I sometimes felt like a servant. Some of them acted as though they lived life with servants, even if they didn't, and I was the most suitable person to play out the role. They charmingly persuaded me to carry luggage, sew on buttons and once I even found myself washing a guest's car. It was a strange turnabout because I had been brought up with servants myself and I remember with fondness some of the cooks and nannies my family employed. During my childhood in Rhodesia we had Black African servants. While I was growing up they were the closest I got to knowing Black African Rhodesians. In daily life in the town of Bulawayo I saw Blacks roughly sent to the back of queues in shops; heard grown men called 'boys' and had a vague idea that Black people were poor. The Black Africans I knew were smiling and friendly. Even with liberal parents, as a child I was not even partially aware of the injustices being perpetrated in the name of White rule. I was unaware that the political system which denied Black Africans the vote was wrong, that across town children my age were scavenging in rubbish bins for food. I can only repeat that I was unaware of this. It was only later that I understood and knew these things in any real sense. Our way of life was ruptured when Ian Smith, the then prime minister of Rhodesia declared unilateral independence from Britain on the eleventh of November 1965 which was followed by international sanctions, tense political negotiations and an intensifying bush war between Rhodesian Security forces and African nationalists. During the tragic years in which Rhodesia became Zimbabwe, although no longer living there, I took upon my shoulders a general guilt based on an increased awareness of the erosion of human rights in the country of my birth. My guilt wasn't just the product of political awareness. It began early. It centered on a baby girl called Joy.

*   *   *

My mother was out playing bridge and I was at home with my nanny, Esther, and her baby. I was four years old and looking forward to going to school the following year in January, when the school year started. I'd been playing barefoot in the sand near the garage. The game was called tickling curly wees. These were ant lions, insects that made conical wells in the sand, hoping to catch ants. I would tickle the sand to make an ant lion think my stick was an ant. The ant lion would show itself when the sand trickled down into the well. Then I would say a nursery rhyme, like Humpty Dumpty, out loud, and walk in circles around it until I turned to teasing another ant lion. I wished that I could be at school so that I could play with the other children. Dad said that I was very grown-up but not quite grown-up enough to be at big school. I wouldn't mind if the teachers got cross with me as Mum said they would. I just wanted something more to do. I stomped on a mound of sand and flattened it.

I went to see if Esther needed help with her baby. She would let me play with Joy so that she could get on with the housework or talk to her friends. I didn't see why she could have her friends over when I couldn't. She had told me to go and play as she was feeding the baby, sitting on the back doorstep. She wasn't shy about breast-feeding. I remember thinking that Joy made a lot of noise for a girl. She had a tiny nose and tiny fingers and short curly hair. She would take one of my fingers and hold on to it with her whole hand. In the heat she usually wore nothing but a nappy. She had the longest eyelashes I'd ever seen.

There she was, lying on a rug, gurgling. She looked as if she was cycling upside down. I had been given a tricycle for my birthday and I rode it happily, but I was always saying I wanted a big bike, a proper bike. Esther laughed at this. I had never seen her ride a bike although lots of Africans did. I saw them through the car window. However, most of them were walking. They'd walk long distances then sit under trees for hours and they would lie stretched out in the park, near the fountain. I was only allowed to ride in the garden, not on the road. That got a bit boring. I hadn't any brothers and sisters like other children and Esther never wanted to play. At weekends my dad played with me. We played ball and took our Alsatian dog, Jani, to the parkland area around two dams in the suburbs of Bulawayo. He didn't want to play dolls with me. Said that was for little girls. I told him I'd like a baby sister so that I could play dolls with her. He laughed, but I was serious.

When I left off playing with curly wees and went to Esther, she looked as if she was in a good mood, the sort of mood when she would let me play with Joy. She was cleaning brass and had her friend Violet with her. I didn't like Violet because she was always saying she'd tell my mummy when she thought I was doing something naughty. Who did she think she was? She was not even my nanny, after all. She made me feel I was doing something naughty even when I wasn't.

'Missy Ruth, you put your hat on,' said Violet looking crossly from behind her glasses. She and Esther both had scarves on. My own floppy hat was hanging at the back of my neck, stopped from falling off by elastic which usually went under my chin but was now half throttling me. I put the hat on to keep Violet happy and because I wanted Esther to let me play with Joy.

They were jabbering away to each other in their own language. I knelt down beside the baby and made sure her bonnet was on properly. She looked at me with her brown eyes, no tears at that moment, and she gurgled. I gave her my pointy finger and her own little fingers curled around it. She tried to suck it.

'No, no, baby, you mustn't suck my finger. I've been playing with curly wees and I haven't washed my hands.' I pulled my finger away and went to wash my hands in the kitchen. As I was going back I had an idea. 'Esther, the baby needs to be in a pram.'

'African babies no need prams, Missy Ruth,' replied Esther. African mothers carried babies tied to their backs with cloth or a shawl.

'Ah, ah, haikona kudaro (don't do that). Prams are for Europeans,' added Violet. They thought my suggestion was funny.

'Well, you're wrong,' I told them and went to fetch my big dolls' pram from the house. It was just perfect. It had clean white sheets and a laced pillow. I parked it in front of Esther whose hands were smudged with Brasso. 'I think Joy should go in the pram. She is hot and sweaty. It's the best pram in the world.'

Esther shook her head and made a clicking sound but she got up, went to wash her hands, bent over Joy with her legs wide apart, picked her up and jiggled her on her hip for a bit. Then she lowered the baby into the narrow pram.

'No pillow,' cautioned Violet and the pillow was taken out.

Still, I had what I wanted. I pushed the baby to and fro until she fell asleep and the two women chatted on. I didn't know how they found so much to talk about. And I talked to Joy even although she was asleep. I told her all about my dolls and teddies, my mum and dad, and I pushed her along the back path and around into the front garden. I told sleeping Joy all about the bougainvillea she could have seen if she was awake and the bees' nest, the swimming pool, the cactus that flowered only in the moonlight. The ground was a bit bumpy but she didn't seem to mind. Then I took her back, but Esther and Violet had gone. Esther often walked back with Violet to her neighbouring khaya (meaning home but in this case used to mean servants' quarters), so I wasn't worried.

The sun was very hot and I decided to take Joy inside. She woke up when I pulled the pram in over the back step because that was really bumpy. For a moment, I thought she was going to cry but then she decided not to. I let her hold my finger for a bit. Then we went into my bedroom which was cool, out of the sun. Esther had made the bed and put the toys on it the way I liked them. My favourites were Trudy, the rubber baby doll in a carrycot and Squiff, the red dog, that couldn't stand up, and my toy panda bear that dad said I should call China. There were others, but I didn't have a lot.

I put the pram beside the bed and pulled Joy out of it so that she was lying on the bedcover. I played 'This little piggy went to market' with her toes. She was quite happy. She smiled at me. I took off her bonnet and my own hat and I noticed that she had a very wet nappy. So, I got a plastic table mat from the dining-room and put it under her. That way she wouldn't wet the bed because, if she did, it would make Esther and mum very cross. She was still cycling upside down and gurgling.

'There's a pretty baby. I have a good idea. I'm going to make you a house.'

There was a game I used to play, with blankets and chairs. I made houses, ships, boats. I got the chair, with thin wooden arms, from a corner of the room and then a blanket from the cupboard. I arranged the blanket over the chair.

'Imagine this house, baby Joy. It's bigger and better than any house you've ever had, better than a hundred khayas. You are going to live in it. 'magine.'

Holding her under the arms and bent over with her weight, I pulled her onto the blanket. She was happy in her new house. 'This is the biggest and best house you ever had.'

I turned to get the table mat from the bed because the blanket mustn't be wet either. Then somehow she was lying on the floor; she'd fallen under one arm of the chair, her new house ruined and the blanket was trailing from the seat. She was crying so loudly I felt my ears were going to burst and I tried to hide from the noise by burrowing amongst my furry animals on the bed. And then Esther came and she was yelling at me. It was like I was the worst person she'd ever met. I was crying and cuddling China and all my toys at once. Especially China.

Not long after that Esther went to Johannesburg in South Africa to marry a miner. That was in 1956 when I was five. I didn't need a nanny after I started school so we employed Alfred. He cleaned the parquet floors, down on his knees with brushes; he cleaned and cooked. One night, two years after Esther and Joy had left, Alfred came to tell us that Esther was at the back door.

'How are you?' Mum asked. She was smiling. I think she liked Esther.

'I'm well, Madam. Thank you, Madam.' Esther was also smiling. She looked different. She was wearing a beret instead of a scarf. She had on a shirtwaister dress, which looked like she had got it from a posh madam. She was wearing shoes which were closed except for a peep hole for the big toe.

'Are you on holiday?'

'No. I came back to find work. Joburg, she is no good. The miners, they think about money, nothing but money. No worry about health and being happy. And there are many skelms (rogues), Madam.'

'What about your husband? Did you get married?'

'We marry but he no good. Just like mining, the beer and beating up his wife.'

'I'm sorry to hear this, Esther.'

Esther shrugged. 'But Missy Ruth, you grow up. You tall and big and strong.'

'I go to school now,' I boasted.

They talked some more and I was hardly listening until I heard mum ask about Joy. That's what I wanted to know too. I was trying to work out how old Joy would be.

'She very sick, Madam. She have cancer. I take her to the big hospital. Then last year she die. Very sad, Madam.' Esther looked down at the ground. I thought she was going to cry.

I burst into tears myself and ran into my bedroom. I was crying my eyes out and squeezing China when dad came in. He tried to comfort me but I yelled at him, 'It's my fault. It's my fault she is dead.'

'It's nobody's fault.' He tried to put an arm around me but I pushed him away.

'I killed her.'

'Hush, Ruth. It's nobody's fault.'

How could he say that? Didn't he know that I dropped Joy on her head when I was four years old?

* * *

'Really, Ruth. You do live in your head. How long have you been standing over the sink?' It was Max. He'd come home from work to collect some papers. As he talked he shuffled the papers, as if he had more important things to attend to.

'Probably as long as we've been married.'

'Oh, it's like that is it?'

'Like what?'

'Do I detect a hint of resentment … of rebellion?'

'It was meant as a joke.'

'Then I'll take it as such.' Max didn't attempt to laugh but went through to his study. He was obviously in a hurry and didn't want to become involved in any sparring.

I still describe my marriage as before Grace and after Grace. She was the woman who nearly wrecked the marriage in 1990. Before Grace we were still in love enough to ride challenges, with Nicky arriving and, in some ways, binding the relationship. Even so, it was not all straightforward. It took just over two years to conceive a child, during which time I became obsessed with falling pregnant. I've spoken to other women who say they've had the same obsession. It's a deep, primaeval need to hold a baby in your arms and call it yours. A craving. A longing that, if allowed, can overwhelm a relationship and damage a couple's sex life. It threatened to undermine seduction. Then one night we conceived Nicky. Nicholas was the name Max wanted for his son and heir. We were both proud, both overjoyed and the next seven years were probably the happiest in our marriage.

Then Max seemed to have hit a mid-life crisis. He changed his entire wardrobe and his taste in music. He started having an affair with Grace, a secretary at the legal firm in the nearby town of Hawick where he was a partner. Grace was blonde and frivolous. She was made to be the other woman. Grace, I thought, was all sex and no sense. The result of this affair was that Max and I discussed divorce. We went over the pros and cons like some intimate debating society. Whatever we put forward as a solution, the sticking point was always Nicky. He was due to go to boarding school the following year but, all the same, he should have two parents. We never got as far as speaking to Nicky himself. Max decided to follow the path of duty, to drop Grace and I had nowhere else to go. We continued the marriage but the trust I had in Max had gone. The love had virtually died but there was familiarity and there was a certain endurance; some might call it discipline.

We slept in separate bedrooms, across the upstairs passage. This was ostensibly because I was a problem sleeper, waking at all hours of the night or morning. I kept a kettle in my bedroom. I would get up and drink tea, and smoke, meditating. This was the only room in the house where smoking was allowed. Our arrangement of separate bedrooms was to be altered that weekend because we needed an extra bedroom for a friend of Henri's. Her friend was someone we didn't know. We had not expected to need an extra room and had originally asked the number of friends we were sure we could accommodate.

Henri – short for Henrietta – was an old friend but always an unlikely one. She was wealthy and at the age of fifty had not married. She was sometimes excruciatingly outspoken. Not for her the social taboos of no politics and no religion in conversation. She was conservative with both a small and a capital 'C'. She worked as a furniture restorer in Glasgow but I had bumped into her when we were both shopping in Edinburgh about three weeks beforehand. I happened to mention I was having a birthday celebration and that Jack and his family were coming up from Devon for the weekend. She promptly invited herself and later invited her friend.

For all that she was bombastic and tactless, and openly in love with Max, I was fond of Henri. It was she who had found me a job in Edinburgh in 1978 when I was a new immigrant and struggling to make ends meet. I was keen to get a job as a newspaper journalist but had got to the point when I was grateful for anything. Henri introduced me to Ken Scott, the manager of a printing works who needed a receptionist/typist. I worked there until I married Max and came to live in the Scottish Borders. Meeting Henri in Edinburgh took me back to the days when we used to see more of her, to the Winter of Discontent in 1978/1979 when Britain was in the grip of strike action, the snow fall was exceptionally heavy and my own country of Rhodesia was on the brink of becoming Zimbabwe. Those were difficult days, brightened by Max as he was then.

'Are you really going to be fifty-three? You haven't changed a bit.' Henri slapped me on the back. We were standing outside a department store on Princes Street, the main street in the city of Edinburgh.

'Thank you, but there is the odd wrinkle and my hair is going white at the temples. See?'

'You always did have fabulous red hair. And no freckles.'

'I'll phone you, Henri.'

Henri didn't see the small signs of ageing that had crept up on me. She didn't want to see me as older because that would implicate her. We were twenty plus years older than when we first met. She thought she could ignore the changes. Yet, she must have noticed the marks of wear and tear; the crow's feet, the faint lines across my brow, the thinning and slight slackness of my skin; the woven patterns of skin covering my hands. My legs were still shapely although there were exploded, swollen veins on parts of them. It seemed that ageing included remembering how things used to be. Birthdays were a time for counting the years backwards. 'Fabulous red hair and no freckles,' I repeated in my thoughts, standing by the sink.

Max appeared in the doorway, holding his briefcase. 'I hope this is going to be a birthday party and not a reunion of Zimbabweans,' he said.

It will be both.'

'When you Zimbabweans get together it can be somewhat exclusive. I don't want Henri and her friend overwhelmed.'

'Can you imagine Henri ever being overwhelmed by anybody?'

'At least we'll have Susannah and George to balance things out, although they might not be too pleased with me.' He was looking smug.

'Why?'

'George borrowed a substantial amount from me when he set up his business. I've decided to foreclose on the loan.' He smiled a small, self-important smile.

'Did you have to choose my birthday party to do that?'

He didn't reply but crossed the kitchen and went out the back door. I remember so well how he used to turn his back on me and what I had to say. He wouldn't do it for very much longer.

Although I was uneasy about the loan, I let that subject float to the back of my mind and thought instead about his reference to a reunion. Jack and Sally were both Rhodesians. Or, had been. I use Rhodesian as a specific, historical term that could, however, be considered dated. When Rhodesia became independent Zimbabwe in 1980, did we automatically change our identity and become Zimbabweans? I can't answer that question. At times I am as happy to call myself a Zimbabwean as I am to call myself Scottish.

Neither sits well but they are social devices. At heart I am still a Rhodesian because the description belongs to my past and to fact.

Jack is my cousin and when I was a teenager I was half in love with him. He was someone to look up to. He was so strong, incisive and handsome. He had the body and looks of a film star. Tanned. Active. Sure-footed. Whereas my father had been giving me my first sips of shandy, Jack gave me my first proper drink – vodka, lime and lemonade. My mother didn't know about the spirits and Jack laughed at what she might say.

* * *

Jack boasted that he was ready to fight. It was 1969 and there were a growing number of insurgents/freedom fighters coming across Rhodesian borders.

I saw him in the light of the cooking fire. His massive thighs beneath khaki shorts; his hair-coated suntan showing even in the semi-dark. He was muscle and sweat, the sort of man that made the most feminine part of me defensive while, at the same time, being attracted to him. He used to spend days in the bush with a gun, though guns were prohibited in the Matopos where we were all staying in rest huts for a few days. Our party was made up of my parents, Jack's parents, his sister and her two children.

All day we had been touring the park, in our car and on foot. The rocks were one of the most startling things about this area which was earmarked for pleasure, walking, climbing, yachting on the dams, game-spotting. Nobody talked about the inhabitants who had been moved to make this one of Rhodesia's foremost resorts. It was an area of rocks, thorn trees and water. Great, rotund, granite boulders stood poised to fall, but did not. It looked as if you could place a finger on a rounded rock and its massive bulk would roll down hill at the touch; but it was held in a frieze of falling; a magical balance. These rocks in their powerful shapes patterned the horizon of land that the Black Africans held as sacred. The green and brown veldt was dotted with the reds, purples and oranges that were the spring colours of the Msasa trees. We had spotted duiker, steinbock, klipspringers and I'll never forget the sight of majestic sable in the long grass at dusk, beasts strong enough to defend their young against leopards. We had stopped the car and had walked up to Bambata Cave.

Since Bambata, I have only pleasant feelings about caves; even spiritual feelings; its cool rock archway led into deep containment and there was sand beneath my feet; on the walls faded pictures of elephants; high up, images of eland buck in red and yellow; ochre matchstick men depicted living out everyday life. Then there were paintings of mythological creatures, imaginative portrayals of animals we've never seen or heard of.

Our folks (parents) were sitting outside the rondavel (chalet), their circle lit by a gas lamp that attracted flying insects. They were nattering over shandies and Jack's sister was inside with her children, undoubtedly on the look out for mosquitos. Her husband hadn't come with them this time. Jack and I stood over the braaivleis (barbecue) fire that burned in a brick rectangle. Jack damped down the flames, flicking water on them from a tin pot that stood on the ledge. My mother and aunt had prepared salads and sauces which stood ready on a light, fold-out picnic table. Some of the visitors in a neighbouring rondavel had a radio on and Bing Crosby singing 'Pennies from Heaven' drifted into the night. The radio could not blot out the astringent sound of cicadas or the chattering of monkeys a little distance away in thorn trees. In the end, nothing could penetrate the vast darkness around us.

We stood, dwarfed by it, beside the braaivleis, on a stretch of dust track near to our parked cars, flanked by high, dry grass.

'We haven't seen any snakes,' I said. I hated snakes, although in my seventeen years of life in Rhodesia I'd seen only house snakes that my father had set free in the empty plot across the road, telling me that they were 'pretty harmless'.

'You are kidding? Only last year I found a ten foot python in my hut here. Hell man, it was a whopper. You should have seen it.' Jack threw his hands wide to indicate the length of the python. 'Those things can squeeze a man to death. It was on the bedroom floor and it could have been in my bloody bed. I always check the bedclothes before I get into my bed here. I can tell you I'd rather have a woman in there, any day.' In those days, you couldn't talk to Jack for very long without the subject getting around to women. I found this a bit embarrassing, at the time.

'But what did you do with the python?' I asked.

'Took it for a walk around the hut. What do you think I did? Got an axe and chopped its head off.'

I didn't think to wonder if his story were true.

Jack was drinking his beer, with great gulps, leaving froth on his clean-shaven face. He drank as if he were in a bar with men. He was scornful of the lime and water I was drinking and he poured some vodka into it, saying something about lovely girls being allowed to grow up.

'Divine providence guards a drunk,' I quoted my mother's rather naïve view, feeling an immediate warm effect from the alcohol, unconscious that while I was defying my mother's attitude to alcohol, and especially to women drinking, I had just fallen in line with Jack's wishes.

'What's divine providence got to do with it?'

'Oh, it's just what my mother always says, whenever we pass a drunk weaving about in the road. They always seem to escape being hit by passing cars.'

'Agh, man, take someone like me. I can drink with the best of men but I'm never too drunk to be off my guard.'

I was experiencing a moment of feeling like an adult. The symbols – vodka and cigarettes – had brought me out of the realm of lime juice and in touch with the image of myself as sophisticated; someone whom I thought could command respect. I blew smoke into the big, exhilarating African night sky. It seemed to waft up from my lips to the stars and half moon. I'd had that same experience of communion with the African night sky the week before when a group of friends and I came, squashed in one car, to another part of the Matopos, singing, with a pack of beers and packets of crisps, crashing through the bush where we knew there were leopards, up the granite rock where Cecil John Rhodes' grave stood and the graves of Rhodesian pioneers, shouting our freedom to the wild, baffling the lizards and rock rabbits in their hiding, hurtling back home before our parents discovered our absence or suspected anything. I contemplated telling Jack about this. However, he would probably think it child's play. Or, give me a lecture about the wild and how dangerous it is. He was, after all, five years older than me.

I extinguished the cigarette on the ground.

'I believe you've decided to go into the army, Jack,' said my mother, walking up to us. I was conscious that my breath smelled of vodka. She must have seen the cigarette but she didn't comment.

'Got to fight for what we believe is right. Grub's nearly up, Aunt Dorothy.' He was putting pieces of cooked meat onto a plate. 'Teach those bastards a lesson.'

I saw my mother recoil at the word 'bastards'. To her mind, Jack was a nice enough young man but she didn't approve of his language.

'On the politics front, it's not just the Brits who are against us. You think South Africa is our friend. There's all this brotherhood of man stuff about bringing petrol to Rhodesia, sanctions-busting, but I tell you they'll sell us down the river. Mark my words.' He was pointing a finger at her, another thing she didn't like, but she put up with it from him.

Then he stopped talking because there was a sudden crash from nearby and a rubbish drum went hurtling over on its side. Jack rushed over and scattered a group of screaming, scavenging monkeys who fled from him, into the bush.

*   *   *

3

I felt two paws scratching at the back of my thighs. It was Brindle, our terrier, who seemed to think I'd been standing over the sink for far too long. I quickly finished off cleaning the baking trays, put the dishwasher on to wash and went outside to take Brindle for a walk. We went along the road because there were sheep in the fields that Max owned. He leased the land to a local farmer. I spun around as Brindle went sniffing down the bank of the burn that ran alongside the private road. What didn't Max own around here? He owned the cottage where Jack's family was going to stay, the house at the end of the road, a section of the slopes of the conical hill that dominated the horizon on the far side of Auld Oak Hall. He did not own the dog. I had bought her. In fact, there was a family tension because I liked dogs and he liked cats. Silly to think of it but it was symptomatic of the way Max and I had dragged on together those past fourteen years.

I told myself not to think like that but recently what he would call rebellion was rising in me. He had brought me Todd, our cat as a gift when I was suffering from depression and, in private, all I could think of at the time was cat hairs and having to hoover them up. All the same, I acknowledged the spirit behind the gift. What he chose to give me over the years always surprised me. His gifts startled me. For instance, he once gave me a super-tall, deluxe ironing board and, on another occasion, he gave me a toolkit. I saw these as, at best, challenges to change my ways and, at worst, disappointing. I did not let him know what I was feeling. I seldom took up these challenges but avoided them, giving the ironing to Heather and storing the toolkit away in the garage because I was never a DIY person. Then there were the things that I asked for, like perfume and books. Although I hinted, he never gave me these. He never gave me what I asked for. Was I ungrateful?

Brindle was coming out of the water. It wasn't very deep, despite the recent rain. The weather had been taunting us those past weeks. The day before had been wintry and wet with bursts of sunshine. That day there was a growing warmth but with a chill wind to remind us that we could slide back into cold weather. I was hoping that there would be sunshine on the Sunday because I was planning a birthday barbecue.

Although I had been preparing for all week for guests coming to stay – planning the menus, freezing dishes, shopping and cleaning – there was still a fair bit to do. I hurried the dog through the rest of her walk and got into the car to drive to the greengrocer in Jedburgh. Fruit and veg was the shopping that I really enjoyed doing. I drove speedily alongside a fast-flowing river, past Zoe and Hank's entrance gate, past a secluded hamlet, between tall trees and ancient hedgerow and onto the road to Jedburgh.

Zoe and Hank were Americans who had come to the Scottish Borders a couple of years before. Hank worked in the knitwear industry. They were my good friends and their daughter, Cherie, was Nicky's girlfriend. There were some things I couldn't agree with them about. They were religious fundamentalists and I couldn't go along with that. After 9/11, they would speak out stridently against all Muslims. I understood their feelings but wouldn't do that myself. With Zoe, I tried to steer clear of the subject of religion but it wasn't always possible. I was always very wary of sectarianism and racism. Having been brought up in Southern Africa, I had seen more racial hatred than I could bear. I also knew how to detect racism. When I first came to Britain in 1976 I felt that people were not aware of racism in this country. That has changed. Nowadays people complain of having to be too politically correct. All the same, there has never been much chance of seeing Black and White racism in the Borders because there are few dark-skinned people living here. Yet there was, and is, fear of incomers. Initially, there was suspicion of me and my accent until I had been in the Borders so long that I became a familiar face.

Jedburgh was one of the towns where I shopped. The other was Hawick, further south. I thought of Jedburgh as a bonnie wee town. It had a high street of bright-painted buildings and quaint small shops. There were butchers and bakers, restaurants, gift shops and a sweetie shop that displayed jars full of old-fashioned sweets. And, of course, there was the greengrocer. I parked the car in the car park behind the High Street and walked through a narrow alleyway to get to the High Street, looking at my watch, wondering how I was doing for time. Thus, not looking where

I was going, I almost collided with a man in a blue suit with tie loosened and top, shirt buttons undone. He looked agitated.

'Niall. Is it you?'

'Mrs. Heriot-Ross. I'm sorry; I'm in a frantic hurry. I'll see you tomorrow.'

That was the first I'd heard of the arrangement for Niall to come and look at Max's computer the following day. I wanted to tell him it would not be convenient as we were having guests. He didn't give me a chance but hurried on. I was annoyed with Max for asking Niall to come on the eve of my birthday celebrations when we should be focusing on our guests. I was as offended by this as I was by his intention to talk business with George and Susannah. Max was devoted to his computer. He would spend hours on the internet every night. At least, that was what he said he was doing in his study night after night. I would hear him coming up the stairs to bed while I was lying in my own room, trying vainly to sleep.

Walking through the alleyway, it occurred to me that Auld Oak Hall wasn't, at the time, a very happy place to bring guests. Except for Nicky, who was determinedly positive and relaxed. For Nicky, life was going to be good because he would see it that way. I thought that, as well as rushing around preparing meals and making beds, I should be working at creating an atmosphere that would make my visitors feel comfortable. I decided not to criticize Max for asking Niall around. This would be a start.

Yet, there was something troubling me, something out of my control that might make the atmosphere less than comfortable. Jack. My cousin had been low in spirits ever since he, Sally and the children left Zimbabwe. Sally and I had had a long conversation about it on the telephone a few weeks before when Jack was, for once, out of the house.

'He's given up looking for work. He has just given up altogether,' said Sally who, herself, had a dog-grooming job with a vet in Devon, where they lived.

'His age must make it difficult for him to find a job.'

'The job is not the issue at the moment. It's the children. He hardly notices them any more and they are hurt and perplexed. He sleeps late, sometimes until two in the afternoon. The rest of the time he sits in the lounge, motionless. Sometimes he gets angry over little things.'

'Have you asked for professional help?'

'He won't go to the doctor. He has always been so fit. He's looking forward to coming up to see you. It's the first time in months I've seen him look enthusiastic.'

'Maybe I can help?'

'He'll pretend nothing is wrong.'

Is that what it was going to be like that weekend? Pretending nothing was wrong. I didn't fool myself that I, Ruth, could heal everyone's wounds but I could give them food, company and a chance to relax.

The greengrocer's was full, the produce displayed lavishly along the walls and on a central counter. The fruit and veg were not only food but also decoration for the table. I piled oranges, peaches, strawberries and raspberries into my basket then picked out the best tomatoes to make small tomato roses. Potatoes. Parsley. Coriander. I had to get a second basket.

'Are you all set for the onslaught?' asked a voice behind me.

I turned around to see that it was Zoe, with her fuzzy hair pulled tight in a pony-tail, and with her strong American accent.

She, Hank and Cherie were coming to our celebration barbecue on Sunday.

'I'm doing all right but I can't rest on my laurels.' I placed my two, full baskets on the floor. 'I'm praying for sunshine.'

'Aren't we all?'

'It has been a slow start to summer.'

'Instead of blethering about the weather, why don't we go for a coffee? There is something I want to talk to you about, in confidence.'

Behind the till Mrs. Grant was beaming. 'And how are you the day, Mrs. Heriot-Ross? Having a party?'

'A barbecue on Sunday. Can you put it on the tab please, Mrs. Grant?'

'Nae problem.'

Zoe and I had a chat with Mrs. Grant, a large, ruddy-cheeked woman who packed our fruit and veg in the shop's bags like a professional. We took our purchases to our separate cars and met up in the restaurant on the corner. I made a mental note that I still wanted to get some sweets for the children. The restaurant prided itself on serving meals made with fresh produce and it doubled as a place to meet for tea or coffee with the option of newly-baked cakes. Its walls were white and studded with paintings by local artists, for sale. Zoe was there first and had found us a table. The place had that post prandial feeling that comes after lunches have been served and customers were idling over hot drinks. The table was pine and recently cleaned, with three real, red carnations in a small white vase at its centre. I wondered what Zoe was going to say to me, bearing in mind that she quite often confided in me about things that other people thought were common knowledge. She didn't waste time. 'I want to talk to you about our children.'

She fiddled with the ashtray, swivelling it around. This made me want a cigarette although I knew better than to light up as she was very anti-smoking. This was a part of her deep religious feelings. Tobacco and strong drink were frowned upon.

'Don't you mean the young people?'

'If you want to be pedantic, yes. I'm concerned that their relationship is becoming too serious.'

'It is serious. I admire them for it. They could teach some others a thing or two about loyalty and commitment.'

'That's just it. They're too young to commit themselves the way they seem to want to do. Nicky is around to see her every single day, but I guess you know that.'

'He is smitten,' I said, wondering if this was really a conversation we needed to have.

'My daughter is just out of school. She has only begun to gather experiences. Don't get me wrong. I like Nicky and I think he has honourable intentions towards her but he is very young too.'

'Are you suggesting we try to split them up?' I asked. I thought privately that Zoe was, on this occasion, being a spoil-sport. Love doesn't happen without rejoicing and young love is very precious. Added to that, if she wanted to prise them apart, I would have a hard time explaining to Nicky that it was the right thing for them. In effect, I didn't think that we would be able to separate them. On the contrary, we might just succeed in cementing the relationship. Listening to Zoe, I thought something in this conversation did not make sense. 'Is this everything that you wanted to talk to me about?'

'Well, actually, there is more. And it's even more confidential than what we've been saying already. The thing is … we're thinking of returning to the States at the end of the year. Cherie doesn't know this. Since 9/11, we've been feeling … homesick. I suppose that's what you'd call it. Feeling we want to be with our own people in the difficult years that lie ahead. We are, after all, American and any threat to our land is a threat to us. It's about solidarity … although we've been very happy here.'

'I, for one, will be sorry to see you go.'

'Are you sworn to secrecy?' She clutched the empty ashtray.

'Of course.' So this was why Nicky and Cherie needed to be prepared. 'Keeping up a relationship from different parts of the globe could be difficult.'

'That's my point.' She sighed.

'How do you propose to prepare them?'

'That's for you, and us, to think about.'

After Zoe and I parted company I went to the sweet shop and bought Smarties and a box of assorted chocolates for the adults. Then I took the road home. I was so busy thinking of what Zoe had told me that I almost missed taking in my favourite view. As I reached the crest of a steep hill I could see the gentle expanse of the valley with curvaceous hills on the horizon. There were few houses to be seen as it was a rural view of trees, fields of sheep and the river running through. Here, Mother Nature preserved her peaceful command. Such views were and are precious, in a world where population increase and migration leads man to expand and build, careless of natural heritage. As I see it, the space and beauty of the Borders is under threat from major commercial developments and from ill-situated housing developments, although the scenic view I had that day is yet intact. There, on an outcrop was Fatlips Castle which looked like an outsize, and very wise, owl sitting on a grassy perch. Fatlips was a landmark for me. Coming back from Carlisle, Edinburgh or Newcastle upon Tyne I would spot the castle and know that I was near my base. There are several theories about why it has this intriguing name. The one I liked was that full upper lips were a feature of the Turnbulls who used Fatlips as a watchtower. Turnbull was an outlawed reiver. Under the arc of the cloudy sky it was hard to believe that this was once a land of lawlessness when reivers, Scots and English, rode and raided, stealing sheep, cattle, horses with no regard for the law. That is only four centuries ago. Now it is a land of work and husbandry where convicted criminals are sent to Edinburgh to be locked up and where the highlights of the year are the Common Ridings in the summer when local people celebrate themselves and their history with ride-outs, ceremonies and partying.

I drove slowly down the hill until trees eclipsed my view and I turned into a country lane between hedgerows. Through my rear view mirror I could see Zoe's car right behind me. I waved through my open window. My thoughts returned to Nicky and Cherie. They were so dear in their innocence. I don't mean in a sexual way. I presumed that Cherie's religious background would rule out sex. And, even if it didn't, making love would be a consummation rather than a groping, what's-in-it-for-me affair. Zoe would be horrified if she read these thoughts. At the time, I didn't question whether or not I was being too romantic about the pair of young lovers. What I could see clearly was that Nicky had sought to protect himself from the staleness of his parents' marriage but he would have been upset to learn that he was the main reason we had stayed together. To a large extent he was independent but he still needed support. Now I had a secret that I had to keep from him; news that would devastate him when he heard it. I decided I wouldn't tell him yet but feared that the mere fact of my holding a secret would undermine our relationship.

I hooted as I saw Zoe's car turning into her driveway behind me and she hooted in response.

Nicky and Cherie were at Auld Oak Hall when I got back. Cherie had recently had her hair braided and she looked pert and cosmopolitan.

'We thought we'd lend a hand,' said Nicky.

'That's very nice. I'll be doing the salads.' I didn't mention that I was going to arrange flowers because that was a job I savoured. I wanted it for myself.

'Good. A bit of lettuce and tomato,' he said.

'Tomato and onion salad with avocado dressing, Italian pasta salad, potato salad with chives, green pepper and orange, celery with cucumber and grapes. And then there is the broccoli mousse which I've already made.'

'Salads don't need to be so elaborate. All they're going to do is eat them.'

'If you want to be helpful, you can take the stalks off the strawberries. I'm running a bit behind hand now.' I gave them the punnets of strawberries and a couple of bowls.

Brindle was in her basket in a corner of the kitchen and the cat would be lurking somewhere. Todd added a great deal of tension to my cooking as he was always ready to eat what I left out when my back was turned.

'Watch out for Todd,' I cautioned.

'Todd won't eat strawberries,' said Nicky, eating one himself.

'Have you had lunch?' I still hadn't had time for lunch myself.

'Yes. It was very nice, thanks Mrs. Heriot-Ross,' said Cherie.

'We had some of the broccoli mousse and some ham,' Nicky informed me.

My heart sank. Eating the ham was all right. There was plenty of that but they had broken the ring of my perfectly-moulded mousse. I opened the fridge to look at it. Sure enough, it looked bitten. If Cherie hadn't been there I would have exploded. Instead, I internalized my feelings and carried on with the business of chopping and cutting salad veggies. Time was now of the essence. I wanted the buffet laid out on the table by five o'clock. The guests were coming from six o'clock onwards. In that spare hour I would do the flowers, shower and dress.

They helped me to put out all the dishes on the long, glossy, mahogany dining-table. I arranged the fruit in a large aquamarine pottery bowl. When we had finished, I impressed upon them the need to keep all the dining-room doors shut because of Todd. That was all I could do. They were grown-up now. Still, I kept checking.

Cherie was eager to help with the flowers and I gave in. Nicky wandered off somewhere. We trawled through the garden with baskets. Together we picked roses, irises, lupins and gypsophila. And ferns from under the holly tree. She seemed to get as much pleasure from the task as I did. The sight of a pretty young girl inhaling the perfume of a pink rose is something I have stored in my memory. I chose that moment to ask her, 'What do you see yourself doing in the future?'

'I don't know. It will be with Nicky.'

'Nicky wants you to fulfill yourself as an individual.'

'Nicky is my destiny.'

I would have gasped if such a response hadn't seemed so crass. I realize now that I was afraid for her. I couldn't bear for her to put her trust so implicitly in one person, even if that person was my son. Nicky didn't know what career he was going to pursue either. He was on holiday from Edinburgh University where he was studying philosophy and he hadn't much of a clue what he was going to do after he got his degree. For him, time had a different meaning. Things would happen without planning. I was tempted to give Cherie a mature woman's advice on developing her special talents but a part of me was in awe of her simple belief. Love conquered all. Yet, if it failed, the loss could be crushing. Who was I to bring cynicism into her world view?

'I know that you play the piano and sing in your church choir. Would you think of being a music teacher?'

'Mum wants me to do that.'

'But, you…?

'Don't know. Look at this rose here. It's almost perfect.'

I left her arranging flowers in the kitchen and took a couple of small vases across to the cottage for Jack and Sally. I put the vases down on the gravel for a moment and turned the key in the lock. Taking the vases inside, I saw that Heather had cleaned well. No dirt, dust or cobwebs. Hospital corners on the beds. The cottage was cosy. I opened some windows to let in the light breeze and relieve the stale air. There were two bedrooms, a living-room with a wood-burning stove, a kitchen and a bathroom. Heather had laid a fire and the log baskets were full. Jack and Sally and the children probably wouldn't need a fire at that time of year but the weather was so unpredictable. I put one vase on the windowsill and one on the slight, flap-top table, and then sank into an armchair. We had furnished the cottage with cast-offs from the Hall. My African pictures had come to rest here as they didn't hang easily alongside Max's family portraits and landscapes in ornate frames in the house. I looked up at Gerard Benghu's painting of an old African man. His eyes would follow me, whatever angle I adopted. On other walls were humbly framed paintings of thorn trees and boulders and the dry African bush. I remembered the Mimosa trees outside my bedroom window at our home in Bulawayo where I grew up. Thorn trees with yellow, powder-puff flowers and yellow weaver birds painstakingly building their hollow-ball nests. The thorns of these trees were razor sharp, like chiseled bones with painful tips. I would dance beneath those trees. I liked to dance. That was one of the things that attracted me to Scotland – the reels and country dancing.

Max and I lived in this cottage for a couple of months while the Hall was being renovated after he inherited it from his uncle. Those were halcyon days. Carefree days, when the burden of owning property had not caught up on Max and, newly married, we played house. After that, he gave up cooking and immersed himself in paper-work in his study. He still played squash and bridge, the game that was my mother's reason for living. It was her obsession with bridge that put me off the game. Yet, it kept her alive. That, and her weekly visit to the hairdresser.

I could see my parents living in this cottage. I had asked Max about it and he thought it was 'feasible'. He probably looked on caring for his in-laws as part of his duty. However, mum and dad had gone through the upheaval of moving from Rhodesia to South Africa and were reluctant to change continents. Also, dad was attached to his medical team as he had a history of heart attacks and now suffered from arthritis as well. They were in their eighties.

Dad's first heart attack happened in 1968 when I was in lower-sixth at school.

*   *   *

The heat was like a clamp on my body, dragging down my energy; sweat soaked the thin cotton of my school uniform. My friend Samantha's bike was bucking. She was doing crazy things.

38

Front wheel down again, she was up on her pedals, straw boater perched on her head. School rules were that we had to wear our hats at all times when in uniform out of school grounds. Was it because they were afraid we'd get sunstroke? Yet the boaters didn't cover the back of the neck where the sun could do its worst. Did they regard the uniform as incomplete without its hat? They wanted us to look like young ladies. As a prefect I was supposed to stop any errant young ladies without their school hats, in any part of town. I was meant to stop Sam fooling around on her bike but she was way ahead of me. Then she stopped. 'Come on slowcoach. I'm dying for a fag.'

'Haven't any. Will you stop messing around? You'll get me into trouble.' I'd reached her and was catching my breath.

'Oh, no. Here really does come trouble.' With drama, she clenched her teeth and gripped my arm. Bearing down on us were the bad five, the most notorious rule-breakers in the school, hatless, riding three and two abreast across the width of the cycle track. Skirts unlawfully short. Ringing their bells. Hands nowhere near their brakes. Hair flying.

'Get the bloody hell out of here. They're not going to stop,' yelled Sam and we launched ourselves and our bikes onto the rough grass between the track and the road. The problem was that our bikes became interlocked and we landed up a tangled heap on the prickly grass, the bikes on top of us. Sam's hat had fallen, intact, beside her. Mine was in the road. And I could hear a car coming.

'Sam, get these damn things off me.' She and I were both squirming to ease ourselves out from under the bikes. I was expecting the imminent crunch of straw.

'Don't kick me,' she wailed.

'I've got to get my hat. My mother will kill me.'

'Don't mind me,' Sam squealed as I pulled myself free. She turned onto her stomach in the dusty grass, holding up her head with her hands. 'Don't get yourself killed. There's a car coming, Ruth. There's a car.'

I was transfixed, eyeing the hat, seeing the car, a prefect naked without her hat. Maybe it was the headmistress's car? Or, one of the teachers? Then the car drew to a halt and out stepped Tony Masters, a sixth-former at a nearby boy's school. He walked over to the hat, picked it up and blew on it to remove the dust. 'I think you've dropped something.' He handed it to me. A prince in school uniform with his mother staring daggers from the driver's seat. 'Anyone hurt?' he asked.

I shook my head. Sam hid her face under her hair. There was a blast of a hooter from a car which had been forced to stop behind the Masters' car.

'Must go.' He leapt into his chariot, agile, sandy-haired, blue-eyed, husky-voiced. I could see why Sam fancied him.

I went to pluck the bikes off Sam who was bewailing the ignominy of being seen by Tony in such an undignified state. She had managed to graze her knuckles and a shin.

I noticed a large streak of oil on my dress. The bicycles weren't damaged. Nevertheless, we were not a pair to be proud of as we cycled slowly down the road heading for the African stall that sold packets of ten, cheap cigarettes.

We weren't allowed to smoke at my house. Dorothy, my mother, strongly disapproved. We walked at a leisurely pace along the side of the road, pushing the bikes and smoking at the same time. It was a road with a single width strip of tar and not many cars passed along it. With bravado, we ignored the possibility that the people in the houses on either side of the road would see us smoking in uniform. We were both fed up with the way our teachers had been treating us. Most of them jealous, middle-aged women.

We were well into lambasting them when I saw my mother's car coming slowly down the road. We quickly stamped out our fags well before she stopped beside us.

'What happened to you?' She leaned out of the window, one blonde curl bothering her forehead.

'Two bike pile-up on the cycle track,' said Sam mournfully.

'Is either of you hurt?'

'No. Our pride is,' I confessed.

'Forget your pride. Look at your uniforms. Get Alfred to put yours straight in the wash, Ruth.' A fly crawled up her arm and she swatted it away in annoyance.

'It's grease.'

'Then I'll just have to deal with it when I come back. I'm off to the hairdresser and, at this rate, I'll be late. Your father will be home soon.' She drove off. The reference to my father being home was a barbed comment meaning that we needed someone to keep us out of trouble.

'Do you think she remembers that we're sixteen?' I asked Sam indignantly.

'And never been kissed!' Sam gave a false trill of laughter. She was delving in her pocket. 'Have a piece of gum. It'll freshen your breath.'

We walked on, chewing. Not many people were in a great hurry in that country, especially not in October when it was so hot that it was difficult to achieve anything more than a dive into a swimming pool or a rest in the shade of a tree. There was a woman sitting in the dust under a Jacaranda tree near our house, a baby in her arms. It was Alfred's wife, Elizabeth. Unlike Joy, I'd never held

Alfred's and Elizabeth's baby but it was a great honour that they had asked me to name their first-born. I'd called her Jacqueline but she was rapidly becoming known as Jacko.

'Not much shade around the khaya, Elizabeth,' I said.

'No, Missie Ruth. This tree, she is good.'

We went along the path behind her, through the back garden, past the khaya we never entered, but which I believed was made up of a concrete-floored bedroom with adjacent washroom and loo. The couple used to cook over a wood fire at its doorstep. We went to the back door of our house and were greeted by Alfred who was peeling potatoes for our supper. He had a broad grin. He was always grinning. I never knew what he had to be so happy about, apart from having a wife and baby daughter. The thing about Alfred was that he seemed perfectly satisfied to be on his knees polishing the parquet floor but when he was in his pristine, starched cook's outfit with cap, he was in his element. Very proud.

Sam and I went into my bedroom and changed into our swimming costumes. The sun was blasting through the burglar-barred windows, even through the drawn curtains. We raced out to the pool, dragging our towels and flinging them on the dry grass as we leapt into the water. It was a tie. The shock of the cold water sent me surging back up to the surface and I swam furiously for a couple of lengths. Sam was doing handstands in the shallow end, her long legs sticking out above the water before she arched and emerged upright.

Alfred brought out a jug of iced lemon juice and two tall glasses with a butterfly engraving on them, carrying these on one of mother's best trays. He put this on the garden table under the bougainvillea.

Out of the pool and drinking the lemon juice, there was a

short-lasting chill on our skins that made us wrap our towels around us. Sam evidently thought it was time to broach a subject that had been on her mind. We were both wearing sunglasses so we could not see each others' eyes.

'I saw the way that Tony looked at you,' she said abruptly.

'But you didn't see the way I looked to him. You were hiding under your hair. I was totally embarrassed. Totally.'

'He looked at you as if he had just discovered you, never mind your silly hat.'

'You mean he'd just discovered what an idiot I am.'

'Ruth, you know very well that I'm crazy about Tony Masters.'

'Well, stay crazy. I'm not about to scoop him up.'

'Now, you're being pathetic and you think you can get away with it.'

'Look. I promise I won't go after Tony, knowing the way you feel. Is that all right?'

'On your honour?' She pulled her sunglasses down to the end of her nose and glared at me.

'Best friend's honour.'

We were back in the pool when I noticed my dad coming through the gate. He was wearing one of those totally embarrassing safari suits that men wore in that country to rescue them from the heat of a jacket and tie. Safari suits consisted of a light-weight, open-necked jacket with matching trousers or shorts that could reveal very knobbly knees above stockinged socks. He had this weird hairstyle. He had a copper-coloured fringe going right around his head, with a close-shaven bit underneath that at the back. Along with this went the freckles and slight buck-teeth. Brown eyes.

He greeted us warmly and we waved from the water that was lapping against the sides of the pool after Sam had dive-bombed me.

'Can't join you.' He pointed at his brown briefcase. 'I've got marking to do. We'll have lunch when your mother gets back.' He strode into the house and we heard his classical music go on in the patio. I thought it must be Beethoven. He liked Beethoven. He always worked to music.

We lay on our towels which were some protection against the thorns, in the sparse shade. I looked up to the great African sky and at the cerise blooms of the bougainvillea.I said aloud a quotation that came into my head. 'The apparition of these faces in the crowd: Petals on a wet, black bough.'

'What are you on about, Ruth?'

'It's a poem by Ezra Pound that my dad showed me. Beautiful, isn't it? The bougainvillea made me think of it.'

'If you say so. Here, do you want some more suntan lotion?' Sam's best subject was maths and she couldn't really see the point of English literature.

There was a silence and then she said, 'If I get it, you like your Dad but you don't like your Mum.'

'It's not that I don't like her. It's just that she's so bossy. She even bosses him around.'

'Maybe he needs it.'

'I don't think so. Look at your family. Your Dad's the boss, isn't he? In most people's families it's like that. I'm getting the wrong message about husband and wife power sharing.'

'All I can say is that the way my family functions is not all it's cracked up to be. Marriage is for the birds anyway.'

'What about Tony Masters?'

'I'm not thinking of marrying him. Fancying him is different.'

I was about to reply when I saw Alfred running across the grass. 'Missie Ruth. Baas sick.'

We dashed inside to find my father lying on the patio floor, clutching his chest, breathless, sweat dripping down him. His lips had turned blue. Beethoven was still playing on the record player.

'He's having a heart attack. Call an ambulance,' said Sam. It was she who took command. Alfred's face was ashen, as was my own. I did not know what to do. I couldn't bear to lose him. I entered another world where I was numb. I fell on my knees, trying to comfort him but he was beyond my reach.

Then mum came in and moved me abruptly out of the way. 'It's no use dithering, Ruth. Get up and do something. I'll call an ambulance.'

'I've called an ambulance, Mrs. Pearson,' said Sam.

'When?'

'About three minutes ago.'

The music had ended and there was just the scratchy sound of the needle on the record.

* * *

I was startled out of my reverie when the phone in the cottage rang. It was Nicky telling me that Sally had rung to say that they were having car trouble and were running late. Nicky said he and Cherie were going to walk across to her house. Nicky had a car but the walk was very short and I guessed they liked to prolong their privacy. I didn't dare to ask if he would be back for dinner as I had learned not to try and pin him down. For the same reason, I hadn't asked Max when he would be back that evening. Max would probably be late. I hoped he would remember to buy the booze. That was, traditionally, his task.

Concerned about what the cat might be up to, I went back to the house and checked that the young people hadn't left the dining-room doors open. I wondered if I should try and do a balancing act and cram the salads in the fridge but decided against it.

The grandfather clock in the hallway ticked on in the silence. I had the house to myself. Outside, the sheep bleated and the farmer trundled across a field in his tractor. Henri and her friend were due to come after work, at about eight. Susannah and George would arrive the following day. I went to shower and began thinking about leaving Auld Oak Hall, something I'd done on and off for years. Since I had turned forty, every time I had a birthday I would stop and wonder why I was still there. Every birthday I vowed it would be my last at Auld Oak Hall. This time it was a more persistent thought. I could leave when the party was over. It came into my mind that this was not going to be just a birthday party or a reunion. It could also be a farewell party. It gave me a thrill of excitement to think that I might leave Max after all those years of oppression, of duty. I had it within my power to fly, at least to dance. Nicky was old enough now. Yet, a part of me knew that he would never be old enough. The elation passed. I would ask Adeline if she could put me up for a while. She was coming on Sunday.

Ever since I had come to Scotland in 1978, Adeline had acted as a substitute mother to me. She was elderly now. She painted cityscapes of Edinburgh. Her paintings were her children, she would say. She had been widowed quite young but never looked for another husband, choosing to remain faithful to Iain's memory. She lived in a high-ceilinged flat in Edinburgh's New Town, amongst great urns and vases, statuettes and magenta, patterned rugs. Entering was like going into a stillness and an eloquence. She would appear wearing one of her pale, long dresses with shoes like ballet shoes and a shawl slung around her shoulders, her hair wispy and grey and her skin soft and delicate. Adeline had the eyes of understanding and the voice of a wise woman. She was everything my own mother was not.

I curled the mascara through my lashes, now wearing my blue summer dress with its deep décolletage. It was mid-calf length. That was the length I liked, although I thought it must be unfashionable as most women were wearing either long or very short skirts in those days. I had kept my figure. Even Max had to admit that.

I moved my make-up and toiletries into a corner of Max's bedroom to give Henri space in my room and went downstairs to await my guests.

4

I sat in the conservatory. Everything was ready. Preparations complete except for the annihilation of a cobweb on a glass panel. Heather and I had missed that bit. I wondered where the spider snare-maker was. Would I see it running across the tiled floor towards my sandaled feet? I lifted them onto a padded stool. I didn't mind spiders as long as they didn't touch me. I thought I ought to get up and destroy that web but it was so light, filigree, well-made.

Max would notice the cobweb and disapprove. He would attack it as he did anything he didn't like, good or bad. With his judgmental actions, Max had made many enemies. For example, there was Grace. He had not only ditched her as a lover, he had fired her from her secretarial post. And then there was his legal partner, Graham Thomson, with whom he had been having a long-running argument over some property in Jedburgh they co-owned. He didn't tell me about this but I read about it. I used to secretly read Max's personal diaries after I discovered the affair with Grace and realized how little he told me of what was going on in his life. He was always like that, preferring to do things rather than talk about them. Were the diaries an attempt to redress the balance?

Max and I met in Edinburgh at a bridge evening. I had been invited to make up a set by one of Adeline's friends. I hadn't wanted to play bridge because my mother's addiction to it had put me off but I was lonely in Edinburgh and I wanted to meet people. Besides, I was practically penniless and was looking for a job so that I needed to establish a network. When I was introduced to Max I forgot all about that because I was instantly attracted to him; his blue eyes, wavy black hair and his smile. As bridge partners, we won the game easily and he invited me to a meal at his flat the following week to meet some of his friends.

* * *

The Max I still remember, as he was at the beginning of our relationship, put a finger lightly over my lips and with his free hand drew me a little way through the doorway so that my back was against the pale ochre-coloured wall. I could smell wood burning in the fireplace through in the sitting-room. It wafted up and around the carved wooden door that was open and, therefore, shielded us from being seen by the guests. He didn't say anything but placed his lips on mine, at the same time loosening my belt and unbuttoning my coat in a slow motion, sensual way. I opened my eyes and touched the large, loose curls of his dark hair, drawing my hand downwards over his chest, feeling under his sweater to the flesh beneath the fabric of his shirt. We made no sound but we could tell this would be the night.

Just then someone came through to shut the door.

'You're letting in the cold, brother.'

'On the contrary, I've just let in the sunlight.'

'Oh my, what a charmer. You'd better watch out for him, Ruth. At least, I presume it is Ruth. I've heard all about the incredible red hair. I'm Max's twin brother. Pleased to meet you.' Lawrence extended his hand.

I was curious to compare his looks with those of Max. He was slightly taller with fair, straight hair. They had different-shaped eyes, but blue eyes. Max had wide eyes whereas Lawrence's were almond-shaped. Their mouths were the same and their voices uncannily similar. Further than that, I did not go. Max took my coat with the smoothness of an accomplished host and we went through to the sitting-room. In it was a small group dressed as though they'd come straight from work, except for Lawrence who was wearing loose clothing, socks and sandals. He seemed like the odd one out. The other two guests bristled with a sense of themselves. At that point, I had already met Henri. She was then in her late twenties, eager, outspoken, affectionate and argumentative in turns. By contrast, the qualities I valued were femininity and gentleness, and voices with timbre. I felt that I could only take her in small doses.

I greeted Henri and turned to the stranger who had stood up revealing that he was well over six feet tall.

'Good day. I'm Wilf. It's a pleasure to make your acquaintance young lady.' Grinning, he turned to Max. 'Hey, Max, where've you been hiding this fine example of womanhood or shouldn't I ask?' He chuckled.

I didn't much appreciate what he said but I did like his laugh. I contented myself with raising my eyebrows and pre-empting Max's reply. 'We haven't known each other for very long.'

'Yup, that explains it.' He winked at Henri who told him to belt up and sit down. Undeterred, he offered me his seat and himself sat on the edge of an armchair. 'I'm from Sydney, Australia, and I'm studying physics in this fine city. And studying the Sheila's, as well. Phew. There's some talent here.'

'Daddy always says that Scotswomen have panache,' said Henri. She crossed her plump legs, swinging a foot so that her classic blue shoe fell away at the heel. In those days, she was not a furniture restorer but trying vainly to adapt herself to office work.

'I just wonder how Daddy gets his information on Scottish women,' Wilf teased her and she threw a cushion at him.

Max ignored this behaviour and turned to me. 'Ruth, I'm afraid you've missed the nosh. I didn't know if you were coming. The meal has been demolished by these appreciative customers. Where have you been?'

'A friend was having problems. I'll explain later,' I said, knowing that I couldn't explain because the friend had been speaking to me in confidence.

Lawrence interrupted, telling Max that he had no manners. He was at least to give me a sandwich. I was so hungry I could have kissed him. He went off to get it himself and, needless to say the conversation turned to food, which made me even hungrier.

I looked at Max across the room, sitting on a tapestry stool, legs apart. The flat had been furnished with elegant cast-offs from his parents' mansion. Deep, old-fashioned armchairs, small tables that had been lovingly polished by his home help, Mrs. Phillips. She was one of the first people Max talked about after I met him.

I watched him chatting to Wilf. The dark undulations of his hair were backed by the glow of the fire but his face … I noticed a flicker of petulance in his expression that I promptly decided to forget.

Lawrence brought my sandwich and sat in a chair next to me, putting up an invisible screen across the room by earnest and total concentration on my needs. What with the long-awaited food and the hefty whisky Max had given me, I found the similarity of the twins' voices and mouths riveting and confusing. I embarked on a standard line of questioning. 'What do you do, Lawrence? No, don't tell me. Let me guess. You're an artist.'

'No. Although I used to play the guitar in a folk band.'

'Let me see … you're a former hippy turned theology student.'

'Close.'

'I give up.'

'I work for an international aid agency. We go wherever war or famine or natural disaster has brought poverty, sickness, starvation, death. Incidentally, I've never been to Rhodesia. We organize appeals and oversee the supply of aid. The state of some of these people would break your heart.'

We didn't know that Henri had been listening until she interrupted, saying. 'Natural disasters are one way of keeping down the population. Some of these people breed like rabbits.'

I winced. Lawrence's eyes narrowed but he remained calm. I rested my head on the back of the chair and closed my eyes. The last thing I heard before I fell asleep was Lawrence, ignoring her remark, answering her questions, admitting that sometimes corruption prevented aid getting to the people in need. He was giving her facts and figures…

…I woke, still dressed, lying between green pinstriped sheets that smelled faintly of soap powder. The ceiling was high and corniced and long, beige curtains hung from the window. Directly opposite me was an old, gilt-framed painting of a girl standing at a gate. I turned on my side, noticing that my boots had been taken off. Max was sleeping next to me. His lashes were thick, casting shadows on his cheeks. He was clutching his pillow with one hand. His lips were slightly open, his sweet breath directed towards me. I traced the lines of his face with my eyes. The duvet covered most of his body so that I didn't know whether or not he was naked.

I whispered his name. He stirred and turned over with a groan and, as he did so, he brushed my face with his fingers.

'Ruth?'

'Yes,'

We made love for the first time.

Afterwards, we did not go to sleep but lay there, talking. We made confessions as some new lovers do. I told him about Bruce, the rugby player I'd nearly married in Zimbabwe. He told me that he'd had a fiancée who had been killed in a car accident just before their wedding was due to take place.

*   *   *

It was early spring 1979 and the snows of the winter had been threatening to keep on falling. Yet it was a clear, bright, if cold day when we drove to Max's parents' farm, east of Edinburgh, where we were ushered into the mansion house.

Max's mother's eyes were not smiling. They were little balls shooting around my inferior clothing and my lower middle class background. It was as if she were playing with one of those games that you jiggle until the silver-quick ball falls into the hole. She wore a skirt in beige checks with a silk blouse and I noted the emerald and diamond brooch on her ample chest. I tugged at my hair to cover the African beaded necklace I was wearing. She, in turn, noticed this. It seemed as if she were going to notice everything. I was not going to be able to hide. Max had left us alone and had gone into the farm courtyard to see his father. Before Max went, she told him with absolute authority that lunch would be served on the dot of one. She didn't really need to tell him. Lunch was always served at one. Breakfast was at seven. Dinner was at eight. No later. No earlier.

'So, your mother's name is Dorothy. Isn't that strange? My home help's name is Dorothy.'

I felt that some response was required. But, what? Was she trying to put my family on the level of servants or was she genuinely intrigued? My mouth went dry and I had the feeling that I shouldn't stir in case I gave myself away. I cleared my throat. 'Yes. It is quite a coincidence.'

'She is an absolute treasure.' She made a light fist in the air to emphasize this. 'God knows what I would do without her. I'm so frightfully busy without having to see to the cleaning and cooking myself. And poor dear, she needs the job so badly. Husband's always out of work. Hits the bottle, rather.' She stared at me as if she had right judgment on her side. 'I keep telling her she'd be better off without him but she can't bring herself to leave him. I think she still loves him, poor dear.'

The conversation was dragging until Monica found and seized an opportunity to tell me about her family. Her parents were titled, Sir Andrew and Lady Ferguson, and Monica was one of six children brought up in this very house. The title had gone to her brother Herbert, the oldest son.

We were in a large drawing-room. Very elegant. Dorothy had

clearly dusted and had shone the silver photograph frames standing on a Chippendale table on one side of the room. A grand piano stood beside the French doors. 'Do you play the piano?' I asked.

'My mother used to play - and Lawrence too - but now it hasn't been used for years. Father would sing. He had a good singing voice. He led the singing in church. Dear Papa. I can see him now sitting in his favourite chair, smoking his pipe while we children lined up to receive our collection money before church. Mother would be wrapped up in furs. Such a serene person. Even with all of us to look after. Of course, there was Nanny Steele. Wonderful woman, if a bit strict. Then we'd all climb into the motor - we still called it that - and Daddy would drive along the country lanes to the church. I remember the little blue hat I used to wear to the services. Of course, we all had to wear hats to church in those days.'

'We had to wear hats to school.' I was desperate to say something.

'You would, wouldn't you? In that sort of climate.' She clearly found this a very uninteresting thing to say. Perhaps it was better if she did the talking and then I wouldn't risk saying the wrong thing? It was five minutes to one by the grandfather clock.

Monica decided to make an effort to get to know me. 'But, my dear, you must tell me about yourself so that I can appear knowledgeable when Max gets in. Your father, what does he do?'

'He's an English teacher in a high school.'

'Oh,' she said, 'I thought only women did that.'

The inner door moved slightly and I was half expecting Dorothy to announce lunch early. But there was silence followed by the sound of clawing at the back of the sofa on which Monica was sitting. A grey cat flung itself over the top and stood on her lap, purring.

'Pussums.' She pulled a hand along the ridge of its back so that it arched in response. 'This is Happy and her friend is called Princess. She's around somewhere. Isn't this one too, too sweet? You see, she's very clever. She has two different-coloured eyes.'

The cat was now lying full-length on her lap and it stared at me with one blue eye and one brown eye, out of a deeply-suspicious, furry face.

'I wouldn't touch her if I were you,' warned Monica.

'I'm not going to.'

'My precious can be a little fierce with strangers. Can't you, pussums?' She squeezed Happy who responded by leaping off her lap, landing with a gentle thud on the carpet; then the cat lay back, indulging in some leisurely licking, eyeing me occasionally.

The men were in the kitchen and I could hear that Max's father had a loud laugh. Monica explained to me that she thought I'd prefer to have lunch in the kitchen rather than having to mind my p's and q's in the dining-room. I was privately feeling awful because Max clearly adored his mother and, so far, I did not like her. I was thrown by her power games and did not have her values. I told myself to try to like her, for Max's sake. I talked myself into feeling positive while soaping my hands in the bathroom. Monica was hovering outside the bathroom door. She had come upstairs with me as if she were worried I'd steal something. I would loathe having to live like that.

When we went into the kitchen, a large room with an oak table laid for the meal, she took me over to the cooking area where Dorothy was putting the roast beef onto a platter with Yorkshire puds tucked around it.

'Let me introduce you to Dorothy, my right-hand woman. Dorothy, this is Trudy'

'No. My name's not Trudy. It's Ruth. Ruth Pearson.'

'Don't worry, Mrs. Pearson. People usually call me Dot. I've been telling Mrs. Heriot-Ross that for the best part of twenty years. Pleasure to meet you ma'am.' She was a short, skinny woman with leathery skin and a hoarse voice. She carried on putting the final touches to the meal.

'Will you women stop nattering and sit down to eat. I've had a hard morning's work. Max, introduce me to this charming young woman and fetch the wine, there's a good chap.'

Max's father, Walter, was good-humoured and guffawed a lot. He was easy to get on with, partly because he was full of flattery and winked at me several times. He had big blue eyes like Max. Walter was always bringing the conversation back to farming but he was also aware of bigger issues. Inevitably the conversation got around to Ian Smith and UDI. Max, who had been relatively silent up until then, looked at me with sympathy. 'I don't think Ruth wants to talk politics,' he said.

Monica, however, was bursting to say her piece. 'Well, I must say it's an out and out absurdity to suggest that Rhodesia is ready for majority rule. People who say that haven't been there. I have. You've lived there. Surely you agree with me, Trudy?'

'No. Actually, I don't.'

'I think they call it Zimbabwe-Rhodesia now dear.' Walter saw that I was in difficulty.

'Whatever they call it. You know I'm not good with names.'

Walter took over the conversation and began to talk about Monica's prize roses. Max joined in. Not only did they want to steer us away from politics, they also wanted to keep us from talking about dark-skinned people. The conversation would most certainly have turned to Lawrence who had left the country with a Muslim doctor and was thought to be living in Paris, secretly because her family in India didn't approve of the match either. However, try as they might, Walter and Max couldn't stop the conversation turning to Lawrence.

'My dear, don't get yourself wound up. The boy will come to his senses. Have some more wine. Max, fill up your mother's glass.'

Max went across to her with the bottle but she put her hand over the rim of the crystal glass. Then he did something that impressed me very much at the time. He put down the wine bottle and took her hand in both of his. She responded by nestling her head in his waist.

'How could he do this to me,' she moaned.

'Damn him,' said Max under his breath.

'Ever since he became a wretched teenager he's been trying to prove he can do better than his family can,' said Monica. 'I wanted him to get a proper job, like you Max. But no, he had to go and be a do-gooder. He had to live in a commune instead of in a civilized flat. And, as for those hippies he got involved with … all along, he's been trying to save the world and prove that we are not good enough.' Monica was almost in tears.

After dessert we went through to the drawing room for coffee. Walter had to get back to the farm. Before he went striding off in his wellies, he came over to me, gave my arm a squeeze and told me that I was a charming young woman and that no-one should say otherwise.

Max took his mother's arm as we walked through and he sat next to her on the sofa. She passed me an ornate, dainty cup made of bone china with a gilded, curved and arching handle. We had begun to talk about Max's squash games when suddenly she held up a hand to interrupt further conversation. 'Dorothy,' she called shrilly. 'Dorothy.' With urgency.

Dorothy must have heard because she came scurrying through from clearing up, and washing dishes.

'Dorothy, I want you to go through the house and find every photograph there is of Master Lawrence and put them in the study where I'll deal with them later. Start with this room.'

'Mother, don't you think you're over-reacting. Her family is just as much against the match. The two of them might be forced to abandon any thoughts of marriage. They might even be in danger if her relatives think she has challenged the family honour.'

'Don't you start, Max. It's not just this match as you call it. Lawrence has been trying my patience for years. I'm disinheriting him. As far as I'm concerned, he does not exist. You are my only son.'

So it was that, by default, I came to be accepted into the Heriot-Ross hierarchy, even if my name was not Trudy. In Monica's eyes, Max could not have made a choice as bad as his brother's. Max, compared with his now 'non-existent' brother, could do nothing wrong.

*   *   *

I will forever remember my wedding day in the summer of 1980. I especially remember the hope that was sprinkled on us like handfuls of confetti. It was very formal. Monica had seen to that. Formality crossed with gaiety, to use an old-fashioned word for an old-fashioned ceremony. That day I changed my surname from Pearson to Heriot-Ross, stepping into a new role with courage borne on the wings of love and elation. Even Monica had become temporarily tolerable in my eyes. She and Walter were hosting the reception. Mum and dad flew over and were staying in Max's flat. In my own flat, sliding my diamond engagement ring up and down on my finger, I sat on my bed in my new silky underwear with my wedding dress beside me. The headdress and veil lay on the pillow, a beaded band and a puff of netting. I had bathed and was attuning myself to what was going to happen that day. I was following a trail of love, and sharing its consequences with friends and family; and boldly contemplating giving myself for life to another. Together we would go to live in that imposing house in the Borders that Max had inherited from his uncle. I had given up my job. Moving into a new region would put the seal on the fact that my parents and my country were always going to be far away. Yet, far from feeling insecure, I saw this as an opportunity to put down roots in a way that I hadn't been able to do for a long time. I would be out there in my jeans, tunnelling through the earth with my bare hands, breathing in the fresh smell of the moist soil. Planting, weeding, turning the earth. Then going indoors to my study to try my hand at fiction writing. I looked at my painted fingernails. I pulled my engagement ring up and down and it was reassuring on my skin.

Dad was coming to fetch me in the chauffeur-driven, hired Rolls Royce that Monica had insisted upon. Monica had taken over the organization of the wedding because mum was not in the country to do it, as the bride's mother usually does. Monica's view was that there was only one way to arrange a wedding and that was the right way. The bride's and bridesmaids' cars were to be Rolls Royce. The men were to wear kilts or black tie. The women, evening dress. The Ceilidh band was to be one she had used for functions before. I won on the colour of the bridal gown in cream with the flowers that were to be predominantly lilac, and the bridesmaids were to wear lilac dresses. Max had taken the view that as his mother was a superb organizer she should be left to get on with it. It's the guests who make the party, Max added. I thought that made sense. He always sounded so practical and so sure of himself.

Beth, my flatmate and one of my three bridesmaids, came in to do my make-up. I glanced at my watch. Three quarters of an hour before the cars were due to come. Dad would be with me and mum would go in Max's car. Beth carefully removed all wisps of hair from my face. It was a warm day and she was wearing a light, scalloped top, her breath close to mine as she worked. We'd moved the dress and it was hanging on the back of the door while I continued to sit on my bed, my bathrobe now wrapped around me.

'How do you feel?' she asked.

'I'm not sure how to describe it. Floating, and I haven't touched a drop.'

'Love affects your brain. Getting married without love must be a very dour experience. You'll be all right. Just lift your head up a little. I'm nearly finished.'

Beth took her tins and brushes away and I inspected her handiwork in the chipped mirror on the back of the wardrobe door. I slipped out of the robe and into the dress, zipping myself into the tight bodice and I glided around the small space, negotiating the wardrobe and bed like a clockwork dancing doll. Then I did my hair, something I'd allowed no-one else to do. I coiled it around at the back of my head in a loose roll and pinned it firmly. I was just putting the headdress in place when there was a knock on the door. Dad came in. We nodded our greetings.

'Here I am, about to leave your name behind. Who can resist a name like Heriot-Ross?'

'Frightfully swish,' he said.

'Frightfully.' We laughed.

Dad became serious. 'The important thing is that you love him. Marriage is about the law and it should be about religion. But love is central. You do love Max?'

'Yes, I do. Why do you think I'm going through this performance?'

He didn't get a chance to respond to my remark because our cars had arrived, and we travelled in convoy through the streets of Edinburgh, out to the country church where Max and Lawrence had been christened and confirmed. There was a white ribbon on the bonnet for all to see, and I smiled out at anyone who wanted to 'look at the bride'. We arrived at the church with ten minutes to spare. Guests were still going in, being greeted by ushers. My stomach was churning and, sensing this, dad put his hand on mine. The bouquet rested resplendent on the leather seat beside me. Within a few minutes, Monica came bustling out and dad rolled down his window. She was in navy blue, wearing a long dress and light jacket, and a navy hat with hat band in beige and navy. She wore a diamond necklace. Under her arm, she carried a matching beige and blue purse. She looked flushed. The best man was there, but Max hadn't yet arrived. She told us not to come in until he did. She went to speak to the bridesmaids, Beth, Dianne and Constance, and then she hurried back into the church. The service was due to start at three o'clock.

We were still waiting when my watch showed twenty past three.

'They'll come. Don't worry.' Dad was trying to calm me.

'I hope they haven't had an accident. Or, perhaps he has

changed his mind?' I reasoned that if he did change his mind, it would be better now rather than later. I pulled out an embroidered handkerchief from my small silk pouch and wiped my palms.

'It's no use speculating. They'll get here all right. You mustn't let this unnerve you,' said dad.

'What do think is up?' Beth mouthed. She had come round to my window. I opened it and she repeated her question.

'I don't know. I'm just wondering if he has changed his mind,' I said.

'He'd be a fool if he did that,' she said loyally. 'I'll go back to the others. Tell them there's no news.'

I stared at the emptiness of the long country lane and at the graveyard surrounding the church as if the graves could give me an answer. Graves speak of stories ended, suggesting little of the beginning and middle of a person's lifetime. What was going to happen to me on my wedding day? What would be the end of this part of the story? Little did I know that the insecurity of waiting for Max had only just begun. I didn't tell dad but, for the first time that day, I wondered if I wanted to go through with it.

At twenty two minutes past three we saw Max's Porsche speeding along the road and it came to a screeching halt outside the church. He leapt out and rushed mum along the path to the church door. Mum was looking anxious and was clinging to a feathery, pink hat as if it might fall off in her hurry. They disappeared through the doorway. Soon after that Monica appeared and came up to the car.

'The tailor gave him the wrong jacket and he had to dash back to get the right one. Poor Max. You can come in whenever you're ready.' She was away again.

'Am I ready, Dad?'

'That's for you to say.'

I gathered up my skirts and climbed out of the car. Beth, Dianne and Constance, smiling with relief, and still fresh in their lilac gowns, joined us as we walked between the graves, up the few steps and into the church. It was three thirty. I watched Max's back on the slow walk up the aisle on dad's arm.

At the reception in a marquee in Monica's garden I channelled all the tension into furious dancing which mum thought was unladylike. Walter, nice man, rivalled me with loud whoops and a swinging sporran. There were a lot of jokes about how it's the bride's prerogative to be late, as if in the group consciousness I was the one to keep two hundred people waiting. At that moment, all was forgivable.

*   *   *

I was waiting for my guests in the conservatory. Being summer, the day was still light although there was some darkness in the clouds. I heard a car come up the drive and thought it must be Jack and Sally. But no, it was Max himself. For once, he was not late because the guests themselves were late. What is more, he came into the kitchen carrying a box full of wine, spirits and beer.

'You're all dolled up,' he said, almost as if he were criticizing me.

'I wanted to make an effort for our guests.'

'My wife always looks nice.'

Previously, I would have taken this as a compliment but now I knew better. His emphasis was on the fact that I was his wife, an extension of himself, and therefore I was likely to look good. It was subtle but annoying, although I didn't say anything.

'I've bought champagne for Sunday,' he said, lifting out the bottles from the box.

It was obvious how far I'd gone along the road of disliking Max for I thought only of him playing the dominant host, popping the champagne corks of his benevolence. Conducting a ceremony to show that he was the master.

This was a man who could pour a glass of champagne with a hand so steady that you would never know that he had betrayed his wife, had exposed his son to the secret of his lover by bringing her into the home as 'daddy's friend', had alienated his friends by his arrogance. He was so dark beneath a bright, successful mask. Yet, after what happened to him, I ought really to have felt sorry for him. He was not going to live on with all his faults. His life would end that very weekend. Even the need to keep up appearances would become, abruptly, insignificant.

*   *   *

'You've missed a bit,' he said. I was still sitting in the conservatory. He was standing, in his work suit and tie.

'It's only a spider's web and it looks quite pretty, there against the glass.'

'It does not look good. When was the glass last cleaned?'

'Heather did the parts that she can reach on Monday. I think I was working.'

'You think. Be more accurate, Ruth. Either you were working or you weren't.' He disappeared into the kitchen, coming back with a feather duster. He tore at the web and soon it was down, leaving a blank on the glass where it had been. The feather duster was covered in dusty, tangled threads.

Just then we heard a car coming up the gravel drive. We both went out to greet Jack, Sally and the children. The family spilled out of the car, travel-weary, pleased to have arrived, all except Jack.

'We've had car trouble. It's overheating.' Sally was the first to speak. With cropped brown hair, she must have been a dress size twenty-four, or more. She was, as always, outgoing and vivacious but - something that hadn't been there previously - her face had a worried look. 'I'm so sorry we're late. We had to stop every so often to top up the engine with water. Jack thinks there's a leak, although he can't see it.' The children were clinging to her skirt.

Jack finally got out of the car. It was as if he had been preparing himself for some sort of ordeal. Yet, he came over to me and hugged me so hard it hurt. He still had a fine physique.

'Great to see you,' I said in response when he'd finally released me. I looked into his eyes and saw among golden flecks, the deep colour of fear. Or, was it anger?

'Sabona. Kunjani? (Hello. How are you?) He used an African greeting.

'Sitshonile,' (I'm okay) I replied.

I could sense Max thinking 'now it starts' but he didn't remark on the greeting. Instead, he suggested the men take the luggage to the cottage and then have a look at the car. He told me to give Sally a cup of tea or coffee and the children something to drink. First, he would go and change out of his work clothes.

We poured into the kitchen, Pip tumbling in ahead of us. Robbie was still hanging on to his mother. I put the kettle on and they sat around the large, round, pine table. Brindle put her front paws on Sally's thigh, as if she sensed that Sally worked with dogs. Todd was lurking somewhere out of sight. As long as it wasn't in the dining-room. Robbie climbed up on his mum's lap and I told Brindle to sit. The dog gave up, in the face of competition, and went to lie in her basket.

Pip was the one I needed to do something about. She had

already explored the conservatory and was itching to see the rest of the house. I had some puzzles and games that I had kept from Nicky's childhood and I brought these out and spread them over the table. I was in luck. It turned out that Pip loved jigsaw puzzles. She chose one and I hoped that all the pieces were there.

'You live in a lovely part of the world,' remarked Sally.

'Devon is very beautiful as well,' I replied.

'They're not Zimbabwe,' said Jack morosely. 'At this time of the evening we could be watching the African sun go down.'

'The sun goes down in this part of the world, too. And we get extra daylight in the summer.' In trying to defend my adopted country, I hadn't quite understood Jack's mood. It would have been better just to let him have his say.

'You don't get the dramatic African sunsets. Blood red, purple and orange.'

The conversation ended there because Max came downstairs in jeans and open-necked shirt.

'Where is Nicky?' he asked.

'Probably with Cherie,' I replied.

'Are they joined at the hip? It's not good. They're far too young.'

'It's not as simple as that,' I said, nursing Zoe's secret.

'Auntie Ruth, are you sure you've got all the pieces here?' asked Pip. She called me auntie although I was strictly speaking a second cousin.

'I can't be sure. That puzzle was Nicky's so it is a little bit old.' The puzzle was of Edinburgh Castle. 'Tell you what, Pip, would you like to watch some TV in the sitting-room? Robbie could watch with you.'

That idea seemed to go down well with the children and Sally did not object. So, with the children perched in front of the TV, a suitable programme chosen, and the men having gone out to look at the car, Sally and I were able to talk.

'It's a cop-out really, sending them off to watch TV but we'll soon think of some better entertainment,' I said.

'It's an educational programme. Can't be bad for them. While I've got the chance, I want to tell you about Jack. You've seen what he's like.'

'He seems very intense.'

'He's worse at home. He won't go anywhere, won't do anything. He has only come up here because of you. He has never recovered from having to leave the farm in Zim. Although it was my farm, he was completely devoted to it. Being confronted by so-called veterans of the war was enough to make anyone bitter, and angry, too, but we have to carry on for the sake of the children. And he's not giving them any support.'

'They seem all right, from what little I've seen of them.'

'Pip, yes. But Robbie is so shy and withdrawn. It hurts me to send him off to school each day. The thing is that I think Jack is seriously depressed. He won't go to a doctor. Maybe you can help him, Ruth?'

I thought a bit. 'You and I, and Jack, have all left our homeland. We know what it means to have our childhood snatched away from us, not to mention your time as an adult on the farm. We understand what it means when not even going back can soothe the homesickness.'

'The wound won't heal.'

'That's why I've become so attached to Auld Oak Hall. It's to do with roots. That's why I will find it difficult to leave.' The last sentence just slipped out. I had meant to keep my thoughts of leaving a secret from her.

'You're not thinking of leaving?' she asked, raising her eyebrows.

There we were, two survivors - two people with memories of African drums, footprints, sun, flowers, animals, art – now living in Britain. Sally was wearing an African print shift dress that clung in places to her oversized body. She had on an African seed necklace and wore canvas shoes. I offered her another cup of tea, which she accepted. Neither of us said anything while I poured it but when I put her mug in front of her, she said, 'You can't just not answer my question, Ruth. Are you planning to leave?'

'Your question is too direct, too black and white. I have, I do think of leaving.'

'I know you and Max have had your problems in the past but he seems nice enough.'

'He's one thing to the outside world and another thing behind closed doors.'

'But isn't everybody like that?'

'Not to that extent. For a long time, I have been staying with him because of Nicky. But Nicky is twenty-one now. The worst thing is that Max won't let me be myself. I am his wife and, therefore, an extension of himself. But that's enough said on that subject. I'd rather you didn't speak to anyone about what I've said.'

Sally promised to treat our conversation as confidential. She sat sipping her tea, shoulders hunched, deflated. She really did have enough to contend with already and I could tell she had wanted to come to a cosy family home for a weekend away and had hoped to off-load some of the dilemma of Jack's mood.

There was a lull in the conversation as Nicky walked in. His red hair was tousled and his T-shirt was hanging lank about his hips. He was wearing wellies.

'Where have you been?' I asked.

'Out and about.'

'It's my guess you were in the river.'

'What a good detective my mother is. Yes. Walking along the river. No booze. No fags. Just nature.'

'You and Cherie?'

'Yes. I'm not telling you any more, Mum.'

I realized I had to hold back with my questions. 'You remember Sally?'

'Of course. Nice to see you, Sally.'

Nicky was taking off his wellies and lobbed them into the back porch. 'Where are the kids?' he asked Sally.

'Watching telly, I'm afraid. I'll go and see if they can't do something else.'

'I've got paper and paints, if they want them. They can paint at the table in the conservatory. Or, they can have their food now, before the others,' I said.

Sally bustled through and Nicky strode, in his socks, out of the kitchen and upstairs to his bedroom. Pip came through eagerly to get the poster paints, brushes, water and paper but Robbie told his mum he was hungry and I took him through to the dining-room to help himself to the buffet. It wasn't a huge success because all he put on his plate was bread and a piece of ham. I suggested to Sally that I grill some fish fingers and he smiled a shy, approving smile. Pip said she'd like some, too.

Robbie looked so like his father. He had the same solemn eyes, the dark hair and the seemingly permanent tan. Pip didn't resemble either of her parents. She had straight blonde hair and high cheekbones. She did, however, have the same lively air that Sally usually had.

I was feeding the two children when Henri and her friend

arrived, Henri having driven from Glasgow. She burst in the door, without ringing the bell. She was as bombastic as ever. She wore a red and green floral print dress with tiny, red buttons down the front, bursting to be released. 'You don't know how glad we are to see you,' she said in a loud voice.

I was getting up when I noticed the man who was with her and I felt a flush come up into my face. Henri introduced us. This was Bernard, a landscape artist. That's how she described him. When I shook his hand it was gentle and strong, all at the same time. Behind my back, Henri and Sally were introducing each other. Bernard, the artist, was of medium build with a comfortable pot belly. He had a mop of brown hair, greying at the temples, and a beard also edged with grey. His eyes were small but twinkling, a penetrating golden brown.

The greeting came to an end because Henri was telling us about their near miss on the road. Apparently, they were making good time when they were slowed down by a bus in front of them. At what she thought was a safe moment she started to pass the bus. However, she had underestimated its speed. When she was three-quarters of the way past the bus she realized that she was facing an oncoming car and she wasn't going to make it back into the left-hand lane. It was only due to the wits of the driver of the oncoming car that he stopped and let her through. 'When something like that happens, you realize how close accidents are,' she said. 'And Bernard didn't say or do anything.'

'It wouldn't have helped,' he said. I noticed what a rich, deep voice he had.

'I think that deserves a drink,' I said and gave them drinks, still in the kitchen where the children had decided to paint. It wasn't long before Max and Jack joined us and we got down to the serious business of eating. It was still daylight, but the dining-room was letting in just a shaded light, so I lit some decorative candles and placed them on saucers along the middle of the table. All the dishes were on mats to protect the surface that Heather had shone to a mirror-like quality. Likewise, she had polished the antique cabinet that stood against the outer wall between the low, sash window and the glass, outer door; and also the one beside the glass door that led into the conservatory. The only low seating was a *chaise longue* beneath the window. This room looked out onto a field, in the middle of which stood an ancient horse chestnut, frequently encircled by crows; the field was then empty of livestock.

I hovered, taking the hostess's place at the end of the queue, while they heaped food onto their plates appreciatively and, each carrying a napkin and fork, went to find a seat either in the conservatory or the sitting-room. I took some hot rolls out of the oven and put them on a silver tray and, carrying this and a butter dish, went through to the sitting-room to hand them out. Henri and Max were sitting on the sofa, Max squeezed against one sofa arm and Henri sitting very close to him in the middle of the sofa.

'Good grub,' said Henri to the room, accidentally spitting out a bit of pasta as she spoke.

'Have a roll, Henri, Max?'

'My wife would be a good cook,' said Max. 'Were it not for all the emotion she invests in it.'

'I'll take that as a back-handed compliment. You're a good cook, yourself, Henri. In the past, you have given us several memorable meals.'

'There should have been many more. Your wedding changed things although I, for one, have made a point of keeping in touch.

Of course, I always thought I should be the one to marry Max. I hope you don't mind my saying this, Ruth?'

'I'm used to you saying what's on your mind, Henri,' I said.

Max seemed to be having difficulty swallowing his food but when his throat was clear, he said, 'You asked me several times and each time I said no.'

'You said you'd think about it and then you went and got engaged to Ruth. All I can say is that if ever your marriage comes unstuck, you've got me to fall back on.'

'If ever the marriage comes unstuck, as you put it, I'll still be thinking about it, as I said.'

I was offended by Henri's brash statements even though I told myself I didn't care what Max did after I left. Henri simply spoke without thinking. One thing I was sure of was that if I did leave him it would not be Henri he would turn to. My replacement would be young and sexy, not overweight and gauche like Henri.

I withdrew my interest in the conversation by taking the now mildly warm rolls through to the conservatory. Henri would have taken my moving off as a sign of disapproval and so she should. However, it wouldn't deflate her. She doted on Max and had done so for years. She had made it very obvious. She was impervious to his rejection of her advances. The nasty thought crossed my mind that she could be Max's nemesis. He wasn't getting any younger. I wondered why I had invited Henri but then I remembered that Henri had invited herself.

In the conservatory Nicky and Sally were talking, seated on the wickerwork, cushioned sofa. Jack and Bernard were sitting eating, each on an individual, wickerwork chair. They took rolls and buttered them.

'What's happening about the car?' I asked Jack.

'I thought it was a leak but there doesn't seem to be one.' He spoke as someone who had just emerged from a reverie. 'Max and I will look at it again tomorrow,' he said.

'Do you know anything about cars, Bernard?' I wanted to include him, to be sociable and because I wanted to hear his voice. It was deep and vibrating and he had a Scots accent.

'I've seen a few car engines in my time,' he said, looking at me directly. 'That having been said, mechanics are not really my thing.'

'My father always said he would insist on my learning the mechanics of a car before I took my driving test. He didn't stick to that, thank goodness,' I told them.

'How is your father?' Sally had been listening in.

'Bearing up. He hasn't been the same since his last heart attack and he's riddled with arthritis.'

'My parents didn't live to see us leave the farm,' she said.

'You had a farm in Zimbabwe?' Bernard was interested.

'I'll leave Jack to tell you the story. That's all he ever thinks about nowadays,' said Sally.

* * *

I know Jack's story off by heart so I'll tell it as he told it. I think I can get his turn of phrase:

That evening, in the year 2000, with a beer in one hand, Jack watched the sun setting over the farm as usual. He saw the great African sky display of purple, red and yellow, beyond the orange trees in the orchard, and it threw the fruit into relief. 'It was all magic. It was God in his heaven and all was right with the world. Well, God could have told me a thing or two. But he didn't. For that half hour, I was like a crazy clown, not heeding the warnings.

Oh yes, we knew what might happen. For years we'd lived on a knife-edge, wondering whether we weren't bringing up the children in the middle of a volcano. But the thing was we loved the place, man. We were literally incapable of leaving until we had to. We were bloody lucky really. It was a narrow escape.'

Thus, he was watching the sun go down and Sally was doing the books at the bureau her mother had left her. Pip was four and Robbie, three. They were playing outside, within the security fence with the 'piccanins' from the compound. Jack's foreman, Winston Ndhlovu, came shuffling up, looking troubled. 'He always took off his hat when he was talking to me and he looked like he was going to pull it apart in his hands this time. By his face, I knew that we could be expecting trouble. He told me a band of about twenty men calling themselves veterans of the war of liberation, wielding axes and knives, had been spotted in the area near old Armstrong's farm and a group of them was coming this way. I would have gone to help old Armstrong but I had to watch my back. I couldn't leave the family, and the workers and their families. It would have been irresponsible. Sal and I discussed it.'

'It was while we were eating our evening meal, great big steaks and chips, that we heard by bush telegraph that old Armstrong was dead. He'd been murdered.'

Jack made a quick decision. He called Winston in and told him to be ready for the veterans. He was going to talk to them and, he said, Winston should be there to translate.

'Yebo baas,' said Winston but he was as shocked as Sally had been when Jack told her of his intention.

'You must be mad, Jack,' she had said.

'I'm not going to evacuate the farm. So, what else can I do?'

'But you're asking for trouble, Jack, and I don't want to lose you. Besides, what about the children? We have no right to risk their safety.'

'That's why I'm telling you and the children to leave. Tonight.'

'Not without you.'

'I'm not asking you. I'm telling you. Winston says the bandits are over by Dead Man's Kopje. That means they're not near the road. You can ring me when you get to Harare.'

'Where will we stay?'

'The Jackson's will put you up. I'll warn them you're coming.'

'How many so-called veterans are there?'

'Winston says about twenty.'

'You'll never hold out against that lot. What weapons have they got?'

'Mainly sticks, farm implements, axes and stones.'

'No guns?'

'Not that I know of. I won't show mine. What I've got are my wits.'

'This is crazy.'

Reluctant as she was to go, Sally wanted the children out of danger so she, Pip and Robbie packed the car hurriedly and started the one hundred kilometre journey south to Harare. She kissed him as if she would never see him again. Jack watched them go off down the dirt track into the dark night. When the car headlights disappeared in the distance he locked the gates to the security fence and went into the house with the dogs. They had three dogs, two Alsatians and one Rhodesian Ridgeback. They were called Fighter, Bomber and Titch. The latter was a joke as the dog was huge and the story is that Rhodesian Ridgebacks are capable of fighting off lions. However fierce they could be, they were still family pets and Jack resolved to keep them out of sight of the mob that was coming, for their own safety.

Before he went to bed, Sally 'phoned, saying that she and the children were with the Jackson's, safely in Harare. They hadn't come across any roadblocks, which suggested to him that the invaders were not well organized. He slept with his rifle beside his bed, which was nothing unusual in those days. It was a fitful sleep and he kept hearing noises in the night. He would get up, grab his rifle and go to the front windows. He could see nothing because it was pitch black outside. Whatever he had said to Sally, he was tense and nervous.

Jack got up at five-thirty in the morning. What he would usually do was put in a couple of hours work on the farm and then come in for breakfast. That morning he had breakfast early and fed the dogs. He had decided to call the police, despite misgivings because they were known to have difficulties with their vehicles and, politically-speaking, they might side with the invaders. Nonetheless, he 'phoned them and the officer he spoke to said they would see what they could do.

Then it happened. He heard singing and chanting. Going onto the stoep (verandah) he saw a ragged crowd snaking its way through the fields of maize, waving their sticks and their fists in the air. Now the anticipation was over, Jack steeled himself for confrontation and, at best, negotiation. They were a motley crew but they were young and able-bodied. Jack felt his fifty-four years. But then, perhaps they would respect his age, in the African way. Slowly, he went to the security gate and let himself out. As if from nowhere, Winston joined him and the singing stopped.

'I get the workers to chase them away, Baas,' whispered Winston.

'Too dangerous. We don't want to start any violent action. We will talk. Ask them who their leader is.'

That question seemed to bring about some consternation within the group but eventually one man stepped forward. He had a face full of anger and his fists were clenched. He was dressed in a sports T-shirt and khaki trousers and wore trainers. Some of the others were barefoot and in rags.

'Winston. Ask him what his name is.'

The man gave an aggressive reply. 'He says it's not for us to know his name. He represents the veterans. That is all,' said Winston.

'Ask what they want.'

'He says this is their land. You colonials have no right to it.'

What they wanted was nothing short of the farm itself; the cattle, milking sheds, maize fields, orchards, the farmhouse. While Jack was patiently explaining that his wife's father had paid good money for the farm the police arrived. There were three of them and they got out of the car at a leisurely pace. They spoke briefly to Winston and to the invaders' spokesman and then lined themselves along the security fence to wait. It seemed they were going to take a back-seat. The police presence, however, did seem to restrain the invaders because when, later that day, the police had gone, they started brandishing their axes. Negotiations were breaking down at the end of the first day. Talks were going in circles. The invaders still expected Jack to sign over the farm to them. Meanwhile work on the farm had come to a standstill as, apart from Winston, the workers kept a low profile. They had their wives and children to protect. As the sun went down the invaders retreated some distance and set up camp for the night. Jack went in behind the security fence and locked it. This night's sleep was even more disturbed than the one before. He spoke to Sally on the 'phone and admitted that he did not know how things were going to go.

The next day the invaders were back at the gates, singing again. When Jack went out they made fists in the air. They had a new spokesman, a man wearing pink-framed spectacles and holding an axe. The negotiations again went around in circles. By late afternoon Jack was getting more and more anxious about not being able to get on with farm work yet he was not complacent about the threat 'these people' posed. Their mood was turning ugly.

Then, when Winston had gone away to his quarters to check on his family, a small group of invaders tackled Jack and threw him to the ground, face down. He had no means of protecting himself and he expected the worst. 'I thought I was a goner,' he said afterwards. 'The worst thing was I couldn't see what they were doing. But I felt it.' They tied his hands together behind his back with some rope and they started beating him with sticks. 'I thanked God they were not using the axes.' And then, suddenly, the beating stopped. Jack turned over on his side and watched. Winston was talking to them in their own language Aching and bleeding as he was there on the ground, he saw them turn and walk away across the farm and into the bush. They moved on to the horizon and were gone. He lay there until Winston came and cut the rope around his hands.

'What did you say to them Winston?' Jack forced the words out from his pain.

'Baas, I tell them we support the Government.'

'That's not true and, anyway, it wouldn't stop them.'

'They haven't stopped, Baas. They have gone to get more comrades and guns. They will be back, I'm telling you.'

'Get me up, Winston.'

Winston helped him struggle back to the house and the foreman's wife came in to treat the baas's wounds with herbal medicine. When he was feeling more like himself, Jack called Sally to tell her what had happened and what was going to happen. She and the children returned but fear had come to settle on the farm. Independently and together, Jack and Sally decided to leave and to come to Britain where the children would be safe from Zimbabwean strife. It was a decision Jack would have to keep making all his life.

*   *   *

Jack was not crying but he was near it. And he was angry. Bernard was deeply affected by Jack's story and curious about Zimbabwe. He kept plying Sally with questions about the landscape and the way of life. After a while he went outside with me for a cigarette. We lit up. He inhaled deeply and I noticed his fingers were stained with nicotine. Soft, artist's hands, but big with chunky knuckles.

We were silent for a moment, and then he said, 'We've just heard a tragic story and I was the only one to respond.'

'You're right,' I said. 'The thing is that we've heard it so many times before. We're more worried about Jack not having anything else to think about, to talk about. He seems to find it impossible to live in the present.'

'I would be depressed too if I'd had to go through that. He was brave. How long ago did it happen?' Bernard persisted.

'Four years ago. The thing is there's a gap growing between him and his children. They're now so British and were too young to remember much of their departure from Zimbabwe.'

'I wouldn't be so sure.'

'It's like bereavement isn't it? People come through bereavement in different ways. Sally, I, and many Rhodesians have had to come to terms with losing our childhood homeland.'

'I have some relatives in Harare. They'd rather die than go through what you've been through,' said Bernard.

'I sometimes wonder whether I should have stayed.' This was true.

'I remember Smith declaring UDI. What I thought at the time was that it was a brave and foolish thing to do, to tell the motherland, Britain to go jump. That's to put it politely.' He gave a half-laugh.

'I'll never forget it.'

'You must have been a schoolgirl.'

*   *   *

On the morning of November 11th 1965 we went to school as usual; dad to teach at his high school and I to mine. Mum was playing bridge at the Hall's. Mrs. Hall was a most important member of the community as her husband was the managing director of an engineering company. I cycled along the track that led to the school and Sam came bounding out of the crowd of milling schoolgirls to meet me. I remember she was elated that morning because her parents had just bought an Alsatian puppy and she was describing to me how gorgeous it was, with great big soft puppy paws, wanting to play. It didn't have a name yet. Quite a few people in Bulawayo had Alsatians as they were considered good guard dogs.

Assembly was as usual. Pupils sat in rows on the floor in the gym. The headmistress was large, formidable and very strict. She conducted all assemblies and no-one dared even fidget. She had prefects standing along the sides of the hall, myself included. We sang rousing hymns. 'Fight the good fight with all your might' was one that frequently came up. The rows of young, white faces, each a potential Christian soldier. There seemed nothing out of the ordinary about that day, a day that, in effect, would change our lives. A fiendishly hot day, a day spent sweating in the classrooms with windows wide open. A day when our Latin teacher burst into tears and walked out of the class. Sam and I spent break-time eating cream doughnuts bought from the tuck shop and discussing the teacher's walk-out. We felt sorry for her.

Each day we started school early in the morning and ended at lunch time. Swimming was the last lesson on our timetable that day; taken by Mrs. Knox, one of the gym teachers. She came from England but was as brown as a person of mixed race. Except on formal occasions, the gym teachers wore different coloured gym tunics, a whistle on a band around their necks and rubber slip-slops (that's what we called flip-flops) on their feet. Mrs. Knox wore her long hair severely tied in a ponytail on top of her head. We liked Mrs. Knox but we didn't like being made to do length after length of the pool. She knew that, and she didn't waste much time on the slow swimmers. There was a girl called Anne in our class who was her star swimmer. Mrs. Knox was training Anne for the inter-school championships. Butterfly was Anne's best stroke. She would rise and plunge, water fanning out behind her; while we did the required number of lengths, then gathered in a little group, wallowing, discussing why the Latin teacher had got so upset. And we talked about Sam's new puppy (later to be called Independence or Indi for short).

Mrs. Knox warned us that there was to be an important

broadcast and that we'd have to get out of the pool when she told us. At the appointed time the school siren sounded. Mrs. Knox blew her whistle frantically and the whole class clambered out, assembling on a stretch of grass, sitting around a transistor radio. Mrs. Knox was fiddling with the knobs, her ponytail hanging down over one side of her face.

Ian Smith, the Rhodesian Prime Minister at the time, with his war-scarred face, scrawny neck and thick Rhodesian accent, declared unilateral independence from Britain.

When the broadcast was over we'd practically dried off in the sun. Mrs. Knox did not comment on the broadcast. I suspected that the teachers had been told not to discuss politics at school. Everyone knew something big and important had happened but we were not clear about the consequences. There was the usual flicking of towels and goofing around. And there was a lot of teasing of a girl who had a crush on her friend's brother. This was news that appeared to rival the Prime Minister's speech.

It was at home that evening that I realized the full import of Ian Smith's action. Dad and mum were against UDI from the start. Had he known dad, the Prime Minister would have called my father a starry-eyed liberal. And mum went along with dad. They had never voted for Ian Smith and yet were fiercely patriotic. They were also full of respect for Her Majesty the Queen and dad had fought with the Allies in the Second World War. They were very sombre that afternoon and hearing them talk about the repercussions of that day, of that act, I began to feel desperately afraid. I phoned Sam and she told me she had a plan that she would tell me about the following day.

I didn't sleep well that night and awoke feeling stiff and battered but curious to find out about Sam's scheme. She said she would tell me at break-time. When the siren went for the break she tugged and pulled me out onto the verandah and sat me down on the cool step. She looked from left to right and behind to see if anyone had followed us. Her face was not only serious; it was showing a determined fighting spirit. She drew a map in the sand with her ruler.

Together we formed a plan that would save our families from the British bombs that we were expecting. It involved organizing tents and supplies and finding a campsite safe from wild animals. We would go to the Matopos until we were out of danger. This elaborate planning kept us going for some time, until, day by day, unable to get our parents to adopt our plan, we were persuaded that there would be no bombs.

*   *   *

The blood red velvet seats sloped down to the stage with lots of leg room between them. The cinema had an elaborate proscenium arch and lavish velvet curtains. Red, again. It was the only cinema in Bulawayo. It was November 1965, a week after UDI was declared. It could be said that the drama was off screen. Defiance, confusion and consternation had followed the Prime Minister, Ian Smith's announcement that the country was to break away from Britain. By all accounts, Ian Smith thought the British Government was two-faced. The British Government under Prime Minister Harold Wilson thought Smith was prevaricating and wanted complete assurances from him that Rhodesia would introduce the vote for all. At that time most Black Africans did not have the vote. Wilson wanted universal suffrage to be immediate and it would mean majority rule. As there were far more Blacks than Whites in the country this would mean a surrender of power by the Whites. The Rhodesian Government was dragging its heels and the Blacks were turning to communist powers for arms.

Daily life had gone along as normal since the Declaration, much to my surprise because Sam and I were convinced the British were going to bomb us. All the way through the film I was waiting for the sound of explosions. I considered the cinema a prime target. School had gone on as usual. Mum continued to play bridge. It was almost as if we were clinging to normality but, in stage whispers. My parents talked deep into the night. In reality, something terrible had happened. Britain had always been the motherland. We were like children leaving home after a quarrel. The green hills, the pomp and splendour of Britain had been ours by proxy. Cecil John Rhodes had been British and there were Rhodesians of pioneering stock who had braved a wild country and war with the natives, riding in ox-wagons to set up homesteads, city halls, shops and businesses in the name of the Empire. Rhodesians still believed the Empire was great, while Britons at home were retreating, and lambasting the suppression of indigenous populations. A small, isolated White group, we were left living in a time warp and now everything we regarded as daily and routine was under threat. Clearly, Ian Smith had the majority of the White vote or he would not be in power. He, like many Rhodesians, had fought for Britain during World War II and, like so many, he had risked his life, as an air pilot, 'for King and Country'. Many Rhodesians, my father included, had divided emotions. As young men they had fought for Britain; now they were defying the very country their fellow soldiers had died for.

We went to the cinema that Saturday afternoon, as a distraction. A western was showing, not normally the sort of cinema mum liked to watch. She had grumbled at the prospect but had come along 'to be sociable'. The auditorium was full of people and the front rows were filled with loud-mouths yelling comments to each other, parading 'I hate Wilson' stickers on the backs of their shirts, crackling crisp packets, showing off. We sat in the back row. Mum went in first, then dad, then me. I was fourteen at the time but dad made sure we still did things as a family. We sat down without crisps or popcorn or drinks.

There were many familiar faces amongst the people still filing in. Sam was sitting halfway down with her parents and her two brothers. She turned around and waved to me. I looked to see if Tony Masters, the boy Sam had a crush on, was there; scanned the heads for his sandy hair. But I couldn't see him. Mum's friends, Mr. and Mrs. Hall, arrived and we stood up as they eased past us to get to seats next to mum. I never thought I'd see them at a western but I guessed entertainment was scarce in Bulawayo and people needed light relief. A teenager in the front row shouted, 'Get on with it'. 'Why are we waiting,' grumbled another. Then came the chorus, 'Why are we waiting' and the front rows were stamping their feet. This continued after the curtains had opened and they went on to make loud comments all through the film, especially when there was a shoot-out or a stagecoach runaway.

I couldn't help comparing the western, drama depicting the days of pioneering in America, with the days of struggle and trek which brought the pioneers to Rhodesia. The pioneers from Britain must have been brave and adventurous, despite the bad press they get now. They risked disease and death to set up outposts of the Empire. The daring nature of their enterprise must have been a bit like risk-taking in the Wild West. They, like us, must have been supported by the knowledge of the motherland, Great Britain. How would pioneers guess that the motherland would change so dramatically while they were away in Africa? And the missionaries who came to Rhodesia still believed they had God on their side. They believed they were sent to convert the heathen natives. Missionaries are still at work, helping and educating Africans to this day.

Needless to say, the film ended with the hero riding off into the sunset. The curtains closed and music struck up. The cinema manager was going through the accustomed routine and playing 'God Save the queen' – our Queen, Elizabeth II. Normally, everyone would stand to attention. This time, however, there was consternation. 'God save our gracious Queen' Some people stayed seated defiantly; some sat because they did not know what to do. 'Long live our noble Queen'. The front rows began to empty with lots of nervous laughter, kicking of shins and banter. 'Long to reign over us'. The whole atmosphere was one of hurt and confusion. 'God save the Queen', but in the end, about a third of the cinema audience was standing out of respect for Her Majesty.

I took my lead from dad. He had shot to his feet the moment he heard the music of the Anthem. Mum and the Halls stood too. I felt embarrassed but I stood by dad's side and we stayed standing right through to the last 'God save the Queen'. Only when it had ended did we move a muscle. I looked at dad's face. It was angry and determined all at once. 'Never forget your allegiance to the Queen, Ruth,' he said afterwards.

Later on, management stopped playing the National Anthem in cinemas and other public places in this country under a rebel regime, Rhodesia.

5

'**Y**ou have a knack of making me talk about myself, Bernard. What about you? For instance, what kind of paint do you use?'

'It varies. Pastels mainly, and oils. But I'm not on a sales trip. You have many fine paintings already.'

'You won't mind my asking, why are you here with Henri and where is your wife?'

We were still standing outside near the kitchen, even although we had finished our cigarettes.

It was almost dark and the lights had gone on in the house.

'I'll answer your second question first. My ex-wife, her name is Fiona, and I have been divorced for some time,' he said in an almost matter-of-fact way, then dismissed the subject, probably as too deep for the time being. 'Your second question was why am I here with Henri? The answer is because Henri is a collector of my paintings and because Henri presumably wanted to bring a man. Also, you did not object to having me.'

'I don't object at all.'

The outside light, above the kitchen door, had been turned on and we saw each other smile.

'You won't mind if I take some photographs of the estate while I'm here?'

'Go ahead.' It did occur to me that he should ask Max's permission but I let that pass.

Just then somebody, probably Pip, let Brindle out of the back door. Instead of racing to where we were standing on the gravel, she ran down the front drive, barking furiously. A rustle in the darkness suggested that something or somebody was slinking away in the foliage that lined the driveway. Somebody could have been hiding behind the great clump of bamboo next to the outhouses. We went down the drive. Brindle was right down at the oak tree by then, ceaselessly barking. The tree was a magnificent silhouette in the moonlight. The moon was nearly full in a sky of sparkling stars. Then Brindle stopped barking and ran back to us. Whoever it was, he was off her territory. After some moments of hesitation, we decided that we had been imagining the presence of an intruder and that Brindle had been giving a false alarm. As we were walking back over the gravel my ankle gave way and I stumbled, clutching on to Bernard for support. He caught me and it seemed logical that we should then hold hands until we reached the back door when, by mutual consent, we let go and went inside.

The house was alive with activity. Sally was taking used dishes through from the dining-room to the kitchen and already had the dishwasher on. Henri had painted a large and eccentric donkey on some card and she was whirling around blindfold in the conservatory, playing 'Pin the Tail on the Donkey' with the children. The tail was a brown shoelace. The donkey was hanging from a picture hook, the picture having been temporarily removed. Bumbling around, egging the children on, she was like a big schoolgirl.

Max was sitting in the conservatory, drinking a liqueur, and he offered one to Bernard who politely refused but sat down to talk to Max. Under the conservatory lights, the plants were shining with the oil that Heather had rubbed on the leaves. Pride of place went to the gigantic yucca plant that thrived in the warm atmosphere and the light. There were Red Grenadier pelargoniums, blue and white lobelia, exotic leaves in large ornamental pots. The donkey hung above a pot containing lavender, which was in danger of being kicked by Henri. Briefly, I was aware that anyone lurking behind the hedge would have a view of us as though we were on a stage, acting out a brief moment in history. I wondered again what Brindle had been barking at. I glanced around to see where she was and saw her sleeping peacefully in her basket.

Pip let out a mixed squeal and giggle. Henri had pinned the tail on the donkey's ear and she stood, with the blindfold around her neck, pretending to be flabbergasted. Then she grabbed Robbie by the shoulders, overwhelming the shy child. 'It's your turn, laddie,' she said, firmly tying the scarf around his head, putting the shoelace tail, with the pin on the end, in his hand and twirling him around. His mouth gave him away. He was reluctant to take part. It was Pip who persuaded him to play the game.

I thought I'd better go through and help Sally clear up. When I got to the dining-room I saw that she had nearly finished the job. All that remained was to store the leftover salads and meat in the fridge and to wash the empty serving dishes.

'Where's Jack?' I asked her.

'He was helping me here. Then he went to bed.'

'Bernard and I were having a fag outside the kitchen door. We didn't see him.'

'No. He has just gone now. Asked me to say goodnight. I must put the children to bed soon, too.'

'Oh, don't. They're having great fun, although Henri is a bit overpowering for Robbie, I think.'

'Pip gets hyper if she doesn't get her sleep.'

Just then Pip came bursting through, triumphant because Robbie had pinned the tail on the donkey's rear end. Sally judged that a fitting end to the game and we gave the proud and bashful boy a tube of Smarties as a prize. Sally took the two of them across to the cottage, saying they'd all come across in the morning. I noticed that she had cleared away the painting equipment, leaving two, presumably finished, paintings out to dry. Robbie's one, that he had signed, was of a man's face. It wasn't his dad, or Max, or Bernard. The face and body were black.

The others were now in the sitting-room. I could hear Henri's loud voice as I went to join them, sitting in one of the armchairs with Brindle at my feet. Todd had taken a liking to Bernard and was sprawled in his lap. Henri was lambasting the war in Iraq. She went on for another half an hour or so, dictating her views, riding roughshod over what any of the rest of us had to say. It had been the same in our Edinburgh days during the Winter of Discontent, when Britain and Henri were contemplating the election of their first ever woman prime minister, Margaret Thatcher. Then, Henri had been divided between her support for the Conservative Party and her suspicion of a woman coming to power. Nonetheless, she had been just as forceful in expressing her opinions. Then, as now, they were urgent times.

George and Susannah tried to change the subject to their winter skiing trip to Switzerland, and to amuse us with a description of how Susannah had broken an ankle when she fell whilst attempting a black run. They had tales to tell about the après-ski and about the characters they had met. One of them was a French woman from Paris, whose name was Florence something or other, who was there with her son. According to them, she had been very charming. I wondered what was up with Max when he laughed too loudly at George's description of how he fell off the button lift, unlike Susannah, escaping injury. Later that evening I would understand the coincidence, understand who Florence was and how he related to her. Meanwhile, the conversation was being bulldozed by Henri. These ski tales were but an interlude because she soon steered us back to politics, back to Iraq. I heard her but will let you imagine what she said because, as an immigrant, I do not feel I have the right to recount such criticism of the British Government. She let her words ride on her emotion. It was a way she had of becoming intense, obsessed by this subject. She wasn't listening to anyone else's opinion until Nicky arrived with some light relief. He came in, having been playing music in his bedroom. 'Don't forget, you lot, that love conquers all.' He smiled.

'That's a bit simplistic, Son,' said Max.

'No. Love is all you need. Have you forgotten the Sixties, Dad?' He whistled for Brindle and went to let her out the back door and into the garden. Then he came back into the room. Todd seemed to take this as a cue to stretch out on Bernard's lap, leap down and stalk off through the cat flap and into the night. I set about making coffee.

I was getting out the mugs when I realized Henri had followed me and had shut the interleading door, presumably so that Max, Bernard and Nicky couldn't hear us.

'I've got a letter here. It's for Max, but I want you to see it before I give it to him.'

'If it's for Max, then it's not for me to see.'

'But it concerns you and he won't show it to you.'

She held out an ivory envelope with one word written in calligraphic writing – *Maximilian*. My curiosity got the better of me. I took it and drew out the letter carefully. Henri must have steamed open the envelope before then. It was a short letter on a piece of ivory-coloured paper, executed in the same elegant handwriting. The whole thing had an old-fashioned feel about it.

1ˢᵗ July 2004

My Dearest Maximilian,

My love for you grows more and more the longer we are apart. All those wasted years! To think we had it right when we got engaged in 1976. I knew we were in love but I was (just like me) trying to be sensible. That was what led me to make the decision that we were too young to marry. How difficult it is to make decisions in life and to make the right ones. Jean-Paul always said that I wasn't afraid to make decisions; the problem is, he would say, that I make the wrong ones. But, he added that he couldn't agree that I had made the wrong decision in marrying him. All this said with a smile. He did, at least, have a sense of humour. I must confess that I do miss him. Where would I be without you and my children?

I wonder how Ruth feels. Does she know that we are seeing each other? You tell me that your marriage has grown stale but I would not like to hurt her. You also said not to email or phone. Does this mean that you are still keeping me a secret from her? I can keep the secret, but not forever. I think that by sending this letter through Henri I will not be risking her finding out.

Hurry up September! It is not so far away now Mon Cher. You just tell me what you would like us to do while you are here and we will do it. I've warned the children to keep, as you say in English, a low profile. You see, my childhood spent in England still stands me in good stead. What would I do without being able to talk to you in your mother-tongue? You know I laugh at your French. I must be fair; it's not really that bad! But no more words now, my love. Imagine a kiss. That is better than a thousand words.

Loving you always,
Florence

I was stunned, silent for a while, re-reading snatches, before I blurted out, 'Max lied.' I struggled for breath. 'He told me that Florence had died in a car accident.' Reading that handwriting, seeing that name was like being drawn into a place of unreality. The best way to describe it is by comparing myself to someone who can't tell the difference between a character in TV soap and the actor as a person in real life. It was as if my favourite character had been killed off and the next day I met the actor in the street, alive and well. No walking corpse but a healthy human being. My sense of what was real had become severely distorted by this 'resurrection'. The story he told me before we were married must have been untrue. Florence had not died at all. She had broken off the engagement and he could not face the public rejection so he 'killed her off' in his imagination and had lied to me.

'Florence is as alive as you or me and living in Paris,' said Henri.

'And she is expecting to see him again,' I said slowly. 'Why have you shown me this, Henri?'

'Because I didn't want to be a courier for an underhand relationship.'

'He said he went to France to see Lawrence. How could I be gullible enough to swallow that story?'

What little trust I had in Max was ebbing away. I felt a great weight entering my body and draining down to my legs making them awkward and artificial. My hands were shaking as I put the letter back in the envelope and secreted it in the pocket of my apron, which was hanging behind the cupboard door. It would be safe enough there.

It surprised me that Max hadn't mentioned seeing Florence in his diary. Now that I realized this, I felt I could not trust even the diaries. At the same time, reading Florence's letter made me aware of how much I needed to pry.

'Where's the coffee? Are you women gossiping?' It was Max himself. I looked at him as though he were a character in fiction, in a movie or television series, anything other than flesh and blood. At that moment, I couldn't give him a human nature. I couldn't voice my reaction to the letter. His lies were consuming. He was the fabrication of himself. To cover up my feelings, I tried to become practical and get on with the job in hand but I let Henri carry the tray of coffee mugs because my hands were shaking too much.

I don't know what they said while we were drinking coffee. All I could think of was the letter and when to confront Max. I also thought of Bernard holding my hand as we were walking up the drive together. Somehow that seemed a moment of sanity to me. The worst thing was that I had to share a bed with Max that night. When Bernard wanted to go up to bed, the rest of us went to our own beds as well. Henri wanted an extra pillow, a glass of water and to be shown where the bedside light switch was.

'Are you going to give him the letter?' she whispered as I was about to leave her room.

'Tomorrow.'

She seemed very keen for me to tackle Max. Was she looking forward to the argument that would inevitably follow? Why had Henri come to me with the letter? Did she really want to see our marriage flounder?

I hovered outside Max's bedroom door. The daft thought came to me that I should knock. I brushed that aside and entered quietly, hoping he would be asleep. A bedside light was on at my side of the bed. He was awake, sitting up in bed, a T-shirt covering his torso. The rest of his body was concealed by the voluminous maroon duvet.

'I've been thinking,' he said as I struggled to undress and put on my nightie with as little flesh showing as possible. 'I have a mind to build an extension with extra bedrooms. It's absurd not having enough room for this small number of guests.'

'Haven't you enough property already? Four houses in the Borders, not to mention a farm, property in Jedburgh and three flats in Edinburgh.' I slipped under the duvet and lay on my back near the edge of the mattress, my arms crossed.

'You're missing the point. Property needs to be maintained and upgraded. I could build out beyond the sitting-room. Two bedrooms and a bathroom. To finance it I could sell the property in Jedburgh. God knows, Graham wants to release his capital. That would more than pay for the extension. Or else I could use George's loan money. Then you wouldn't have to share a bed with your husband and practically fall out onto the floor while you're doing so.' He laughed, scornfully, pulling the duvet further up against his chest.

'I'm finding this a little strange,' I said.

'Don't worry. I'm not going to touch you. Far be it for a husband to touch his wife,' he said sarcastically.

'And it's all right for a husband to touch another woman?'

'Don't start that again. What is a man expected to do if his wife won't give him conjugal rights?'

'You forfeited the rights you had when you betrayed me.'

'Have it your way. I just hope you're not going to disturb me tonight with your strange sleeping habits.'

'I'll try not to. But before you go to sleep, there's something I want to speak to you about. Tomorrow, in private.'

'I'll write it down. Appointment with wife.' He mimed writing in the air. 'Now I'm going to sleep. Be a good girl and turn off that light.'

I slept for some hours then found myself wide awake with Max sleeping noisily at the other side of the bed. He was obviously having a dream that involved some conflict. I left him to his restless sleep and went downstairs where the house was awash with the early light of dawn. I made myself a cup of tea and dared to light a cigarette in the kitchen. Using a saucer as an ashtray, I inhaled deeply, concentrating on nothing but that and my tea for a few minutes. Brindle had opened one eye but refused to have her sleep disturbed. She was used to me and my nocturnal ways.

I went to the cupboard and got out Florence's letter and read it again. As I held it in my hand, I started to feel odd. The calligraphy was so perfect and the English so good. I began to think it was just someone's concoction. After all, Max had told me the woman was dead. There was no address. Was that just casual? Max knew her address. It was dated July 1ˢᵗ, a little more than two weeks before. How did Florence know that Henri would be in touch with Max? Is that why Henri had invited herself for the weekend? My mind began to spin. I was confused. A woman who had been reported dead was alive and had seen Max in the spring when he had been to France, alone. And she expected him to visit her again. Max had once shown me a photograph of Florence. She was extremely pretty, with long auburn hair and the wide-eyed look of a child. I had felt sad at her passing and sympathized with him. He had never gone into graphic detail about her death. A car accident. He hadn't said where or how, or who she was with. It had seemed crass to ask questions. All the time Max was making it up. But Max was a lawyer. He was supposed to seek the truth. It was his job. That's what flummoxed me about the lies he had told me over the years, about the lies he told when he was concealing his affair with Grace. Max was so solid, secure and approachable in appearance and so devious and false in essence. Who was this person I had married? Who was I?

I felt like tearing up the letter but instead folded it and put it in its envelope in the apron pocket. I flung the cigarette stubs in the bin and washed the saucer, spraying the kitchen with an aromatic room spray. Then I went to bed and slept for a few more hours.

*   *   *

By the time I got down to the kitchen that Saturday morning Max had gone to work and Nicky was preparing breakfast. Hot croissants for the majority, and bacon and egg for Henri and Sally. Robbie timidly asked for a boiled egg. Sally was laying the table. Radio Two was on and the doors were flung wide open. Brindle rushed to greet me. It was a warm, welcoming, living scene. Even

Jack seemed to blend into the busy quality of it. It was how I liked the kitchen to be – full of eager eaters and a meal prepared by my son. However, I was startled when I noticed that Nicky was wearing my red apron, the one with the letter in the pocket. I looked at him intently, trying to see if the letter was still there but could see no ivory corner sticking out of the pocket. I didn't know whether to ask him openly or to sneak up to him, give him a hug and, at the same time, feel in his pocket. He saved me the trouble of deciding.

'There was a letter in this pocket addressed to Dad and he'd gone to work so I put it on his desk.' He flipped over pieces of sizzling bacon.

'Did you read it?' I asked apprehensively.

'Of course not. In any case, what's it to you? What was a letter to Dad doing in your apron pocket, anyway?'

I looked to Henri for some help. She caught my eye and plunged in. 'I gave it to your mother to give to Max. She must have forgotten about it. You do know that this young man likes his egg boiled for three minutes, don't you?'

'I'll do it,' said Sally. 'You've got enough to do already, Nicky.' She found a pan, filled it with water and moved around him to put it on the hob.

Thus, the question of the letter was submerged in the priorities of cooking. Only I, and perhaps Henri, had not forgotten it. After a suitable interval, I slipped out and went into Max's study.

The sun was shining into the room that was dominated by a large mahogany desk with a green leather top. The walls were lined with tall cabinets and glass-cased bookshelves that held volumes of legal case histories, as well as a row of novels that Max particularly liked. Behind Max's chair hung an impressionist painting of the old walled garden as it had been when Max inherited the property. To the right of that was a glass-fronted cabinet, not holding books this time, but guns. They were displayed on brackets, mainly shotguns for pheasant shooting but at the top was a rifle and at the bottom, an antique pistol. Max was very proud of his great-grandfather's pistol, which he kept in working order, taking it with him to a gun club at occasionally. He would often say that he wanted to use his inheritance and that there was no point in living in a museum. He kept ammunition locked in a drawer that was part of the lower section of the cabinet. Spare keys were kept in the tallboy in the dining-room; all keys carefully labelled.

The letter was there, on the desk, facing his chair and I snatched it up, ran upstairs, my heart pounding, and shovelled it into my handbag. I would confront him in the evening. Meanwhile, I had to put it out of my mind, which wasn't easy.

The group had decided we would go out to visit some tourist spots in the Borders, starting with Trees Unlimited, a centre devoted to wood with play things for the children. Max was at work. Jack, who had been silent up until then, said he would stay behind to clean out the car radiator. Nicky said he and Cherie were going shopping. So, that left Henri, Bernard, Sally and the children and me to fit into my four-wheel drive. The trouble was that there was room in the back of my car for three people only.

'I'll sit on Bernard's lap,' announced Henri.

Bernard laughed.

'Don't be silly,' cut in Sally. 'I'll go in the back with Robbie on my lap. The seat belt will fit over us.'

'I was only joking. Bernard wouldn't want to take my weight. You all looked horrified. You should have seen your faces.' Henri laughed heartily. Then she insisted on going in the back, saying she was still shaken by yesterday's near accident. I couldn't imagine Henri being nervous for long. In effect, I was quite pleased with the arrangement because I had Bernard sitting next to me and we talked all the way to Trees Unlimited.

Pip leapt out of the car as if she had suddenly been allowed to breathe, having been squeezed between two large women on the journey. She ran towards the children's play area that was next to the car park, at the entrance to a long, two-storeyed building, which housed an exhibition centre and café. Pip's pigtails were flying as she headed for the swings and she was soon plunging forward and then riding backwards, legs tucked in, scooping the air. Then, almost as soon as she had reached her peak, she lost interest and let the swing die down. She rushed to the slide, the only play thing not made of wood. Meanwhile, Sally pushed Robbie gently on a swing. I felt an impulse to swing myself.

'Watch Pip for me, will you Bernard? She is totally without fear,' said Sally.

Bernard went over to where Pip was now 'tight-rope walking' along a wooden bar and I stayed with Sally and Robbie.

I had been fearless as a child, too. I had been the first to climb up to the big slide in a Bulawayo park; the first to climb inviting trees; the first to race downhill on my bicycle. Mum heard about the latter and put a stop to it, saying that young ladies didn't do that sort of thing. As well as the imprint of mum's interventions on behalf of decorum, I wondered whether the recent, creeping fears had to do with my growing older. Whatever it was that brought them about, I had undoubtedly gained fears in adulthood. Nicky would tease me about it.

'It's good to see Pip's *joie de vivre*,' I said to Sally.

'Do you think so? Sometimes she goes too far. She's had several broken limbs and that doesn't stop her. You'd think my son would be the daredevil. He's quite the opposite, as you see. I worry about them both.'

'Worry seems to go with parenthood. It's not exactly helpful. Nicky is always criticizing me for it.'

'Concern is essential and so is care. When a mother worries it is because she can't do anything about the problem. I can't change the innate character of either of them.'

'This leads us to the old nature, nurture debate. But before we get involved in that let's go and have a cup of tea. We'll also have to find out where Henri is.'

Pip came away in one piece from the play area; and she and Robbie went upstairs in the centre, to where there were games made of wood. Henri, it turned out, had been watching a film about the work of the centre and she'd also been around an exhibition. She'd bought a walnut coffee table that she was going to collect on her way home.

Over tea and cake, we chatted about children. Henri was the only one who did not have any children but she confessed she had thought about becoming a single parent. 'I decided there would be too much responsibility,' she said. Then the children themselves gathered at the table, Pip wanting to know what was happening next. We were to follow the blue arrows that would take us on a short walk around the estate. Pip appointed herself arrow-spotter with Sally, Robbie and Bernard walking briskly behind her along the rough path. Henri lagged behind with me. She clearly wanted to talk to me.

'Have you shown him the letter?' She dug me in the ribs with her elbow.

'Not yet. I've got it here in my handbag. I wanted to think through what I'm going to say to him.'

'You ought to show him, to get it out in the open.'

'Short of going to his office in town, I'll have to wait until tonight. In any case, your part in the matter is over.' I was annoyed.

'I'm not just the messenger, if that's what you mean. I'm involved because I know the contents of the letter and it concerns old friends.'

'What gave you the right to read the letter, Henri?'

'I think Florence wanted me to read it. What you must remember is that I chose to give it to you and not to Max.'

I thought this was a mixed blessing. Did I really want to know about Max's deceptions? The relationship was difficult enough as it was. I wanted the letter to be a fake because I had believed my husband had changed since Grace and was, at least, being honest with me. I still wanted to deny the authenticity of the letter and to believe that Henri had written it herself in order to get to Max, whom she so obviously adored.

'Yes. Thank you,' was all I said and she was completely oblivious to my thoughts.

'That's better, old girl.' She slapped me on the back and hurried on ahead to catch up with the others. I saw her stop and have a short conversation with Bernard who had been taking photographs with his digital camera. He, too, got a slap on the back before she trundled on, rocking over tree roots.

'Do you paint from photographs?' I asked as I caught up with Bernard.

'Generally speaking, yes,' he said.

We fell into step. I wanted to tell him about the letter, about Grace, about Max and his oppressive behaviour, about wanting to leave, about Nicky whose young lover was going to be taken from him. Yet, my thoughts were too full and I was silent.

Eventually, he said, 'There's a coolness between you and Max.'

'Max doesn't show his feelings.' I automatically tried to cover up.

'That's not an honest reply.' He stopped and looked directly at me.

'We try to keep up appearances.' I offered this as an excuse but I was crumbling under his gaze. I even felt the first prickle of tears. 'It's a long story,' I eventually said.

'Let's go back to the beginning and simplify matters. Is there a problem between you and Max?'

'Yes. I'm thinking of leaving him. Have been for a long time.' The tears were trickling down my cheeks and he offered me a clean white handkerchief.

'I'm sorry,' he said, 'I didn't realise you were so unhappy.'

'Fourteen years ago Max had an affair with his secretary which I found out about. We decided to stay together because of Nicky. We have carried on out of duty, but I don't know how much longer I can continue. Nicky has grown up now, but that doesn't make as much difference as I thought it would.' I told him about Cherie going to America. It was the first real secret I confided to Bernard. I thought of telling him about the letter, but stopped short of that.

'Your lifestyle, does that suit you? A big house and lots of entertaining.'

'It's not such a big house and I have my freelance writing business. You've seen only one side of me.' We started to walk again. I'd stopped crying. On impulse, I told him about the lifestyle of my Aunt Marijka and how, in the back of my mind, she would always be my role model.

Marijka was my aunt but not a blood relative. She was my father's brother's wife. She was a dynamic, demonstrative person, Dutch by descent, and she was a potter. The first time I became aware of Marijka in any real sense was on my fifth birthday. My admiration for her was inspired by the present she gave me. The other gifts had been dolls, games, jigsaws, a battery-operated monkey. I accepted them with pleasure, but then my mother handed me a box wrapped in brown paper. I opened it. Embedded in straw, inside the box, was a pottery pig money box with my name written on one side. She had made it for me. It was pale cream, with ears, nose, tail and writing in terracotta. It had a small plug under the tummy so I could raid the bank if I wanted. While I was still a child Marijka's presents continued to surprise me and to awaken something in me. They were not just pottery but also natural artefacts such as a rigid piece of seaweed sprayed gold or a large shell she'd found that allowed me to listen to the sea. They told of another world of richness allied to creativity. They put me under her spell. As time went by I began to write poetry and I sent some to her Cape Town home for her to read. She was very frank. Some she liked and others she sent back with expletive deletives. The way Marijka swore as a part of her conversation fascinated me. Mum and dad never swore or, shall I say, only in the most trying circumstances. Even then, the only word they used was 'bloody'.

Marijka's home in Cape Town reflected everything she was. I remembered whitewashed walls, a courtyard at the back and leading off it a room that housed her kiln. Pebbles and shells were scattered around the courtyard and, in the middle of the paving, was a circular bed for a miniature orange tree. In contrast to the light shining on white outside, the interior of the house was shadowy. Pots were strewn about the public rooms alongside trinkets from the market, and African prints hung like tapestries on the walls that she had painted a colour that was a blend of pink and brown. The prints were a riot of colour combinations, such as purple and yellow, red and orange. She had made curtains of them, which hung over interior doorways. She would pour us tea from a brown pottery teapot into pottery mugs. 'The way you like your tea is just piss,' she would say when I asked for weak tea.

The strange thing about her abundance of creativity was that it came along with destructiveness. She could damn a person in just a few words and she was self-destructive. She would go for days without eating, just drinking out of demijohns of rosé wine. This became a pattern after she had divorced my uncle and after the one man she really loved in her lifetime, Thomas, died of cancer. This was after she herself learned she had terminal cancer and she was living in severe pain.

She had a great many friends; a lot of them people of mixed race, which was unusual in South Africa in that day and age. As I grew up, I saw her infrequently but loved her and her influence never left me, even when I went in a completely different direction.

Bernard, who had been listening silently to my description of my aunt, spoke up. 'You think I might reflect Marijka's lifestyle?'

'I'm not as romantic as I once was. When I was younger, I didn't see her poverty although I did notice her pain.'

'Max would not understand your admiration for this woman.'

'No.'

'You must come and visit me sometime. On your own. Without Max.'

'I'd like that.'

He took my hand and pulled me gently into the trees by the side of the path. With my back resting against a tree, he very briefly brushed his lips over mine. I closed my eyes, waiting for more and he gave me more. It was a long time since I had felt such intensity, a feeling that made me want to give this man something of me that he could take as pleasure.

However, the moment passed and I became aware of my conscience. 'I'm a married woman,' I pleaded with him.

'Are you happy?' He remained standing, very close, and everything in me wanted to submit to whatever would be.

I never found out what could have happened next because Pip appeared through the trees. 'Mum says to hurry up. We're tired of waiting.'

We hurried along the path to the end of the trail where Sally, Robbie and Henri were waiting.

'What has happened to you, Ruth? You look inspired,' said Sally.

I looked at Pip. If she were going to say anything she'd say it then and there. But she was pulling on Sally's arm, ready for the next event of the morning, apparently innocent and ignorant of our grown-up behaviour. 'Let's go,' she said to Sally. 'I want to go.'

Sally's remark about my appearance threw me, even as I smiled at her, not replying. I may have looked glowing but inside I was in turmoil. I had betrayed my husband just when I was about to accuse him of betraying me. Strangely enough, Bernard's kiss made me confident and all the more determined to confront Max. With the letter in my bag, I was impatient for the evening to come, when my husband would be back from work.

I couldn't escape the feelings Bernard had aroused. Sex had

been dormant in my body; sex had been taken away from me at an early age. Max and I had shut out our love life, scarcely touching. I had turned away from him as though he were spoiled goods. And he? Perhaps he had casual lovers? I could not see him remaining celibate for all that time. Living together but separate as we did, I wanted love. Now, this kiss from a man I hardly knew awakened all the feelings I had tried so hard to suppress. It had seemed so natural. For that moment, I had felt as if I had a right to it. Then, for the following hours I tussled with my conscience. I had no right to kiss a man who wasn't my husband. Although the sensation of my body as an object of desire was wonderful, my conscience triumphed. I decided to put a stop to any further physical contact with Bernard.

*   *   *

I drove fast. We were going towards a town called Galashiels that was situated just off the route to Edinburgh. Sally wanted to get a digital camera for Jack, like the one Bernard had. We were heading for Argos in the town centre and we would have lunch in the town.

On the journey Henri was regaling Sally with stories about her father. Henri adored her father. Some said that was why she hadn't married. His name was James Houston and he was a remarkable man, according to her. He had come from a wealthy family and did not need to work. However, instead of going to university, like his peers, he had started working as a bricklayer. Ten years later he was head of a large construction firm, expanding internationally, and he had doubled his fortune.

'He's seventy-nine and he has just gone out and bought himself a sports car,' Henri told us proudly. 'You should see him in it, wearing a baseball cap, looking … well, looking my age. Mummy disapproves. She thinks he is going to have a heart attack at the wheel.'

'It could happen,' said Sally.

'It could happen to anyone,' replied Henri. 'That's what I love about him. He's not afraid to live. Everyone in this nanny state is so worried about seat belts, food additives, vaccinations and God knows what. You wouldn't think this country had been through two world wars.' She then began to boast about her father's valour in the Second World War.

After that, the conversation was divided between the back and the front of the car. Bernard, in the seat next to me, began talking as if that kiss had never occurred.

'There's a fair bit that I could paint here in the Borders,' he said, looking across to the hills lying near the town of Melrose.

'I still see its charm, even after all these years. Yet, there are things I miss about the city. If I hadn't met Max, I think I'd have been a city person. The buzz. The stimulation.'

'You've made big changes in your life. Some people don't move from the village where they were born. Others change continents but take their village mentality with them.'

'I've had a hard time hanging on to my Rhodesian qualities. It's not a very popular culture, as you know.'

'It's the individual that counts.'

'Racism comes in strange forms.'

'If it's any help, I find you exotic,' he ventured.

We passed the Borders General Hospital, on our left, and went around a series of roundabouts before we came to Galashiels, a town that vied with the slightly larger Hawick in a bid to attain the status of capital in the Borders.

The children were starting to become restless and probably hungry. 'Why have we come here?' asked Pip petulantly.

'To buy your Daddy a surprise camera and to have lunch,' answered Sally.

'Is there a McDonald's?'

'I believe there is but we're going to a small restaurant Auntie Ruth knows where they serve baked potatoes. You like baked potatoes.'

'I think we should go to McDonald's. Why are we buying Daddy a camera? I want a camera.'

'Shush, Pip.'

'You can have a shot at my camera, if you like, Pip,' said Bernard.

'Say thank you, Pip.'

'Thank you.'

We drove through the suburbs and found a parking place near the centre of town. Sally decided the priority was food so we went into The Sycamore, a small café where there were plastic flowers on every table and the tablecloths were pink under glass. A wind chime above the door tinkled as customers came and went. We found a table for six and enjoyed a meal of club sandwiches and baked potatoes. Henri dominated the conversation, with more tales of her family and silly jokes that were tame enough but still needed parental guidance.

Bernard and I had ordered coffee when Sally got up saying she'd go with the children to Argos. She seemed frustrated by the effort of trying to keep up with Pip. Henri decided to go with them, saying she would give advice on the best buys. I could see from Sally's face that she didn't actually want advice, but was too polite to say so. I gave her directions to Argos. It is a small town and they couldn't get lost.

'On our own again.' I couldn't help smiling at Bernard.

'Ruth, I feel as if I've known you all my life. I felt it the moment I arrived at Auld Oak Hall and you were before me, married to another man.'

'That's just the point. I *am* married to Max.'

'Fiona and I were divorced ten years ago.'

'Listen to me. We may have our problems, but Max and I cohabit at present, and part of the arrangement is that we are faithful.' I knew as I was talking to him that I wasn't being honest. If I left Max as planned, I would be free to form a new relationship, or new relationships, but Bernard's whole approach was creating a complication I couldn't deal with at the time.

'Is he faithful to you?'

'You should not ask me that.'

'I don't mean to interrogate you, Ruth. It's just that there is something between us. I'm not talking about something as idealistic as soul mates. I'm talking about a strong connection that I, for one, cannot ignore.'

'Bernard, I do feel attracted to you but the timing is wrong. There is something I can't tell you about. So please leave it at that. I would love to be your friend.'

He put a hand on mine and I felt the warmth and contradiction of this.

*   *   *

When we got back there was nobody in the house. No Jack. No Nicky and Cherie. Just the animals.

'It's time for hide and seek. Count to ten, and then come and find me. You too, Bernard,' said Henri who needed a boisterous game as much as the children did. She disappeared into the innards of the house. Bernard, Robbie and Pip stayed in the kitchen, closing their eyes and counting to ten. Then they were gone, chasing through the house with shrieks and warnings.

Sally and I went to the cottage to see if we could find Jack. He was there, sitting in a chair, gazing at the Gerard Bhengu painting of the old African man with his leopard skin clothing and hat, and his stiff, scratchy beard. Jack didn't even greet us. What he said was, 'His eyes follow you. You can be anywhere in this room and he will be looking at you.'

'Do you like that?' I asked.

'It's kind of protective. We're being watched over by a wise old African man.'

'And he has the beginnings of a smile. It's as if he is about to say something,' I said.

'He is looking at good and bad, and not judging,' said Sally.

Jack had fixed the car and seemed to have been sitting in that chair ever since, evidently glad to be alone. He hadn't bothered about lunch although I had told him to eat leftovers. Sally brought out the Argos packet and placed it in his lap. 'For you, because you're such a dear husband,' she said, eager to see a look of surprise and delight in his eyes.

'It's not my birthday,' he said gruffly, opening the bag and pulling out the box. When he drew out the camera he looked at it for some moments while we waited for his response.

'When people getting a gift say 'you shouldn't have', they don't mean it. I do. You should not have bought this for me, Sal. You know we can't afford it, even if my old one is knackered.' His eyes were dull and he was speaking heavily.

'But I thought …' Sally was dismayed.

'You thought you'd try and cheer me up. Get things in proportion, Sally. Would you rather have a digital camera or a farm in Africa?'

'It was my farm.'

'You know what I mean.'

There was a flickering of temper in Sally. 'Can't you at least try to like Britain? It has given us a home and our children a good school. If you took out that camera you could capture this exquisite countryside. It's not Africa but it has its beauty too.' Her speech slowed down as she implored. 'Can't you at least just try, Jack?'

I had kept very quiet and still during this conversation and I wasn't expecting to be included. However, Jack asked, 'And what does Ruth think?'

'I think you've changed, Jack. You used to be energetic and enthusiastic. The old Jack would have thought the camera a lovely present. Sally was so looking forward to giving it to you,' I said.

'But I can't pretend,' he said.

'I bet you that old man in the picture would say that there are times when we have to pretend. I'll leave you and Sally alone now but later on you must come and climb the hill with us. There are panoramic views from the top.' I left, thinking of how Jack used to be.

*   *   *

It was the beginning of winter in 1978. He was tall, muscular, bronzed and carrying a backpack. It looked as if every item of clothing he was wearing was new - khaki trousers, brown open-necked shirt, dark brown leather jacket. Jack was coming through the arrivals gate at Edinburgh airport. Adjusting the position of the backpack. Looking away. Now looking towards us. I ran to him and embraced him then turned around to see Max seeming amused.

'Max, this is Jack.' The two men shook hands and I was fascinated by the difference in the colour of their skins. Victorian British stock burned indelibly by the African sun and contemporary British pale in the airport light. At first, they didn't know what to say to each other. We stood there, jostled by people greeting and moving on, heaving luggage onto trolleys, carrying umbrellas and bags; backpackers on adventures; smart women in coats and wearing loud jewellery; businessmen hurrying to deadlines with briefcases and folded newspapers.

'They told me it would be raining in Scotland,' said Jack in an amateur attempt at weather talk.

'Then your informants won't be disappointed.' Max smiled.

'Come on, Jack, come and see Max's car.' We started walking through the long glass passage to the car park.

'I've come to see you, not a car.' He put his arm around my waist, as he used to do when we were younger.

'And bonnie Scotland,' I said.

We emerged from the passage into the rain. There was Max's Porsche 911 coupé, gleaming silver under spots of rain.

'Gee, is this it? Hell, it's a beaut.' Jack's arm left my waist and he spent half an hour talking to Max about cars, in the drizzling rain, while I sat in the front passenger seat for shelter both from the conversation and the weather.

We drove into the city and took Jack to his B&B where he did a quick turn around and we were off to lunch in one of the streets parallel to Princes Street. Edinburgh Castle stood imposingly above the shops and offices, faces of people in a crowd, the buskers, news vendors, cars, taxis, buses; the city buzz.

'I must have a shot of the Castle,' said Jack. He took his camera out of its case and took several pictures. Then he decided he wanted a couple of pictures of us so Max and I stood holding hands and saying 'cheese'.

'Gee, smiling should be easy. It's not raining.' He pulled us closer together, arranging our limbs like sandbags.

He stood back and, as he did so, there came the sound of a gun being fired. Jack grabbed both of us and hauled us into a crouching position behind a car. 'Heads down,' he ordered. He himself started to peer up to see the lie of the land. What he saw was pedestrians going about their normal business. No one else was crouching down to avoid danger. He was puzzled. 'What the heck was that?'

'That was the one o'clock gun up at the Castle. It goes off at this time every day.'

Max was straightening himself out and concealing laughter.

The only person who seemed to have noticed our dive for cover was an old man standing in a shop doorway. He was scratching the grey stubble on his chin and peering at us through thick lenses. 'Reminds me of when I come home from the War. I could nae hear a dog bark or a car backfire without jumping oot my skin. You'll get over it, son. Give me your hand man. We're unsung heroes.' After shaking hands he walked away, leaning heavily on a stick.

That night we went to the theatre to see Ibsen's 'Hedda Gabler' and Jack met Henri for the first time. She embarrassed him, but not herself, by making a pass at him. He did not really enjoy the play. As he said, he was a man of action and not a man to sit for hours in a theatre seat.

* * *

Jack had done ten lengths to my four. He ploughed through the water with brute strength and total concentration. We were at Edinburgh's Commonwealth Pool. I smelled the chlorine and sank into the sound of children fooling around, which rose like a wet echo to the high roof. I savoured the weightlessness. I floated out from my arms that were stretched out, hands clinging to the pool's edge; the water at its surface lapping against my chest. Jack stopped beside me, flicking water from his hair. His bronzed torso was gleaming wet. He took off his goggles. 'You're not giving up now, Ruth.'

'Just taking a break. I wasn't born to be as athletic as you.'

'Just a delicate flower,' he teased. 'My target is seventy-five lengths.'

Jack was then in his early thirties. As a boy he could be seen slaloming through poles on his bike, clambering up granite rocks, disappearing way ahead; the boy we only caught up with when he'd shinned up a tree and was way above us. The cousin I admired, to my mind, would always be eternally young. Now he was a soldier who killed for a living; in the throes of a war I didn't believe in.

'I dunno how you can live in a place like this where even the swimming pools are caged in.'

'You mean the weather?'

'Yes. But it sort of affects everything.'

'You haven't seen anything yet. Winter's only just begun.'

'And I don't want to see it. In two days I will be back home where I can breathe in fresh air and soak in the sun.'

'Then you'll go into the bush and get shot.'

'Ruthie, you're worried about me. You know what they say, and it's true – when your time's up, your time is up. And that applies to being mugged in a city or shot in the Rhodesian bush war.'

'You know it's going to become Zimbabwe?'

'Over my dead body.'

'I hope it's not going to be over your dead body. If it's not, what are you going to do?'

'It's my country. I was born there. That's what you people who leave are denying. Mark my words; anyone who takes the gap (leaves Rhodesia for good) is heading for guilt and regret.'

'Jack, I don't think we agree on politics. And if you feel so strongly, why are you here?'

'I'll let you into a secret, Ruth. I had a nervous breakdown and my folks advised me to take a holiday, to get right away. I'm not going back into the armed forces. So, now you know.' He chose that moment to plunge back into the water. I could hardly believe what he had told me.

Later, meeting up outside the main doors after changing, we were silent. I was still astonished at his revelation and I didn't know what to say. We began to walk towards the city centre. There was a constant trickle of people on the pavement and a stream of cars on the roads. The buses were moving light-boxes in the crisp, frosty night.

I was apprehensive about taking him to the pub on a side street to listen to jazz and have a pub meal. I loved the smoky, boozy atmosphere and the gutsy music. None of my Edinburgh friends would go to a place like this. It was important to me that Jack should share the pleasure. Once inside the pub, we struggled through the crowd to find a table. We learned that the evening was a tribute to Louis Armstrong and the band was playing songs like

'Hello Dolly', 'What a Wonderful World' and 'Lazy River'. The singer, with long crinkly hair, had a deep voice but not gravely like Satchmo. When it came to playing the trumpet, he was giving it his all. We got some beer and some food and settled down to be part of the mood - earthy and relaxed - only to find that the band was to take a break.

I decided to plunge in with a question I had long been hesitating to ask Jack, a question remote from his revelation of a nervous breakdown, which was a subject I didn't know how to approach. 'Why have you not married, Jack?'

'Never found anyone who would put up with me.'

'No, really. You've had lots of girlfriends.'

'It's kind of like I'm in love already.'

'What do you mean?'

'I'm in love with the bush. So, I'd be having an affair before she and I started. But you be less quizzy about me. Let me tell you about you. I'm going to say something you're not going to like. Are you ready?'

'Yes, okay.'

'Well, it's this. I don't think you should marry Max.'

I reacted quickly. 'He hasn't asked me.'

'Think about it. He's going to ask you. Even I can tell.'

'Why?'

'Because I can see the way he looks at you.'

'No, I don't mean that. I mean why shouldn't I marry him?'

'Now, don't get me wrong. He seems to dote on you but he doesn't know where you're coming from.'

'But, he has been to Rhodesia and ...'

'You don't understand. I mean you ...'

'He doesn't know me as well as you do. Is that it?'

'Something like that.'

Then the music resumed and claimed our attention. The band was playing 'On the Sunny Side of the Street' and that put an end to serious thoughts and discussion.

6

It was raining lightly as I went back to the house from the cottage. It was the sort of rain that sprinkles through bright light. It turned out to be the harbinger of more and heavier rain. I ran over the gravel and reached the dry indoors.

I'd only just closed the kitchen door when I heard a car speeding up the driveway. It was George and Susannah in an open-top Morgan. They parked alongside Henri's car and Susannah, a scarf tied under her chin, strolled over to the kitchen step where I was standing. George seemed unwilling to leave the car, a new acquisition of a classic model in white with red upholstery. The car made a statement about its owners, their interest in timeless superiority. The car spoke to me of indulgence and fun.

'Darling, it's so good to see you,' gushed Susannah. Her curly blonde hair had been tossed by the wind.

'Didn't you get wet?' I asked.

'What's a little bit of rain when you've got the open air and the wind blowing in your face? Never mind that. Do tell us how you are?'

'Fine. Fine, thank you.'

George now came over to us, carrying their bags. 'We would have been here earlier but for those ruddy speed cameras.'

'You should have seen Georgie nipping in and out of the traffic. He's already so devoted to his new toy.'

'Cost a bomb but she's worth it,' said George. 'What with one thing and another, we're now up to our eyes in debt.'

They laughed nervously and thinking about Max's intention, I felt a pang of pity for them. I imagined they were living to the limit, surrounded as they were by material possessions. George ran an antiques shop and their house was crowded with valuable antiques. Susannah was a full-time housewife, although they seemed to have decided not to have children.

'Come in out of the rain and meet some of my other guests. Jack and Sally are in the cottage. We've got a bedroom for you upstairs.'

'Darling Ruth, it's super to be here. A birthday celebration tomorrow. What fun!' enthused Susannah.

Henri and Bernard were stretched out in the conservatory while Pip and Robbie continued the game of hide and seek. Henri knew Susannah and George and I introduced them to Bernard. He stood up courteously.

'An artist. How absolutely sweet,' said Susannah. I could see Bernard cringe. I showed Susannah and George their bedroom, which Susannah pronounced 'cosy' but it would be cosier if I pushed the beds together and got some more pillows. She had brought some potpourri and she needed a container for it. I did what she asked and left them there because they said they wanted to freshen up. I mentioned that they should dress for climbing the hill, if they wanted to come with us, and I went back downstairs.

'When are we climbing the hill, then?' asked Henri.

'I thought we'd wait until the rain stopped,' I replied. I felt I had an obligation to my guests to keep them dry and sheltered.

'Who is worried about a bit of rain?' said Henri.

Getting ready to climb the hill, which was just over a thousand feet high, was a complicated procedure. Everyone needed to have the right footwear, particularly because there was mud on the lower slopes where cows came and went, trampling the wet ground. Susannah and George came downstairs and agreed to climb with us but she had brought only the flimsiest of footwear. It turned out that she had the same size feet as me so I was able to lend her some boots. Henri was the least difficult. She had brought sturdy walking boots. I raided the coat racks in the porch to see that everyone had a light raincoat. When Jack and Sally joined us, Jack carrying his new camera, I guessed that they had come to some sort of resolution and I was pleased. They each took a child by the hand and led the way, following my directions, heading across a field to the stile that brought us to the muddy patch on the lower slopes. The rain was easing up. In the beginning, Brindle stayed with me. Bernard soon moved away from the group to take photographs of the landscape. Pip let go of Jack's hand and climbed on ahead. Henri and Sally, with Robbie, were not far behind her. Jack hung back and we were soon bringing up the rear together. For the first time, I really took in the fact that his hairline was receding.

'There was a time when you'd be up at the front and at the top before all the rest of us,' I said. We had leapt over a small stream, were stepping onto springy, green heather and were weaving around prickly gorse bushes. There were no farm animals around.

'My daughter is doing it for me,' he said tersely.

'What has happened? You've changed, Jack.'

'You've already pointed that out,' he snapped. 'You know what has happened.'

'I'm sorry but you've been in this country for over four years and you still haven't adapted.'

'I'm a sponge, Ruth. I live on what Sally brings in. That's no way to gain your children's respect. Anyone's respect.'

'You *have* tried to find work.'

'I'm always looking for a job but my age is against me. I'm fifty-eight and they don't want to hear that I was in the Rhodesian army.'

'Can you blame them? You need to keep that quiet.'

'I do now. It took me a while to learn the ropes. Then I got a job cleaning public lavatories. I won't do that again. Anyway, they fired me for being too slow.' He stopped climbing and stood, looking me straight in the eyes. 'It's Sal. She has been a star but I don't know how much more she can take. She's always so busy and I'm so useless, dragging her down. The children … Pip is always on the go, never still. She exhausts me these days.'

'They love you.'

'And I them. It's just that I feel like I'm in a different world.'

'Have you been to a doctor?'

'Sal wants me to but I won't go. I don't trust doctors. All they do is pump you full of pills with God knows what side effects.'

'When I was depressed some years back I took anti-depressants and they helped,' I said.

'You seem to have recovered from leaving Rhodesia. You give

me the impression you're in love with all this.' He waved his hand across the view of hills and valleys.

'Yes. I am in love with all this, as you say, but I never forget Rhodesia or Zimbabwe.'

'That's just it. When they bloody changed its name it became a different country.'

'And the stories we hear of the present hardship of the people; elections rigged, houses bulldozed, soaring unemployment, low life expectancy … it's so sad. At present I have no desire to go to Zimbabwe but I often return to my memories of Rhodesia and my childhood there.'

'What would I go back to? Sal's farm is presumably now occupied by so-called veterans. We're here to stay but I'll be damned if I'll pretend to be British. They betrayed us.'

'How can you live in this country thinking this?'

'I'm just a bloody foreigner.'

'Jack, the war is over.'

'You always were on the side of the starry-eyed liberals.'

'If that means I did not support Ian Smith, I did not. It was his damn fool action that led to the chaos that is there now.'

'The change to majority rule would have happened. Only slower.'

'I don't want to argue with you, Jack. What's done is done.'

'You are right. The whole thing is hopeless.'

'That's not quite what I meant.'

We had been scrambling over knotted grass and stones, alongside a dry-staned dyke. I always congratulated myself on using the Scottish word 'stane' instead of 'stone'. It was like the pronunciation of Hawick as 'Hoyick' or being called 'hen' by the locals. These little things helped me feel I belonged, although I doubt whether many people would understand. We came to a fence and another stile. Jack climbed over first and then held out his hand to help me over. There was just the last steep stretch to climb. Susannah and George were approaching the summit. She was wearing pert denim shorts and he had on unsuitable pale trousers that, curiously, were not muddied. Pip was already at the beacon that stood at the highest point. As we looked up we saw Henri join her. Bernard was nowhere to be seen. Sally and Robbie were a short way ahead of us, Sally crouching down over her son.

'He seems to have twisted his ankle but I don't think it is serious,' she said as we came up to them. 'Will you carry him up the last bit, Jack?'

Jack reluctantly lifted Robbie and carried him piggyback to the top. Jack was still a physically strong man. Everyone was there, apart from Bernard. The top was, as the shape of an extinct volcano suggests - a circle of small, rocky outcrops, or mounds, with pathways in between. In the middle was a deep well of earth, grassed-over. The view was liberating. We could see Teviotdale, the Cheviot Hills, the Eildons near Melrose which we had seen close-up earlier that day. Other hills I didn't know the names of. Fatlips Castle. We lay on the grass, basking in the sun. The rain had held off, which made our rainwear redundant and a nuisance. Most of us had our jackets tied around our waists.

Bernard appeared from behind us and started taking photographs of us. I noticed that Jack had taken a panoramic view with his new camera and saw Sally smiling to herself at this. Bernard looked invigorated and unhurried as if he were used to roaming the countryside. There was nothing receding about his thick, brown hair and I was tempted to stroke his trim, tactile beard. Briefly, I regretted turning him away.

'I don't know about you lot, but I'm parched. I'm heading back down for a cup of tea,' said Henri. Having been one of the first up, she was refreshed. The children elected to go with Henri. Robbie's ankle seemed to be better. Brindle went with them.

Jack, Sally, Bernard, Susannah, George and I waited awhile, breathing in the fresh air, with the sense of achievement that goes with climbing even a small hill. Then Sally and I were left on our own because the others decided to descend.

'You spoke to him. What did he say?' asked Sally.

'We spoke about Zimbabwe and about living as a foreigner in Britain. He was very negative.'

'He is these days. I'm trying to get him to live in the present.'

'If only he could get a job. Some work outdoors, perhaps?'

As Sally and I clambered down, I had briefly forgotten the imminent showdown with Max who would be coming home from work soon. When we got back we found that Henri had made a pot of tea and was spreading butter and jam on the scones. Pip and Robbie had a story to tell us. 'She got stuck,' Pip said excitedly.

'Who got stuck? Was it Henri?' Sally asked.

'No. Silly. Brindle. We couldn't pull her out and we couldn't push her in,' said Pip.

The dog was lying in her basket looking perfectly serene.

'She was too big for the hole,' said Robbie, speaking up for the first time since he had arrived. 'She's too fat. You should put her on a diet. That's what Henri says.'

'Did I say that? Oh, well, I suppose I did,' said Henri, licking jam off her fingers. 'The thing was that Brindle was after rabbits. She went into a rabbit hole that was too small for her.'

'She couldn't even bark, she was so stuck,' said Pip. 'Henri had to scrape away the earth with her fingers, to make the hole bigger.'

'It doesn't look as if she has come to any harm,' I said.

'What an adventure.' Sally cuddled her son.

'The only things that have come to harm are my fingernails. I used your nailbrush to scrub them, Ruth. You don't mind?'

'Of course not. Where are the others?'

They were in the garden talking to Max, who had come home from work. They came inside, scraping mud off their boots at the back door. I quickly whipped some cream for the scones and we all went into the conservatory. Max strode around in his work suit and tie, the benevolent, jovial laird who appeared keenly interested in what we had been doing that day. I determined I would not delay in showing him the letter. I had been thinking about this and not paying attention to the conversation so that I was taken aback when he appeared in the conservatory doorway holding the pistol in both hands. He was not pointing it but cupping it, to show it off. He explained to them that it had belonged to his great-grandfather, holding it out so we could see its silver inlay, studded with tiny rubies. He assured us that it wasn't loaded.

Robbie was eager. He wanted to hold the gun that was then in Jack's hands. Jack let him handle it.

'Fine piece of craftsmanship,' commented Bernard.

'If you can't have a swagger with friends, who can you show off to?' said Max.

'It's worth a tidy sum,' said George, taking it and inspecting it.

'I don't think this is a men only thing. Let's have a look,' said Henri, whipping the pistol away from George.

'I used to sleep with one of these under my pillow in Zimbabwe,' said Sally. 'I mean, not an antique as such, but a pistol. We left all that behind, didn't we, Jack?' Jack grunted. 'Thank God, I never had to use it,' she continued. 'Goodness, it's a mighty fine piece of work.' She looked at it in Henri's grip. 'Could protect you from intruders, Ruth.'

Silence followed this remark and seriousness settled on the group. No-one, not even Henri, dared to aim the gun in jest.

'I think it should go back in its cabinet now, don't you, Max?' Even although I badly wanted the thing out of sight, my words were encouraging rather than controlling. I had learned to try and get my way by wiles rather than by orders.

'And you, Ruth? You've never touched it. Here. Have a feel.' Max pushed it into my hands. I quickly cupped them to receive it and held it as if I had been handed a spider. It may have been an antique but it was also a lethal weapon. Max was grinning at my reaction.

Bernard understood my confusion because he said to Max, 'Better put it away now, old man.' He stood up and lightly plucked the gun from my hands, giving it to Max, who then took it back to his study.

Our guests went to wash and tidy up, and I saw a space opening up, which would allow me to confront Max with the letter. However, the 'phone rang. It was Zoe wanting to find out if Nicky and Cherie were with us. She hadn't seen them since the morning and she was starting to worry.

'You haven't told them, have you?' she asked in a low voice as if talking about the secret were a secret itself.

'No. I promise you. I haven't said a word. They've probably gone to a friend's house.'

'I hope you're right...' She put down the receiver unceremoniously and I let the matter of the whereabouts of Nicky and Cherie drift to the back of my mind. Nicky was often away for long stretches of the day and night. He would turn up and say very little about where he'd been. I did, however, go and check to see whether or not his car was in the garage. It wasn't. I still thought Zoe was worrying unnecessarily. The pair of them might have gone to Edinburgh for the day.

It was nearing the time when I should start to cook dinner but I had to speak to Max first. I found him in his study, reading his mail. He had left the door open.

'I need to talk to you, Max.'

'Fire away,' he said, supremely ignorant of my purpose. 'But remember I've got Niall coming at six to look at this computer.' How like my husband to give me a deadline. It was always so. He wanted me to realize that he was a very busy person and that, by implication, I was not.

'And I've got dinner to cook,' I retorted.

'Then perhaps we should do this another time,' he said.

'No. It can't wait. I want you to look at this. Henri was to deliver it to you, but showed it to me first.' I handed him Florence's letter and he took it casually, drawing out the single sheet from its envelope.

'What's this?' he asked, with a patronizing smirk. As he read, I watched his face change from a look of indifference, to an enigmatic darkening, to a brooding anger. I felt that he was cornered, but I underestimated him.

'Where did you get this?' he demanded as if somehow I was at fault.

'Henri gave it to me. I told you.'

'Yes, but where did Henri get it?'

'It would seem, from your dead fiancée.' I enjoyed the sarcasm I put into that phrase. 'The one who has popped up from the grave.

The one who is alive and waiting to see you again when you go to France in September.'

'It's a fake.' He slammed his hand on the desk. 'Anybody could have written it; anyone who can use calligraphy. There's not even an address.'

'What I think is a fake, an utter lie, is your story that Florence died in a car accident. You are a lawyer, Max, and lawyers are not supposed to tell lies. I've swallowed this story for twenty-five years, just as I've put up with your arrogance and greed for all this time.'

'Hang on a minute. I've told you this letter is a fake. Why don't you believe me?'

'Because the facts fit. To start with, your little jaunts to France.'

'It could be that Henri wrote it. You know how she has always had her eye on me as a husband. You've persistently been in her way, Ruth. It could be a plot by her to break us up.'

'It doesn't need Henri to do that.'

He ignored my remark. 'Be realistic, Ruth. Henri takes the facts about my former fiancée and spins a web of intrigue that deals a hammer blow to an already cracking marriage. That leaves me free to marry someone else. Her. It's canny.' He was smiling at me, as if he had the solution.

'If Henri has created this letter, I'll get her in and we can question her,' I suggested and moved towards the door.

'No. Wait a minute. No need to involve our guests. It's not a very hospitable thing to do, accuse a guest of forging a letter.'

'That's because you know she didn't do it.'

He sat down and, very earnestly, pressed his hands together as if in supplication. 'We were very young and she was very beautiful...'

'And now? Is she very beautiful, now?'

He paused. 'Like all of us, she has matured. To get back to the point … we were in love and decided to marry. As you will understand, she had to get past mother. Well, she did that and I gave her one of mummy's antique rings. I met her parents in France and they seemed to approve of me. They'd lived in Britain for some time. Florence was brought up in this country. The wedding was to be in Scotland. Everything was arranged. Two weeks before the wedding was due to take place, Florence called it off. She packed her bags and went back to France.'

'To save face, you concocted the story of her car accident, of her death. Weren't you afraid she'd turn up in Scotland again?'

'I didn't think of that. The story wasn't planned. It just grew in my mind. I didn't tell it to just anybody. Only certain people. I began to think of Florence's disappearance as the result of some kind of accident. Then it became a car accident. The more I repeated this to myself the more I believed it and eventually, in my mind, she died. For a long time, she was dead to me.'

'It's more likely that you could not cope with the shame and embarrassment of being jilted, so you had to lie. But why to me, your wife? And why are you busy resurrecting Florence? Why are you going to France in September? It seems to me that we've been through most of this before, Maximilian,' I said, referring to Grace. I was angry but I managed to keep my voice down in deference to our guests.

Nor did Max raise his voice. Now he leaned back in his chair with a half smile on his face, looking as though he were a naughty child being chastised. 'It's not like that,' he said. 'It's not like that,' he repeated and then added, 'It's not as if we have sex any more.'

'Oh, I see. It's my fault. Our marriage is dead, Max. You've killed it.' My head was throbbing. All the time I was castigating him I was longing for a gentle man who would invite me to lay my head on his chest and who would stroke my hair.

'Ruth, this is not an appropriate time to discuss the future of our marriage when we've got guests.'

'That's it. Always thinking of appearances. In any case, they see through it.'

'That might be so. There's still no need to make a drama out of this.'

He didn't deserve a reply. I gave him a long, angry look. Then I turned and walked out of the door, tears running down my cheeks. Bernard was in the sitting-room reading a newspaper.

'Are you all right?' he asked.

'Yes. I'm okay.' I wiped my face roughly. 'Give me five minutes and I'm going to cook dinner.'

'Can I help?'

'Finish your newspaper. I'll call you.' I did not thank him for the offer but stumbled into the downstairs bathroom where I flung cold water on to my face, staunching further tears. The water ran coolly and I continued to slap it against my face, angry at myself for showing my emotions. I looked at my red eyes in the mirror. The rest of me was a blur that reflected my state. I could no longer stay with Max as my husband. I could not stay and I doubted that I could go. Fresh tears were welling as I held my own gaze. I was crying for Auld Oak Hall. With a conscious effort, I checked the flow. Lamb pilau. We were to have lamb pilau sprinkled with coriander and served with salad and yoghurt. This was to be one of the last meals I would cook in Max's kitchen. As soon as the guests had gone, I would leave. Until then, I would act as if everything were normal. The trouble was I felt exhausted. Here

I was, caught between the prospect of leaving and the prospect of staying, caught in a conflict of wills. What would it take for me to leave? Hadn't Jack and Sally left their home behind? It was like that – leaving all that was familiar and all that belonged in places, in corners of a room. The cooker they used. The fridge that hummed. The dining table they'd eaten off. The place mats. The kettle. The mugs and glasses. They'd left it all behind. Even the dogs. I'd take Brindle with me.

I had done this before – lost an environment and a history.

*   *   *

The doorbell rang and I knew it must be Niall come to look at the computer. I decided to let Max answer it. After all, it was his appointment. I wondered how he was reacting to our conversation. He was probably steely, determined not to let emotion overtake him, ramrod stiff in his effort to act calm. At any hint of strong emotion, Max usually clammed up or became very practical. I did not realise at the time that I was attempting to do the same. There was dinner to cook. I dabbed my eyes with a hand-towel. They were still red. I waited a little until the upset-look cleared from my face. I moved my jaw and smiled into the mirror, controlling my thoughts and feelings. I had already cooked the meat for the pilau so the dish would not take long to prepare.

There was no sign of Jack and his family, nor of Henri. Niall was ensconced in Max's study. I called blithely through the sitting-room doorway to Bernard. 'Do you want a fag?' We went out of the kitchen door and sat on the bench, lighting up.

'You look as though you've been crying.' I was getting to know that he could be quite invasive.

'I'm allergic to something.'

He was silent. The truth was that I longed to tell him about the letter, but if I did I would risk dissolving into tears again. Sally saved the day by arriving in a bright yellow dress to come and help with the meal.

'You ought to give that up, you know. You should think of what it's doing to your lungs,' she said.

'I am going to quit,' I said. 'It's just that it's never the right time.'

'I'm not. I smoke when I'm painting,' said Bernard firmly. 'It's part of me.'

'But you are the pariahs of the world,' she said. 'In the same way, white South Africans or Rhodesians are pariahs,' she added.

'The latter is not so bad any more,' I said.

'I still get the feeling that people think Rhodesians have got whatever was coming to them,' said Sally.

'I don't think that way,' said Bernard, stubbing out his cigarette.

'Some people do think that way. Come on. Now that you've fed your nicotine habit, let's go and cook,' said Sally. She either hadn't noticed my puffy eyes or had chosen not to comment.

The sun was still shining, lighting up the roses and the lawn with its apple and plum trees. I was reluctant to go inside. However, we went in and within three-quarters of an hour had a meal all but ready. I'd made a butterscotch pie for dessert in advance. Bernard made the salad and Sally laid the table in the dining-room. That had to be re-arranged slightly when I asked Niall to stay to dinner and he accepted. Niall had recently lost his wife to cancer and, as he had no children and no partner, he lived on his own.

'I'm just presuming the children will eat what we eat,' I said to Sally.

'Try them.'

'The meat is quite spicy.'

'I can always grill some sausages, or something.'

Henri, Susannah and George came downstairs - having bathed and changed - just as I was about to go and fling on a dress and put on some make-up. Henri was dressed in pink, a dress with an empire line that displayed her cleavage but, overall, made her look like an over-sized child with white hair. This, she had pinned back with a floral clasp that could have come as a free gift in a young girls' magazine. She let George and Susannah go through, hanging back, blocking my way upstairs. 'Have you shown him the letter?' she asked in a stage whisper.

'What letter?' asked Sally, who was passing behind me with the dinner plates.

'Oh, just a letter that Henri brought for Max.'

'Well, I suppose it's none of my business. It's just that you look like you've got some conspiracy going.' However, Sally continued what she was doing.

I turned to Henri. 'He has the letter,' I said. I begrudged having to tell her. I felt now that it had nothing more to do with her. She was just the messenger.

'And what did he say?'

'At first he tried to deny that it was genuine, but then he admitted he had lied when he said she was dead.'

'What are you going to do about it?'

As I looked at her I saw that she was enjoying my distress and that, however much I tried to cover up, it was plain on my face. Henri could have given that letter straight to Max and I would have known nothing about it. It was then that I became sure that her motive had been to cause a rift between Max and myself. I had stupidly thought that after all these years she would have given up trying to claim my husband for herself.

'We are waiting for this weekend to be over before we tackle the issues raised,' I said, rather pompously, pushing past her and going upstairs. I could feel the tears welling up, but I conquered them. Pensive, I began to apply mascara and lipstick in front of the mirror in Max's dressing-room.

*   *   *

I was remembering that night, that awful night more than ten years before when I got back early from Bath. It was a Sunday and I'd been visiting my old school friend, Sam, for five days. Max had seemed keen for me to go but I simply put this down to the fact that he recognized I needed a break. I'd kissed Nicky goodbye, trusting that he'd be all right with his father, although Max hadn't much idea of our daily routine, and I drove down the motorway. I felt carefree yet strange to be without Nicky's seven-year-old needs. Steering him through everyday life had become so much a part of me that I almost imagined he was asleep on the back seat and would bob up with a question like, 'Are we nearly there?' But I drove on in the cocoon of the car, alone. This solitude could have been bliss if it were not so unfamiliar. It was a little frightening.

I was glad to see Sam at the other end of the journey. It was tempting to say she had not changed because her features were the same, but it was presumptuous to think she hadn't done a whole lot of living since I had seen her a year previously. Thus far, Sam had not married. She was dedicated to her job as a vet. There had been admirers but as she grew older she seemed to be hypercritical of men. So much for Tony Masters. I was an old enough friend to ask her about her love life.

'Animals are my great love. People come second,' she said, defensively. 'And children. I like children. How is Nicky?'

'As far as I know, he's fine. With Max looking after him, he's in for a few surprises.' As I said this I had no idea how true it was. At the time, Sam and I laughed to think of a man like Max feeding a child, getting him to school and back, taking him to swimming lessons and to visit friends. All the things that parents do.

Sam was at work and I was sitting reading, on my second day there, when the doorbell rang. I opened the door to her tiny cottage on the outskirts of Bath and stood facing a tall, lanky man with a stoop. Sam hadn't warned me to expect any visitors.

'You must be Ruth,' he said, ducking through the low doorway. 'Sam said you'd be visiting.'

'I'm David. I'm here to invite her to a party on Saturday.' He was now standing upright in the hall and I thought him attractive.

'I'm sure she'd love to come,' I said. 'I'm not going to hold her back.'

'You could come too. There'd be no problem.'

'I don't think so. Thanks.'

At that moment, Sam came back from work, manoeuvred us through from where we were still standing in the hall and put the kettle on. David told her about the party and said he had invited me too, also saying there would be a number of singles at it.

'No. No,' I insisted. 'I have to get back to my family.'

'But you're not due to go back until Sunday,' said Sam.

'I'll go early. Give them a surprise.'

Sam could see it was no use arguing with me so we dropped the subject and, when he had finished his coffee, David left. She came back from seeing him to the door. 'He's nice,' I said. 'Is this one of your dark secrets?'

'I've known David since I got here five years ago. We're just good friends. He's up for grabs if you want him.'

'Don't forget, I'm married to Max.' Although she had been joking, I was slightly offended.

'Of course you are,' said Sam, as if apologizing.

The whole idea of being invited to a party as a single disturbed me. At the time, although marriage to Max wasn't ideal, I took the marriage vows very seriously. I was not going to put myself in a position where I'd be tempted to cheat on my husband. What I later discovered, was not going to make me regret this decision. I took a strong moral stance on this - we had promised to be faithful to each other. It was only when Bernard came along all those years later that my resolve began to weaken.

I was ready to leave late that Saturday afternoon. Sam was out attending to a dog that had been run over by a car and I didn't want to go without saying goodbye to her. She is a good friend, Sam, and I felt privileged to be able to see her, as most of my former school friends were either in South Africa or in other parts of the world. War and politics in Rhodesia had split apart White communities.

She came home and we said goodbye, promising to meet again soon. She told me that the dog, a mongrel called Patch, was going to live but they'd had to amputate its back legs, and it was to use a set of wheels strapped to its body where the back legs had been.

I started the journey home, music blaring, fag in hand. I was looking forward to getting home. The husband I thought I knew, Nicky, and the animals we had then, were so much part of my being and, even, my reason for living. I was not working at the time. With stops, the journey took longer than I expected and I found myself going up the drive in the early hours of the morning, the old oak tree a massive shadow in a starlit, October sky. I parked the car in one of the garages to the side of the house and walked across the gravel to the back door. I unlocked it and let myself in quietly, not wanting to disturb the sleepers. I switched on the light. There were dirty dishes stacked on the worktop above the dishwasher, including two glasses with the sediment of wine in them and I wondered briefly who Max had been entertaining. One of Nicky's toy guns lay on the kitchen table. One of his larger ones, looking like a machine gun. Some post lay unopened on the worktop. I made myself a cup of tea but before I drank it I decided to slip upstairs and take a peek at my sleeping son. I had to put on the passage light in order to see my way upstairs and I waited a moment at the foot of the stairs to see if I'd disturbed them. No. All was still. I crept into Nicky's room and found him lying as if he were in the womb, his head sideways on the pillow, his arms and legs curled up. He was snuffling as though he had a cold, or a blocked nose. And then he said something in his sleep, something I couldn't decipher. A warm feeling ran through my body.

I tiptoed out and hesitated on the landing. I thought I would take a peek at my husband and then go and have my tea. When we were first married he would tell me that he gazed at me while I was sleeping and would wonder where I went to in my dreams. I wanted to do the same. I nudged the door and stepped in. I flinched, as if I had been dealt a blow, because lying on my side of the bed was the sleeping body of a woman. It was Grace.

* * *

After the showdown with Max over Florence's letter, dinner was a disaster. I had over-cooked the rice and, as it was a rice-based dish, this was a glaring culinary error. I thought, at one point, of offering them sausage, egg and chips like the children were having but everybody, even Henri, kept up a pretence that this was a 'delicious' meal. Niall and Bernard even had seconds; the former out of hunger, the latter out of sympathy, I thought. Max and I sat at opposite ends of the table, not even glaring at each other. It was as if there were an invisible barrier between us. Henri sat beside him leaning her cleavage over towards him, giving him her full attention. Susannah and George were at his other side, self-consciously laughing at some joke that excluded the rest of us. Sally was busy with the children and Jack sat morosely. This made me sad because I remembered him as a cheerful joke-teller and a fund of 'bush' stories. Niall was intent on being a model guest but he clearly thought he was not quite part of the group. It was, it seemed, left to Bernard or myself to initiate conversation.

Bernard brought up a subject he had obviously been thinking about. 'I picked up a leaflet about the Waverley railway line. I see the Borders is planning to re-instate the line by the year two thousand and eight,' he said. 'Do you think this is a good thing, Ruth?'

'Absolutely,' I replied and would have gone on but I was interrupted by Max.

'There's no doubt about it. A rail network in the Borders can only benefit business, tourism and the local economy generally. I suspect it won't be in place for some years, though,' said Max.

'There are a lot of people living in the Borders and commuting by car to Edinburgh every day. This adds to the congestion that already exists in Edinburgh. A railway service would ease that,' said Niall.

'With the new parliament in Edinburgh, house prices are so high. People are looking to the Borders for cheaper accommodation,' I said.

'You need to see the wider picture, Ruth,' Max cut in. 'The

railway will connect us to the world. We've been isolated for far too long. They say that the Scottish Borders is Scotland's best kept secret.'

Bernard responded to Max's rebuff of me by challenging him. 'I imagine, that is as long as it doesn't intrude on the privacy of Auld Oak Hall. It's something special you've got here.'

'You said it,' replied Max and the conversation turned to the weather.

We cleared away the dishes. Pip and Robbie were helping too. Pip was keen to learn how to put the cutlery into the dishwasher basket. For her, it was not a chore. It was an exciting game. When that was finished, she looked at me and said very seriously, 'You know, Auntie Ruth, I like trains.' I realised she had been listening to the conversation, only really understanding that we were talking about trains. She had been very patient.

'Now, we're going to do something you'll like. We're going to play a game,' I told her.

I was already playing a game. Some way through dinner I had managed to submerge that afternoon's confrontation between Max and myself. I adopted the relationship I'd had with Max for many years. Detached but familiar. I even managed a pang of jealousy when I saw how Henri was flirting with him. Yet, I kept my thoughts and feelings to myself. I was hostess to my guests for the evening. Nothing more. Nothing less. Even though I'd ruined the lamb pilau. I had fed my guests. Now I set out to entertain them.

'We're going to play charades,' I told them as they were gathering in the sitting-room. Pip and I had written the titles of songs, plays, books, films on slips of paper and Robbie had provided the baseball cap for us to put them in. I handed one of the slips of paper straight to Robbie because it held the title of a children's book that he could relate to. Pip passed around the rest in the cap. Henri chuckled when she got hers and I could see the others thinking how they were going to act out the titles they'd been given. Susannah and George looked weakly at theirs, reluctant to join in.

'Be a darling, Ruth, and get me a glass of water. I've got a splitting headache,' said Susannah.

'You never did much like climbing mountains, dear. Apart from skiing, you're not one for too much physical activity.'

From what they were saying, I gathered that I was disappointing them. It was as if country life and pursuits didn't much appeal to them. A game of charades was to be tolerated and not enjoyed. Sally put a hand on one of my shoulders and went for the water. Susannah said she had brought her own painkillers.

Niall came forward to the space in front of the television, to play first. He looked slightly reckless and I remembered his state of disorientation of the day before. It was not long since his wife had died. He read his slip of paper silently, screwed it up and threw it aside. With both hands together, palms up and opening out, he signed that it was a book he was to portray. Four words. First word. One syllable. Then he left the room and went out of the door, coming back almost immediately.

'Goodbye Mr Chips,' suggested somebody. He shook his head.

'Hello Dolly?'

'That's not a book.'

'Gateway to…something. Going, going, gone?'

'Gone'

Niall nodded

'Gone with the Wind,' shouted Henri, and he gave her the thumbs up. 'That's a film as well,' she criticized and got ready to take her turn. She heaved herself up from the sofa where she'd been sitting between Max and Sally and positioned herself in front of the TV, signing that this was a song. Five words. First word. Then she pointed to herself.

'What about Henri?' asked Sally.

'Me. You,' someone shouted, drowning out Sally.

'I?'

Henri nodded her head vigorously. Signalling that she was now showing us the fifth word, she raised her hand and waved it rather like a traffic policeman.

'Wave.'

'This way.'

'I Did It My Way,' said Jack, abruptly joining in.

'Yes. Bravo.' Henri clapped.

He came forward and Henri went back to her seat, flopping down so heavily that she threatened to bounce Max off the sofa. Jack signed that his was the title of a play. Then he thought a bit, one hand to his chin.

'Philosopher.'

'Think tank.'

'I haven't started yet,' he said and laughed. That was the only time that weekend that I heard Jack laugh. He stayed everyone with his hand and did the sign of a play, again.

'Play,' we shouted.

'Two words.'

'First word. Two syllables.'

He pointed to his head.

'Hair.'

He shook his head and pointed to it again.

'Brains.'

'Head.'

Jack nodded. For his second word he started opening and closing his mouth.

'Head fish. A Fish Called Wanda.'

'That's a film.'

'Gobble.'

He shook his head and made as if to erase everything and start again. First word, he signalled, pointing to his head.

'Head.' The group agreed.

'But two syllables,' said Jack, cheating by speaking. Then he made the shape of a gun with one hand and pointed his finger at his temple.

'Oh. Hedda Gabler,' said Bernard and, of course, he was right.

We then gave the children their turn, Robbie doing 'Thomas the Tank Engine' and Pip miming 'The Sound of Music'. The game continued and went on well past their bedtime. After Sally and Jack had taken them off to the cottage, Niall left and the other guests decided to call it a night. Susannah wanted more water and gave me some ironing to do the following morning. I said nothing to Max and went to the linen cupboard to get out a spare duvet. Taking this and some pillows, I made up a bed on the sofa where I tried in vain to sleep. I was no longer keeping up appearances. I was worrying and fretting about how I was to leave Auld Oak Hall and where I was to go, at my age.

Added to this, I had a gnawing disquiet. Where were Nicky and Cherie? Zoe had 'phoned at about eleven thirty, saying they had not turned up and she asked if they were with us. She was anxious. What she said threatened to disturb me, although Nicky quite often spent the night in Zoe and Hank's spare bedroom and he would also go for days at a time to Edinburgh where his friend, Tim, had a flat. Zoe repeatedly asked if I had told Nicky and Cherie about their plans to go back to the States. I had to keep reassuring her. Despite her anxiety, at that stage, I still expected Nicky to just come strolling in.

At about two o'clock in the morning the 'phone rang and I groped around, trying to find the cordless 'phone as quickly as I could lest its ringing woke the household. It *was* Nicky.

'Do you know what time it is?' I asked, piqued.

'Happy birthday, Mum. There's a present for you from me in the tallboy in the dining-room.'

'Nicky, you haven't 'phoned at this hour just to wish me happy birthday. Where are you?'

'I'm not telling you that. All you need to know is that Cherie and I are safe and together.'

'What is this? Some sort of game? Are you saying you won't come home?'

'We won't until Zoe and Hank abandon their plans to go back to the States.'

'How did you find out about that?'

'We heard them discussing it. So, you knew about it and didn't tell me. What sort of a mother is that?'

'I only heard about it yesterday. Zoe asked me to keep it a secret.'

'Well, now the secret is out and we've gone into hiding. If you want to see me you'll get them to cancel their plans. Cherie and I are agreed.'

'Cherie is a young girl. You could be getting yourself into all sorts of trouble.'

'She's eighteen, remember. You can tell Zoe she's safe and you can tell Dad that, if he cuts off my allowance, Cherie will suffer.'

'Nicky, tell me where you are. We can talk this through.'

He paused. 'You know our terms. You talk it through with Zoe and Hank. I'll call you again at some point. We're serious, Mum.' He put down the 'phone.

By now, I was sitting on my makeshift bed, dumbly staring at the pillow where I would have liked to have lain my head. The question was whether to 'phone Zoe immediately or to wait until later, when they were more likely to be awake. On reflection, I thought they'd be awake anyway so I 'phoned them. Hank answered, saying they were both wide awake. I told him what Nicky had said and he took it calmly. I think he was glad to learn that the pair of them was safe. I said I would go around to see them after breakfast. That was all. If Zoe had answered the call it would have been a different matter. Zoe never kept her emotions to herself. I imagined she was in tears.

I dumped the 'phone on one of the small tables and crawled back into bed. It was nearly three o'clock. But sleep wouldn't come. I got up and went into the kitchen to make a cup of tea. Brindle was delighted to see me, coming over to greet me, squirming as if her tail were wagging her whole body. I bent down to her and she licked my neck. When I had put on the kettle, I picked her up and sat with her on my lap in one of the wooden chairs.

Bernard must have been in the doorway for several seconds before I noticed he was there. He was wearing a T-shirt and boxer shorts and his hair was tousled.

'I'm sorry I haven't got a dressing gown here.' He came into the room and sat down.

'I couldn't sleep,' I said.

'Ditto.'

'Would you like a cup of tea?' I pushed Brindle off my lap.

'Please. Milk and one sugar.' He continued to talk as I made the tea. 'You've got something on your mind that you haven't told me,' he said. It was a statement, not a question. 'I'm here to listen.' I could feel him watching me as I moved around the kitchen in my dressing gown.

'That can't be why you woke up.' I was defensive. 'Did the 'phone wake you?'

'No. I make a habit of waking up in the early morning.'

'Ditto,' I said.

'Ruth, I'm a friend and I will treat what you say as confidential. You're a great actress, playing the hostess while there are things bothering you that you can't sort out by yourself.'

'How do you know that?'

'You're not that great an actress, after all.' He smiled. 'Why did you come out of Max's study in tears yesterday? It took you a full ten minutes in the bathroom to compose yourself. And why did a seasoned cook like you over-cook the rice?'

'Anyone can make mistakes.'

'Because you were upset. That's my guess.'

'I told you Nicky has fled.' I blurted out, still trying to conceal my confrontation with Max. 'He 'phoned. I still don't know where he is.'

'Where does he usually go when he's away from home?'

'My guess is that he is with Tim in Edinburgh. He's flirting with the wrong side of the law. Zoe could make out he has kidnapped Cherie. Although she is eighteen. They're so naïve and this is, effectively, blackmail. I wonder if they realize it themselves.'

'Why don't you 'phone Tim later? Even if they are not with him, he might know where they've gone.'

'I could try it but they will have sworn him to secrecy. They are so in love. That's a strong motive.'

'Do you approve of their relationship?'

'Yes. But this isn't the way to go about things. Nor would I want Nicky to go to the States permanently, to be with her.'

'Could she stay behind?'

'I can't see Zoe agreeing to it.'

'What does Max say?'

'He doesn't know about the 'phone call yet. He's asleep, like we all should be.'

'And you and Max can discuss this?'

'What do you mean?'

'I mean that I sense a row going on between you and Max.' He cradled his mug of tea and held my gaze.

I felt my defences crumble. 'All right. If it's so damned obvious, I'll tell you.' I told him everything and felt relief as I talked and talked. I told him about Florence and the letter. And Max's lie. 'This has made me more determined than ever to leave.'

'And does Nicky running away affect your decision?'

'Nicky is twenty-one. I can no longer live like this because of his needs. He has to be able to cope with his parents splitting up. He is no longer a child, although he acts like one sometimes.'

'I don't know why you don't show more anger about this French woman.'

'I am angry. I've just put it on hold for the weekend.'

'You won't be able to do that,' he said, looking directly at me.

'How do you know?' I was annoyed.

'I just think you are trying to be superhuman.'

'I *am* an adult. In fact, a fifty-three-year-old adult. What am I supposed to do? Break up the party?'

'I meant to say happy birthday, Ruth.'

'Thank you. Already you and Henri know about the letter

and, of course, Max. That leaves Jack and Sally, Susannah and George. No. I think they have enough problems of their own. There is Adeline. She is coming for the barbecue. She's something like eighty-five now. And she's wise. I'm hoping she will offer me a refuge.'

'You can stay with me, initially, if you want. My cottage is remote and private.'

'You're very kind, Bernard. I'll think about it. Now shouldn't we at least try to get some sleep?'

He went upstairs and I went to the sofa, but before I could sleep I found my mind fixed on Rhodesia, on my life there, my experiences, on what I had left behind. I thought of the time when I was a young reporter. The thoughts came to me. I could not avoid them.

*　　*　　*

'I'm going to give you a fictitious scenario. Imagine there has been a fire in a house in the suburbs. Imagine I am the fire chief. Ask me questions.'

We were sitting in the editor's wood-panelled office at one end of the newsroom. He had shut the door against the clacking of typewriters and was challenging me from behind his large wooden desk. It was my first day working for 'The Matabeleland News' in Bulawayo, commonly known simply as 'The News'. I was a very young junior reporter.

'Go on, Ruth. Don't be shy. You've got to be pushy in this business. You've got to be tough.'

I was determined to be tough, tougher than I was, but I was overwhelmed by the big boss, the editor paying me so much attention.

'I've got so many questions that I don't know where to start,' I said.

'Remember you're working to a deadline. There are always deadlines in this game.'

'What is your name and how do you spell it?'

'That's a good start. Let's say, for want of a better one, that my name is Frank Noble and I've been fighting fires for thirty-odd years.'

'Is the fire under control?'

'Yes. My men have it under control.'

'When did it start and what started it?'

'That's good. You're using the basic questions of who, what, when and where.'

'What was the cause of the fire?'

'It's too early to say but it could have been an electrical fault.'

'When did it start?'

'Okay. You're making sure your questions get answered.'

'When did the firemen get to the fire, Mr Noble?'

'It must have been at about six thirty this morning. We were on the scene ten minutes after receiving the alarm call. We've had two engines here and four fire fighters.'

'What is the damage?'

'Well, you can see for yourself. There is very little of the house left.'

The editor waved his arm to indicate a burned down property and he shifted in his chair. For a moment, I couldn't think of anything else to say.

'That's fine for a start, Ruth. But you're forgetting the most important point. Now, what is that point?'

'Who owns the house?'

'You're on the right track. However, that's not what I want you to ask me.'

'Was anybody in the house at the time? Is anybody hurt? Were there any pets in the house? What about African servants?'

'Yes. But one question at a time.'

'Was anyone in the house at the time of the fire?'

'Now, you've got it. Can't you see the headline? 'Twin Boys Rescued from Blaze'. You've found your introduction. There were twin boys, six-year-olds, asleep in their bedroom while their mother was watering the garden with a hose pipe. She tried to turn the hose on the blaze, but to no avail. A neighbour stopped her from attempting to rescue her sons. It was left to fire fighters to bring them to safety. In the end, no-one was hurt. The father had already gone to work.'

'Any servants trapped?'

'The maid was out in her khaya at the back. No. She was not hurt.'

'Animals?'

'The two family pets, two dogs, were in the garden with the mother at the time of the fire.'

'What is the family's name? I especially want the names of the twins.'

The editor leaned back in his chair and swivelled to one side. 'You give them names, Ruth. Fill in the details. The value of the house etc. I've got a meeting coming up. So, I'll have to let you get on with it. I want the story on my desk in fifteen minutes. And don't bother looking for it in today's edition.' He laughed.

'Thank you for giving me your time, Mr Palmer.' I went back to my desk, at the front of a row, near the news editor. The desk tops were strewn with cheap newsprint and there were spikes for unwanted copy. The typewriters were old and heavy. When I pressed on those keys I really felt I was doing something. It was very physical. And when we were all at our typewriters the sound was like a cacophonous symphony. I was totally caught up in what I saw as the romance of journalism. I even loved the smell of the newsprint.

These feelings never left me all the while I was working for 'The News'. I wanted to write and the very word 'writing' had a fabulous aura. During my first years with the newspaper I was compiling a book in my spare time. I was interviewing the children of Rhodesian pioneers with a view to telling their stories. Needless to say, they were very old, as the first pioneers entered the country in 1890. I was compiling the book in the early 1970's so the old people I was interviewing had been young people or children in the early days of Rhodesia. They were in their late eighties and in their nineties. A group of them lived in a nursing home in the town centre. I remember one old lady called Maggie. She was ninety-eight, going on ninety-nine. One day I went to the nursing home at an appointed time. I was going to her room when I met her nurse in the long corridor full of doors behind which the frail elderly had their bedsits.

'Hello, Ruth,' she said. The staff knew me by that time. 'Who is it you come to see today?'

'Maggie. She knows I'm coming.'

'I'm afraid she doesn't know anything, any more. Maggie died last night.'

'But she was all right yesterday. I spoke to her.' I was shocked to think that I could no longer speak to Maggie. She had so much to say. She had lived through dangerous times, and now she was gone.

'I'm afraid she has passed away. The funeral will be next week. Poor old dear.'

She wasn't a poor old dear. She was a strong, courageous woman who had come to this country on an ox-wagon, through the wilds of remote territory where there were lions, rhinoceros, hippopotami, at a time when the native Matabele and Mashona were openly hostile. She had been born and brought up in Scotland like my own grandmother, my father's mother, and had married a doctor who wanted to come out to Southern Rhodesia. 'It was his dream,' she said. I shed a few tears as I transcribed from my tape recorder the words of the last chat we had.

'Some people have said to me…' Her voice wavered but I remembered her eyes being full of indignation. 'Some people like to say nowadays that all we were after was gold. Hah! I ask you? There wasn't even very much gold to be found. And if we had wanted a comfortable life we would have stayed in the UK. Never mind the weather. You know, my dear, we all go in search of something in our lifetimes. We go after whatever it is that makes us happy. All I wanted was to be with Richard, God rest his soul, and I didn't care what it took. It brought me to a strange land…'

I had to rewind the tape a bit because her voice had filled with emotion and had become unclear.

'This is my country now,' she went on. 'And Britain has let us down badly. Even my family, what's left of them, back home… I mean, back in Scotland… they don't understand what it is like to live in Rhodesia.'

There was a long pause. I think she was journeying into her memories.

'Richard was a driven man. He wanted to treat the sick. And there were plenty of those. Malaria and all those other diseases.

He would have treated White and Black if things would have allowed it. He worked all hours. Then, he came home to me… I'm tired now, dear. You can come back tomorrow.'

I made a move to turn off the tape but she was still talking.

'I got malaria myself. I was in a terrible fever. I thought then that I was going to die. I fought the fever. I had so much to live for. There was Richard, my one and only love and there was a whole new country to build, and now look what's happening.'

She closed her eyes. Her face was sad. 'It has been war and peace in my lifetime. And now it's war again. The Communists are coming over the borders to ruin everything we've built up.' She opened her eyes. She was agitated. 'I'm not sure I want to be British any more after what Wilson and his government have done… Scotland is so bonnie. I would have liked to visit it again but there's no chance now.'

There was scarcely a trace of a Scots accent in her speech. There were, however, flattened vowels typical of the Rhodesian way of speaking.

'You won't go will you dear? Stay with me. I'm going to sleep soon and then you can go.'

'I'll come back tomorrow.'

'Stay.'

'I'm not going yet.'

'Richard came out with the Pioneer Column. It was all men. He was there when they raised the Union Jack at Fort Salisbury. He was there right at the beginning. It was a hard life but there was adventure. Can you understand that, Ruth? The bush. The wild animals. The snakes.'

She closed her eyes again. 'I joined him when it was deemed safe for women to come. We weren't married then. We got married under some thorn trees …by a missionary in the heart of Africa… it was very romantic. The hippies would have appreciated our wedding ceremony. I wore white, of course. A long dress with a bustle and starched petticoats. You will understand, we were still in the Victorian era. Those dresses were very unsuitable for the bush, however. Nowadays, youngsters wear hardly anything at all. Not suitable either.'

'You know I've got a wee great-grandchild now. Although there's nothing little about him. Ten pounds plus he was when he was born…' She was drifting off to sleep so I stopped the tape recorder and stowed it in my bag. 'See you tomorrow,' I said as I left the room, knowing she didn't hear.

There was no tomorrow for Maggie but I had three or four other pioneers to talk to, men and women. I foolishly told Peter about these memoirs. It was a mistake. Peter was the only Black African reporter on 'The News'. 'The token Black,' he used to say. Peter was difficult to get to know but I persevered because I wanted a friendship with the first Black African I'd had dealings with who was not a servant.

I remember the day he started work for the newspaper. By that time I had been there about two years and was writing the Women's' Page and was editor of the education section. I had moved to a desk at the side of the open-plan newsroom and he was given a desk at the end of the room, next to Rashid, the Indian reporter. I went up to him where he was seated at his desk.

'Hi. I'm Ruth Pearson.' I put my hand out.

'That's nice,' he said with a small smile, his hands inactive, palms down, on either side of his typewriter.

I didn't know what to do so I stood with my hand held out. Still, he refused to shake it. I let it drop.

'I do women and education.'

'So, while men are fighting on the borders you write about fashion and make-up.'

'It's not like that. Women are becoming liberated.'

'They're not the only people becoming liberated, as you put it.'

'What do you mean?'

'If you don't know, I can't help you. You'll see for yourself one of these days.'

'Well, it's nice to meet you. I hope you'll be as happy on this newspaper as I am.'

That was one abortive attempt to make friends with a reporter who was classified non-White.

However, as time went by, the remarks Peter directed at me became less barbed and we settled into a kind of friendship. He continued to be hypercritical but I accepted that as his manner. I was by now well aware that Blacks were being discriminated against in Rhodesia and was, first of all, curious to know the extent of it and also wanted to make reparation in my own way. Even one friendship with a Black African seemed to me very precious. At the same time he began to treat me as an individual and not just a member of a master, if doomed, race.

I was reluctant to tell anyone about the memoirs because I was shy about my aspiration to write a book. It was in a moment of confiding that I told Peter.

'You're what?'

'Writing a book about the pioneers. They have a whole lot to say about the history of Rhodesia.'

'I bet they have. The original robbers and bandits who stole our land.'

'That's a bit extreme.'

'Extreme? I'll tell you what's extreme. It is conning Lobengula out of his kingdom. It is turning guns on people who have only assegais and shields. It is flying a Union Jack in a place where it has no right to be. It is naming an African country after an Anglophile entrepreneur.'

'They are still people, with their own stories.'

'Stories that belong to 'Boy's Own'. And I don't mean the term 'boy' used for African men.

'I'm sorry.'

'What are you sorry for, Ruth?'

'I'm sorry for everything that has made you so bitter.'

'No. I'm sorry that I can't believe in your book.'

'You go too far, Peter.'

'They were after gold, you know. Those pioneers had the glint of gold in their eyes.'

'Then, why did they stay? There was little gold found. They had individual reasons for coming and individual reasons for staying. No matter what you say, I love this country and I believe that Black and White can live in peace.'

'You are a sentimental woman. I'm afraid to say, it's too late.'

'I need to believe...'

'Believe what?'

'In the future.'

'Have your dreams, Ruth.'

'Do I have your friendship?'

'You are misguided but, yes, I am your friend. Now, haven't you got a deadline to meet?'

Our friendship was rocky, but it kept going until one day something happened that offended him and left a silence between us for months. It started when I was put on a Sunday shift. There was no newspaper published on a Sunday so that there was just a skeleton staff on duty and the news editor took the day off. When I worked on this shift I was expected to cover general news stories although I often took the opportunity of a generally quiet day to work on features for the women's' page. On occasions, the converse could happen. There'd be a major story breaking and no-one else but a photographer and a sub-editor to help deal with it. I was writing up a story on an African woman who had started a women's' group in the townships when the 'phone rang.

'There's been a murder. My next door neighbour has been murdered,' a distraught voice said.

'Can you give me the victim's name and address?' I tried to put some calm into the situation.

'Mr Hutton. His name was Cecil Hutton.'

'When did this happen?'

'Last night. They only discovered him this morning. Our maid told us. The police are here.' He gave me the address.

'Thank you, Mr...?'

'Brown. The name's Brown. You can speak to me when you come.'

'Okay. Bye for now, Mr Brown.'

I put the 'phone down and immediately rang the police. There had indeed been a murder in one of the affluent suburbs of Bulawayo. The victim was an old man. Inspector Geoffreys was at the scene. That was good news because I had dealt with the Inspector before and he was quite friendly towards the press. I telephoned down to the basement for John, the head driver, to have a car ready; asked the duty sub-editor to cover the desk and grabbed my notebook and pen. Mike, a photographer, came with me. We were at the scene of the crime in less than twenty minutes. It was roughly ten o'clock in the morning and it was a blazing hot day.

What struck me first about the house was its immaculate garden. Dahlias and roses lined the semi-circular driveway and there was a lush climbing rose growing up the stone walls of the house. At one end of the driveway were large granite rocks overhung by trees. The entrance to the house had been cordoned off and a police constable guarded the doorway. John parked the car, and Mike and I got out. I asked the police constable if I could speak to Inspector Geoffreys, but before he had time to reply the Inspector came through the doorway.

'I wondered how long it would take for you people to get wind of the story,' he said. He was a very large man with a bald head and suspicious, piercing eyes. 'I see you've brought a camera. Well, it's not a nice picture I can tell you. Multiple stab wounds. It's a sorry affair.'

'Who found him?' I asked.

'It's more complicated than that. The bastards tied the maid to a chair in the kitchen, and gagged her. That was last night. The next door maid found her and untied her, then called her baas. They then went through to the lounge and discovered the poor old fella's body lying in a pool of blood. As I said, not a pretty sight. Come and see for yourself, if you can stomach it.'

He led us into the house, down a couple of steps and into a sunken lounge. There, lying on the floor was the still form of Mr Cecil Hutton, covered in wounds inflicted by a knife, the carpet soaked in blood.

'Fire away, Mike. Let your readers see what the buggers have done. Looks like the old man was trying to get to the telephone.'

'I'll take some pics but I think this is too grisly for our readers. I'd like to take a picture of the maid,' said Mike.

'Was anything taken?' I asked the Inspector.

'My men are having a look through the house right now. My guess is that a lot has been taken, judging by the empty spaces. TV. Music centre. That sort of thing. There's an empty cash box lying over there in the corner. He was more than likely a rich old man. But go and speak to the maid. She'll give you the full story. She's in the kitchen. In a state of shock, mind you.'

I was relieved to leave the corpse behind and go into the large, well-equipped kitchen where Agnes Manyiwa was seated at a table, drinking tea from a tin mug. Her friend, the maid from next door, whose name was Bella, was standing next to her. I sat down in a chair opposite her. She wore a patterned overall and, strangely enough, a worn, woollen beret. Her cheeks were wet and she wore thick glasses. She was a big woman. I felt deeply sorry for her but I had to do my job.

'Mrs Manyiwa, I'm from 'The News'. I wonder if I can ask you some questions.' I spoke as gently as I could. At first, I thought she wasn't going to reply because she screwed up her lips in distaste at the memory and there were tears forming in her eyes. But then she spoke in anger.

'Three men, Madam. Three men did this.' Her voice was loud, as if she were fighting the intruders in her thoughts.

'How did they get in?'

She turned and pointed to the back door.

'We don't lock the back door. I get from here to my khaya.'

'So, they came in the back door. What were you doing? Were you in the kitchen?'

'I am washing the dishes. I have just given Mr Hutton his dinner. I am clearing away and washing up.'

'Did you recognize the men?'

'No, Madam. They have scarves around their faces.' She indicated how the scarves were tied, across their noses and mouths. 'I see only their eyes.'

'Were they White men or Black men?'

'Black men, Madam.'

'Did they hurt you?'

'One of them, he put his hand over my mouth to stop me screaming and warning Mr Hutton. Then they put my hands behind my back and tie them together. They tie my feet.' She started to sob. 'Then they take some rope… they bring it with them… and tie me to this chair. I cannot move. I cannot say anything… 'til morning… when Bella finds me.'

'And when you were bound to the chair, that's when they went through and attacked Mr Hutton? They must have unlocked the front door from the inside and left that way. Did you hear a vehicle drive away?'

'Yes, Madam, I hear an engine but I can't do anything.'

'You must be very sad, Mrs Manyiwa.' I was reminded that she had not only lost her employer, but she had also lost her livelihood.

'Yes, Madam, very sad. Mr Hutton, he is a good man.'

Then Bella interrupted, 'And Joshua, he is gone.'

'Who is Joshua?'

'He's the garden boy. He just disappear,' said Bella.

'He's afraid,' said Agnes. 'Afraid they think he did it.'

'Do you think Joshua had anything to do with it?'

Agnes didn't answer my question because just then Mike came through wanting to take a picture of her. She was reluctant but we persuaded her to pose for the camera. Mike asked her to pull the chair back from the table, to stay seated and to put out her wrists to show where the rope had cut them. She had a very serious look on her face and it seemed as if she might weep again, but Mike got his pics.

Before we drove back to the newspaper office, I went next door to have a word with Mr Brown, our informant. He came to his front door and was very keen to let me come in, but I stayed on the doorstep. Although my deadline wasn't pressing, I wanted to get back to the office to see if any more stories were coming in. He was a small man with a prominent bone structure. He was very caught up in the drama of the night before. From the outside, his house seemed very different from Mr Hutton's, being more of a box-like shape. His garden was less well-tended.

'It's usually a very quiet neighbourhood. Nothing like this has ever happened before,' he said.

'Did you see anything or hear anything?' I asked.

'No. Only knew about it when Bella came to tell us. She was shocked out of her wits, I can tell you. So was I when I saw the body. A frenzied attack, I think you'd call it. Bella and I untied Agnes. If she was White I'd say she was as white as a sheet. She was devoted to the old boy.'

'So, then you called the police?'

'Yes. You know, that other one, he wasn't so good.'

'What other one?'

'Joshua, 'the garden boy'. Bella has always called him a skelm. And Africans have a way of knowing.'

'Did you see him before he disappeared?'

'No. He got out of there quick. As guilty as sin, I would imagine.'

'Thank you, Mr Brown. You've been very helpful.'

On the way back to the office, John driving, Mike and I in the back seat, I started writing up my story. Mike and John chatted about cricket, rugby and things totally unrelated to murder in the suburbs. I typed up my copy back in the newsroom, where things had been quiet during our absence.

It was unusual to have a murder in Bulawayo, so the story - with a photograph of Agnes Manyiwa - made the front page of the following afternoon's edition of the newspaper. The opposition newspaper, the 'Daily Gazette' had not latched on to the story at all. Our headline read 'Pensioner Murdered – Garden Boy Missing' and that was what Peter objected to – the suggestion that the gardener was implicated in the attack. This was quite apart from the offensiveness of calling Joshua a 'garden boy'.

'Where are your ethics, Ruth?' asked Peter. 'You seize the first black man you can find and suggest that he is guilty. You're prejudicing this case.'

'The robbers were Black men. The maid said so,' I protested. Anyway, it was the sub-editors who made a big thing of the gardener being missing.'

'Garden boy is what they called him. A term that Whites can relate to.'

'I made a point of called him a gardener. You will see, in the body of the story.'

'I bet that gardener is bloody terrified. He has no chance now.'

'If he is innocent, the law will find him so. If he is guilty, he deserves to be caught. You should have seen the state of that poor old man, covered in knife wounds, lying in his own blood.'

'I wonder if the police would have taken so much interest if this victim had been Black.'

'Peter, sometimes I just can't cope with your cynicism.'

'You won't have to, any more.' He walked off.

*　　*　　*

After about three hours of sleep, I woke, pleased that it was my birthday. After all, I'd come a long way, despite the pitfalls and the hurdles. At the same time, I hadn't had enough sleep and my confidence was patchy. I was unaware that by nightfall my husband would have been killed; would have died from unnatural causes, would be dead. That morning the knowledge of this was as foreign as I had been when I arrived in Britain for the very first time. I went through to the kitchen in my dressing gown and found the children exuberant because it was my birthday and because there were presents for me to open. I persuaded them to let me shower and dress and I put on my beige cotton dress with its pleated bodice. I had washed my hair and let it hang loose to dry itself. I slipped my feet into brown, woven sandals. We did not expect to do any climbing that day.

'Why do you sleep down here?' Pip had asked me.

I had hesitated. 'Because I don't sleep well and I did not want to disturb Max.'

She had been satisfied with that.

Max was nowhere to be seen. Nor was Brindle. I imagined they had gone for a walk. After he had dressed in the morning, Max liked to go across the fields and along the edge of the woods, tracing a line along one side of his property.

'If you don't mind my saying so, you look as if you haven't slept a wink.' Sally was bustling around the kitchen, wearing my rubber gloves, washing any stray dishes and cleaning the worktops.

'Why is everyone so concerned about me?'

'Who else is concerned about you?'

'Never mind.' I gazed out at the garden and saw the children playing catch, using the larger apple tree as den. I started telling Sally about Nicky, but before I could finish Max came in with Brindle at his heels. At the sight of him, acting out his part as laird as if nothing had happened between us, a rush of anger went through me. I tried to disguise this by grabbing a tea towel and rubbing dishes dry. But I had to tell him about his son's 'phone call and I did so in a harsh and artificial voice which was a parody of my own natural way of speaking.

When I had finished, he gave me a shrewd look and said, 'That's easy. I just cut off his allowance. That'll bring him running back.' He had the arrogance to think he had the definitive answer to the problem, and he moved towards the door as if to block out any objection.

'Nicky has thought of that. He says that if you cut off his allowance Cherie will suffer. He didn't say it would make him come home.'

'That may be so, but it will motivate him to get a job, pretty damned quick.'

'I don't think that is the answer. I think we should talk to him, reason with him. Hank and Zoe aren't going to be blackmailed into dropping their plans.'

'How can you talk to him if you don't know where he is?' asked Max.

'He'll 'phone again. And I'm going to see Zoe and Hank this morning. You don't mind, do you, Sal?' I was eager to bring Sally into the conversation as I thought she might support me.

However, Max was just as keen to get out of the kitchen. I could tell that he was feeling uneasy about talking to me. In the doorway, he turned. 'Nicky has until tomorrow to bring the girl home or I 'phone the bank and cancel the direct debit.' He left, not having wished me happy birthday.

'I told the children we'd call them when you open your presents. Shall I call them now? Or, do you want to wait until the other grown-ups are here?' Sally asked.

'No. No. Call them.' The last thing I wanted was a great performance, but I wanted the children to have fun. They came in, chattering away. Even Robbie was more forthcoming. I let him choose the present I should open first. It was a large, rectangular parcel, a painting of boats and water framed in natural wood, from Bernard. He was clearly very talented. But the children interrupted my appreciation, rushing me to open their own present. It was wrapped in shiny red paper with silver ribbon and rosette, and there was a card. I must have infuriated Pip and Robbie by taking time to read the card and by taking off the paper very carefully so that I could use it again. Inside the wrapping was a smooth glass bowl for salad or for punch. I hugged the pair of them and thanked Sally. Henri had given me a small wooden vase, delicately carved. When I asked her afterwards, she said a friend of hers had made it. Susannah and George had given me a silver sugar spoon and some chocolates. There was a gift of bath salts from Nicky and Cherie and I was impressed by their forward thinking, holding the box to my nose to inhale the sweet smell. As I was doing this, Max came in.

'I've been too busy to go out and buy you a present,' he said coldly.

I noticed he was waving a cheque in the air as though the ink were still drying. He didn't give it to me, but laid it on the worktop beside the other gifts and wrapping. I froze, staring at it, thinking that never had a gift been more grudgingly given. At the same time, he had made out, to Sally in particular, that this was a very magnanimous gesture. He turned, but not before I had seen that his face was grim. 'You might need this,' he said, then left the room, presumably to go into his study.

I looked at the cheque. It was for fifty pounds, a fraction of the sum I was going to need when I left him. I wasn't too worried on that account. I had been saving money from the freelance writing business and from the housekeeping money during the previous ten years. That would cover me, temporarily. And there was a possible divorce settlement. I had already taken legal advice on this and I'd been told not to raise my hopes. Max would be protected because most of his wealth was inherited.

'Max could have made more of an effort,' said Sally, cutting into my thoughts. The children had gone outside.

I suddenly felt very tired. I didn't much feel like discussing my relationship with my husband. I wanted to pretend he did not exist. Yet, Sally's remark demanded an answer. 'Well, did you think that was a nice way to give his wife a birthday present?' I asked.

'I thought it was insensitive.'

'There's your answer.'

'Ruth, you can tell me ...'

'I'm sorry, Sally. I really don't want to talk about it right now. I don't want to spoil the party. Maybe later. I have something I must do. Won't be a moment.'

I took the cheque and went through to Max's study. He was not there. I put the cheque on the desk, where he would see it, and found a piece of paper, on which I wrote, 'Thanks. But no thanks.' I experienced a curious feeling of power as I did this, as if the possibly childish gesture had broken the hold Max had over me. I put the piece of paper on top of the cheque and dumped a paper-weight on both.

The lack of sleep was beginning to tell and I had to wait a while before I got my second wind. Meanwhile, I had to go and see Zoe and Hank. I excused myself from my guests who had all gathered in the conservatory, apart from Jack, who was still in bed, and then I drove down the road to Zoe and Hank's gateway. To get to their front door I had to drive over two wooden bridges that always made me uncertain as to whether or not I would reach the other side. Sheep grazed on the grassy banks. Dead tree trunks rested prone on the riverbank, surrounded by their living counterparts. Their front garden was alive with colour and a clematis bloomed pink around the front door. I was feeling weak as I walked up the path and even worse when I anticipated how emotional Zoe was going to be. I expected Hank to be easier to talk to.

'I don't know what your son thinks he is playing at,' Zoe started off, and then went on to imply that Nicky had kidnapped her daughter. 'It was only Hank who stopped me from calling the police.'

'The police can't do very much about it if we don't know where they are. And we can't do very much about it if we aren't on the same side. We're dealing with two young adults who are very much in love and who have devised this plan in order to stay together,' I said.

'It won't stop us going back to the States. With Cherie. Did you go and tell them the secret?' Her voice was querulous and she was wringing a sodden handkerchief in her hands.

'I can't repeat to you often enough that I did not. They overheard you speaking about it.'

'You are both going off at tangents,' said Hank. 'You have got to look at this situation in the clear light of day. What we've got here are two young people who are trying to force us to change our plans. We've got to think where they could have gone and how to compromise with them. Whether we like it or not, we'll have to negotiate and possibly strike a deal.'

I gave him Tim's number and we decided to ring him. Hank did it. However, Tim said that he did not know where Nicky and Cherie were. They had been at his flat but he didn't know where they had gone after they left.

'So,' said Hank after he had relayed this message. 'We have to wait until they 'phone. Surely Nicky is going to wish his mother a happy birthday?'

'He did. At two this morning.'

'Did he say he would 'phone again?'

'Yes, but he didn't say when.'

'I can't bear it if they don't keep in touch. All this waiting,' wailed Zoe.

'Come to our barbecue as planned. That'll relieve you of some of the anguish of waiting. We'll just hope that they phone there. And you can leave your own answer 'phone on.'

'Zoe will come. I will stay to man the 'phone here.' They had clearly decided this beforehand.

'What do we say when they 'phone?' Zoe was becoming calmer, now that we were deciding on a plan.

'That we would like to talk to them, together and here, about what we can do to stop them being separated,' I said.

'The main thing is that we are willing to talk. Perhaps Nicky can come to the States with us?' Hank said.

He had said it; hearing the suggestion voiced was like a body blow to me. My world was already breaking apart without the prospect of now losing Nicky. I closed my eyes for a moment to try and blot out this possibility. I had nothing to say that would not lead me to come to a complete standstill, or lead me to alienate some of my best friends. I did not answer Hank. Instead I turned to the subject of Max threatening to cut off Nicky's allowance.

'I don't think that's the way,' said Hank, making me feel a bit better. Although I knew Max would do as he threatened.

7

'Do you know what your husband has done? He has announced his intention to foreclose on the loan he made to George two years ago, when he was setting up the antiques business,' complained Susannah.

They were slumped in the sitting-room, looking as though they had been physically beaten. My immediate response was to openly sympathize with them.

'You think he'd be satisfied with the huge rate of interest he has been charging. Now, he gives us some cock-and-bull story about wanting to use the money to put an extension on Auld Oak Hall.' The anger was beginning to rise in George as he spoke. 'I have no idea right now how we are going to pay him fifty-five thousand pounds. This will ruin me.'

'We'll have to give up the car at the very least. Our precious car.' Susannah was mournful.

'I'm not giving up the effing car so that he can build a few more bedrooms. It's probably more a question of taking out a loan to pay off a loan. Plus the frigging interest,' said George.

'Can't you talk to him, Ruth?' Susannah pleaded with me.

Although I had known Max would be foreclosing on the loan, I hadn't expected to become involved. I was reluctant to tell them that anything I did on their behalf would be totally useless. When Max had made up his mind, nothing would stop him. I explained to them as diplomatically as I could that I had no great influence over Max.

'Well, we can't stay. Not after this behaviour,' said Susannah. 'I hate to be rude, as you've been so sweet Ruth, but we must go.'

'Wait a minute, dear. We might just get the old miser to change his mind. He'll not get rid of us as easily as that.'

'I would be glad if you would stay,' I said.

'Well, we will stay for your party but I can feel another headache coming on.' Susannah put a hand to her head.

'I'll get you a glass of water,' I said, turning to go to the kitchen.

'You are so kind, Ruth. Unlike someone else I know.'

* * *

It was around about the time that Adeline arrived that my energy returned. She came up the drive in the tiniest of cars, Natasha, her great niece, driving. It was one of those cars that look as if they have been cut off at the back so that only a wedge-shaped slice remains. I hurried to greet them and to help the old lady out of her seat. Adeline swivelled around and let her feet, in sturdy lace-up shoes, rest on the gravel. She was taking this in stages. I tried to hold her arm but she gestured to me to take her stick. Then she levered herself out of the car into a standing position. She was still elegant, had never lost her figure. She stood in a light blue dress, pouched at the bodice and gathered into her waist. It fell in soft folds down to her ankles. Her thick silver hair was tied back under a straw hat with a wide brim.

'Operation exit has been accomplished,' she said, laughing and taking her stick. 'Now, how are you my dear? Having a happy day?'

'I'd rather not be fifty-three.'

'That's young yet, Ruth. Wait until you get to my great age. But, let me introduce you to Natasha.'

Natasha *was* young, in the full bloom of youth. She had long blonde hair and wide brown eyes. She wore a short denim skirt, revealing shapely legs, and a purple vest top that showed her black bra straps. She moved like a dancer, her long limbs gliding across the grass. Another striking thing about her was that she was very effusive, a bit like Susannah. She came around the front of the car to shake my hand, wishing me a happy birthday, enthusing about the countryside and Auld Oak Hall. Her smile was extravert, encouraging. By her demeanour, she had a way of reaching out to people, as if to say it was all right to be them.

We walked slowly around to the side of the house where we were having the barbecue, a lawn that had an unbroken view of the hill. It was one of those summer days you treasure more because the forecast had been for rain. The men had carried two trestle tables across from the garage and we had covered them with white cloths, starched by Heather, which we pinned underneath the wooden table tops. On these was an abundance of salads and fruit; the baking potatoes were in the oven and the meat was on a large tray near the stone barbecue where the men had congregated as if by some natural force. There were marinated chops, chicken in honey and mustard sauce, South

African sausages called boerewors, hamburgers for the children. Henri had done the flowers for the tables that stood end to end on the lawn. For someone with such a forthright manner, she had a delicate touch with flowers. She'd picked pink roses with gypsophila and ferns, and a sprinkling of purple flowers. She had placed small glass vases at intervals. Although still disgruntled, Susannah had brought party poppers and streamers, which she scattered around the dishes. On the table was the champagne in ice buckets, with long-stemmed glasses lined up. Scattered on the grass was an assortment of deck chairs and dining-room chairs. Adeline needed a straight-backed chair that was relatively easy to get out of. Once she was seated, I offered her a cup of tea.

'I'm waiting for the champagne. You go and introduce Natasha to everybody.' She waved me away. 'We must have a chat, later.'

I did not need to introduce Natasha to the others. She had done it herself. Max and she were at the centre of a small circle consisting of Henri, Bernard and Jack, Susannah and George. The latter two had on their best smiles and were trying to flatter Max who didn't notice because he was so absorbed by Natasha. Sally had taken the children and Brindle for a short walk. Max put down the long fork he was using to turn the meat and was wiping his hands with some kitchen towel, all the while talking, concentrating on Natasha as if mesmerised. I don't remember what they were saying – something to do with her being at university and what she was going to do afterwards. What I saw was a fifty-six-year-old man doing his best to impress, and a twenty-year-old who was too polite to do anything but humour him. She smiled as if this was what she was meant to do in life, and gave the appearance of being completely engrossed in what he was saying, as if she had eyes only for him. Max didn't appear to be aware that this would have been the same whoever she was talking to. I saw, too, behind his shoulder, the look of fury on Henri's face. She was at that moment in a deep pit of envy. It was as if Henri knew she did not have the tools to challenge this competition. The look didn't last long for she caught my gaze and erased the jealousy, writing on her face a casual look instead.

'You won't burn the meat will you, Max?' I said sweetly.

His response was dark and hostile but there was a re-shuffling and Bernard took over the cooking. Meanwhile Jack had gone to talk to Adeline. I went into the kitchen to see how the potatoes were doing. I thought I was alone. However, I was followed by Max and Natasha.

'Really, Ruth, you haven't given this poor girl something to drink,' he said. 'She has driven from Edinburgh to be here.'

'No. Honestly. I don't want to trouble you,' said Natasha.

'It's the least we can do. What can I offer you? Whisky? Wine? Gin and tonic? A cup of tea? Water?' asked Max.

I carried on pricking the potatoes.

Natasha wanted water so he poured some from the tap, put some ice in it and a slice of lime and gave it to her.

'This is very good of you. Thank you so much,' said Natasha as if he had given her the elixir of life. 'Is there anything I can do?'

I got up and put the potatoes, which were ready, on top of the cooker. I was still wearing the oven gloves and holding a skewer.

'You look as though you're going to stab someone with that thing.' Max could have been joking.

'This thing wouldn't make much of an impression,' I said coldly.

Natasha coughed in embarrassment and I put down the skewer, handing her a bowl of potatoes to take outside. She was grateful to be given a task and went out carrying the bowl.

'You should have cooked the potatoes on the fire. It would have saved on energy,' said Max.

'It takes too long that way.'

'Talking of which, this whole barbecue is taking too long. People are waiting for something to happen,' said Max.

'Barbecues are relaxed, informal meals. Nobody is anxious but you. Besides we're still waiting for Zoe, and Sally and the children. When they come we can open the champagne.'

The four of them arrived soon after that, and Max prepared everyone for a speech he was going to make. He stood there, at the head of the table, one hand resting on the neck of a champagne bottle and I stiffened, wary of what he was going to say.

He popped the cork of the first champagne bottle and filled the glasses. Henri handed them out on a tray.

Max began to speak: 'My wife tells me she is twenty-one today. And I would like to believe her, although a woman always lies about her age. There are social lies and other lies. God knows, I come across enough of them in my work. This type of social lie perpetrated by the fairer sex is an example of the forgivable lie. We all indulge in social lies and we call it making excuses. I've done it myself. Mea culpa.' He said this in a light, throwaway manner yet he couldn't have realized it, but he was smiling with one half of his face, so that his joviality was deformed. His fists were clenched and he swayed slightly. Max's mask was slipping. Or, was I imagining it? Temporarily, he seemed at a loss for words. Then he seemed to recover, and he continued, 'But to get back to my wife...she needs no excusing. She's as young as a twenty-one-year-old today and I ask you all to drink a birthday toast. To Ruth.' They all raised their glasses. 'Happy birthday.' They drank then pulled the party poppers and threw the streamers into the open air. Nobody appeared to take Max's speech very seriously but I felt it had been full of innuendo about his own lie. Or rather, his latest lie, or web of lies, about Florence.

The champagne went straight to my head. I started to fade away from my guests. Max's speech reverberated in my mind. Then I drifted away. I looked across at the hill and mistakenly saw it start to move and caught my head dropping into the canvas of the deck chair. As I began to focus again, Natasha came over to me with a plate full of food. She was, after all, a sympathetic young woman. Perceptive. She seemed to know that I needed revitalizing. She even understood that I didn't necessarily want to talk to her at that moment and, having given me the plate she walked away on dancer's legs. I was touched and I began to eat silently. Perhaps the food would counteract the effects of the champagne and the tiredness?

After that, there emerged a part of me that was fully functional. I could hear myself laughing at somebody's joke. There was an air of jollity and celebration of my birthday. All but Jack and Zoe were joining in. Natasha had taken refuge from Max's attentions by Adeline's side, holding on to the back of her chair while Adeline entertained Sally, Henri and Bernard with stories from her past. This left the way clear for Susannah and George to entertain Max with false flattery. It was so obvious what they were trying to do. They were pitiful in their desperation. Wine was now flowing.

When the phone rang, Zoe started and she followed me as I went indoors to answer the call. It was not Nicky. It was my parents from Johannesburg. Zoe went back outside, disappointed. As I talked to mum and dad, I found myself resorting to the role of child, even at my age. Yes, I was eating properly. No, I was not sleeping very well. I said nothing of my intention to leave Max.

This was not the right time to tell them. Yet, dad sensed something was wrong and I had to promise to 'phone him when I would be able to talk freely. Mum gave me a description of her last bridge game, and they rang off.

I went over to Zoe. 'Sorry. Perhaps Nicky and Cherie will 'phone later.'

'It's not your fault, but I think I'll go now and see if Cherie has 'phoned Hank.' Her face was full of anguish. 'I'll let you know,' she said as I walked her to her car. 'If I don't ring it means he has not heard from them. You go and enjoy the party,' she said half-heartedly. I didn't hear from her again that afternoon.

It wasn't that I had forgotten Nicky. It's that I had a simple faith that, whatever happened, he would look after Cherie and, therefore, himself. The thought did cross my mind that they would go and get married, to force our hands.

Max was setting up a croquet game on the lawn down by the old oak tree. Natasha, Bernard, Henri, Sally and the children were taking part. Susannah and George were now looking miserable as if they had lost any hope of winning Max round, but they joined in. I watched the group start the game and then, as it was getting cooler, I went to fetch Adeline's jacket from the car. I helped her put this on and drew up a chair beside her and Jack.

'Your cousin has been telling me about his family's departure from Zimbabwe. A terrible wrench,' said Adeline.

'You loved the farm, didn't you, Jack?' I said, and wondered how often he went over the sad sequence of events in his own head. Was he ever going to be able to move on? Adeline immediately empathized with his preoccupation but began to try and focus his attention on the present. I waited to hear what Adeline would come up with to help Jack. Both Jack and I were waiting. With what wisdom would she approach the seeming stalemate of Jack's situation? It crossed my mind that she would turn to religion as I knew her faith had become much stronger over the years. Yet, for some reason, she steered clear of religion, turning instead to science. She put her head to one side and said. 'I understand there is such a thing as Cognitive Behavioural Therapy that can change unhelpful thought patterns. To sign up for that you would probably have to see your GP.' She wasn't forcing this on him, just suggesting it as an option.

'I don't have faith in doctors,' he said abruptly, clearly having only half-digested her advice. 'Now, if you'll excuse me, I'll go and watch my children play croquet.' He got up and disappeared around the corner of the house.

'Well, that has sown the seed of the idea,' said Adeline.

'Sally has been trying to get him to go to a doctor for months,' I told her.

'Poor woman. Poor both of them. Now, Ruth, for heaven's sake, tell me why you are looking so drawn?'

'Adeline, you are here to be at a party, and not to act as a sponge for other people's problems.'

'It's my age. People mistake it for wisdom.'

'You are wise and I will tell you what's happening with me, but not now. However, do you have a spare room for me over the next few weeks? As soon as Nicky is back, I want to take off.'

'It's like that, is it? I thought Max's little speech was a clue. Of course, I will always have room for you. And we can talk.'

'I'll tell you everything.'

'You know, Ruth, my great thought for the day at the moment is forgiveness. Forgiving people for what they have said and done.

Perhaps you and Max have some forgiving to do. It doesn't need to be in a religious manner.'

'I think it's too late for that,' I said.

'Or, too early.' She was silent for a moment, and then asked, 'When is Nicky coming back?'

'Soon, I hope.' I glossed over the question of Nicky and Cherie because I was still feeling some the effects of the champagne and couldn't face going into the details with anyone. I was also intent on relieving her of the burden of disclosures. At least, that day.

*   *   *

Natasha won the croquet game, a win quite possibly engineered by Max and which prompted him to kiss her on the cheek. She took this all very graciously. She accepted from me her prize of a box of chocolates which it seemed that Henri coveted because she muttered something about cheating. Henri was incensed by the kiss but her outward reaction was centred on the prize that she thought she should have won. She was disproportionately jealous, and immune to Natasha's smiles. That was the only time I saw Natasha look uncertain. It seemed for a moment as if she would offer the whole box of chocolates to Henri but she thought better of that and, still smiling, she helped Adeline into her tiny car and they headed for Edinburgh. The others lined up to wave goodbye. The rest of the afternoon and the evening were spent talking, drinking cups of tea and coffee, and soaking up the sun. I gave them bacon rolls as a snack supper and they ate up the leftover salads. Henri went around in a black mood, half-heartedly helping out. Sally and Bernard set about bringing in the dirty dishes. We put a load in the dishwasher, washed the larger bowls, cleared and cleaned the worktops. Susannah retired to their bedroom with another headache, periodically requesting a cup of tea. George must have approached Max again on the subject of the loan because he took to making bitter, caustic remarks to all and sundry. It seemed that the party mood was waning.

My thoughts were occupied with a new guilt; this time I felt bad for suggesting, albeit to myself, that Jack was somehow to blame for not moving on. He had, after all, suffered something like bereavement with the loss of our homeland. By grieving he was being loyal to his country. It wouldn't mean very much if he could forget it just like that. Put in perspective, four years isn't a very long time. It had taken me at least ten years to start to come to terms with leaving Rhodesia and, even then, I was still, in my memories, living partly in Africa. Also, my homesickness was complicated by the fact that I felt I should not have abandoned Rhodesia. Jack felt he had deserted Zimbabwe. Neither of us dreamed of suggesting that Rhodesia had betrayed us. 'It is as if leaving it has damaged his soul,' Sally had confided. Thinking these thoughts brought to mind some lines from Rudyard Kipling's poem 'The Burial' which was read in the rites at the graveside of Cecil John Rhodes, a poem written especially for the occasion. These closing lines were taught to us in school:

'The immense and brooding Spirit still

Shall quicken and control.

Living he was the land, and dead

His soul shall be her soul.'

What did I think of that now? It had been used as propaganda and I would always remember it, like an advert that gets stuck in your brain to pop up at unexpected moments or something my mother said about how to tie my shoe laces or her often-repeated injunction to consider what the neighbours would say. No. I did the verse an injustice. In its time, and for supporters, it was a reverential piece of work based on belief in the glory of the Empire. Trust in Cecil John Rhodes was founded on a bloody history but it had a time and a place. No matter how often it is rejected as a dark hour in British affairs, it still happened. Colonialism did exist. I had to see the reality of it because it was part of my heritage. Not to do so would be to take bits of my childhood and erase them, leaving a fantasy upbringing.

*   *   *

Peter and I were the only two reporters in the newsroom when word came through of a bomb scare at Dawson's, a local department store and supermarket. The news editor told us to get down there and find out what was going on. We grabbed our notebooks and pens. 'Run,' said the news editor. We had little choice but to work in tandem. We hurried across the wide streets towards Dawson's. It was another hot day and I could feel the sweat erupting as I raced to keep up with Peter, who said nothing. There was a small, multiracial crowd three blocks away from the store; evacuated members of staff and hangers on. Here, I took the lead and pushed my way through agitated people to the front, where the police were standing. I caught sight of Inspector Geoffreys again. He had a loudspeaker and he was cautioning the crowd to stay calm and keep away from the danger zone. I went up to him, and chose a moment when the loudspeaker was at rest, 'Can you tell me what's going on, Inspector?'

'We think there's a bomb in a fitting room of the ladies department. The bomb disposal unit is in there. We also think there's a child somewhere in the building.'

I noticed a young White woman standing with the policemen, wringing her hands and sobbing.

'Keep back, please. Stay together, and keep as far away from the building as possible. For your own safety,' boomed Inspector Geoffreys . He then lowered the loudspeaker again, and said to me, 'This woman lost her son in the store before the alert. My men are looking for him now.'

I went up to the woman, 'I believe your son is in the shop. When did you last see him?'

'They won't let me go back inside.' She looked imploringly at me.

'How old is he?' asked Peter. I hadn't realized that he was directly behind me.

'Who are you?' the woman asked.

'We're from 'The News',' I replied.

'I'll speak to you, but not to him.'

'Peter is very sympathetic.'

'It's all right, Ruth. You get the story.' Peter moved back into the crowd and began talking to some Black employees.

'Are you a mother?' The woman was addressing me. I think I was a distraction. Waiting for her child to be rescued was overwhelming.

'No, but I know what my mother would feel in a situation like this.'

'My child is so much a part of me. I only have one child. I couldn't bear it if anything happened to him.'

'How old is he?' I repeated Peter's question.

'He's seven. His name's Freddy. He's always wandering off. I take it as part of the routine. Then he always pitches up. Only, this time...'

I was aware that Mike had arrived on the scene and was taking photographs of me talking to the woman. Somehow that reminded me that I had to get her name. It was Rachel Tredgold. 'What school does he go to?'

'Jameson Primary. He's not very good at schoolwork but he's good at sport, especially running. The other kids like him.' She looked at her watch. 'It's been nearly twenty minutes. I wanted to go in there but they won't let me. I was in the cosmetics department buying some new make-up when he disappeared. Will somebody get him out of there? What if the bomb goes off and he's in there?'

'Where is his dad?'

'I don't know… I can't think straight… at work. He works for the Rhodesia Railways. He doesn't know anything about this, or he would be going out of his mind, like I am.'

Just then two policemen in khaki uniforms came out of the building. Walking between them was a young boy. It was Freddy Tredgold. He looked proud of himself and not at all worried. Mike took pictures of the reunion with his mother, Rachel.

Inspector Geoffreys lifted his loudspeaker to his mouth. 'You'll be glad to hear that the young boy has been found, safe and well.' There was a small round of applause. 'Keep back, please, ladies and gentlemen. The bomb disposal unit is still in the store and I have every confidence that they are doing their job. Be patient.'

What we were to discover was that the bomb disposal unit had very quickly found the source of the scare. A red shopping bag had been left in a fitting room in the Ladies Department. Inside this bag was an alarm clock, ticking like a bomb. The scare was indicative of how edgy everyone was, with the war on our borders. The bomb disposal unit did a thorough search for any other suspicious packages in the building. Once they had given the Inspector the all clear, he allowed staff back inside, but most shoppers kept away from Dawson's that afternoon, and the crowd dispersed.

Mike had left already. Peter and I started to walk away from the store, past a car park, when I noticed a woman, a brassy blonde, at the open boot of her car, standing beside a trolley filled with two large cardboard boxes, presumably of groceries.

'Hey you, boy,' she called.

I looked around to see who she was calling. It could only be Peter.

'Come here, boy. I need some help lifting these things.'

I hesitated. I felt a deep embarrassment and a deeper understanding of Peter's cynicism.

'Both Peter and I are newspaper reporters,' I said firmly. 'Why don't you ask one of the shop staff to help you?'

'They're all occupied with this bomb scare. They usually do this for me. I suppose I'll have to do it myself.'

'That would never do. Let me help you,' I said.

Together, she and I lifted the boxes into her boot and she had the decency to say thank you. 'I suppose I'll have to take this back myself.' She tottered off on high heels to take the trolley back to the supermarket.

Peter was silent as we walked back.

'I'm sorry. I'm ashamed for my countrywoman.' I said.

He took a while to reply and then he said, 'You don't need to carry the evils of the whole system on your shoulders, Ruth.'

'Friends again?'

'Friends.'

*   *   *

It was a Sunday in 1976. A few years before that, I had moved out of my childhood home and into a flat in the town centre. Now mum and dad were leaving to go and live in Johannesburg, South Africa, to be near to my aunt, Jack's mother, and her husband. So many things were driving them away from their roots in Rhodesia - the shortages of goods due to sanctions, petrol rationing, the war. Many young men were dying for a fruitless cause. Most of all, my parents believed that white liberalism no longer had a place in the extremist Rhodesia of the future. Dad had a part time job in a school in Johannesburg and mum would soon find some bridge players. So, this was our last Sunday lunch together in our family home, which had been sold. Bruce, still my boyfriend at the time, was there although he was going to have to leave early as he had tickets for a rugby match. If mum lived for bridge, Bruce lived for rugby and the game was all the more precious because he was frequently being called up to serve in the army.

'Hey, where did you get that?' asked Bruce.

Dad was holding a bottle of genuine Scotch whisky, rare to find in those days of sanctions and foreign exchange problems.

'This particular bottle has been waiting many years for an apt celebration. Perhaps it's not the most suitable drink for a sunny afternoon. You might like some South African wine instead.'

'No. Hell, man. I wouldn't want it said that I missed an opportunity like this. I'll guard it with my life.' He accepted the glass of honey-brown, neat liquid and took a reverential sip. 'Ah,' he said.

It seemed that it was just the men getting the whisky. Mum and I stuck to wine. We were sitting around a table in the garden, under the bougainvillea, next to the swimming pool, just the four of us. Mum sat looking strained while Alfred solemnly loaded up the table with cold meat and salads.

'Not that dish, Alfred. I told you to put the potato salad in the blue dish.' Mum made him take it away and went into the house to supervise the switching of the dishes, saying, 'If you want a thing done properly, do it yourself.'

'Your mother is very sad about leaving the house and about letting Alfred go, I might add.'

'We're all sad, Dad.'

'We must look on it as a new beginning.'

'But you've been in Rhodesia for so long.'

'Close on thirty years.'

'I'm presuming the sale of the house has gone without a hitch,' said Bruce. He was now onto his second glass of whisky.

'No problems there. You've seen all the packing cases. All that is left is for the removal van to come and we're on our way. We've sold the cars and there's a new one being delivered to the flat in Johannesburg. Ruth is taking us to the railway station tomorrow.'

'You know you're deserting us in our hour of need. I mean, I'm risking my life for you people and all you do is desert. You take the chicken run and you scarper.'

'Bruce. Go easy. My parents wouldn't be leaving Rhodesia without some heart-searching.'

Bruce helped himself to another whisky. 'You're too gentle, Ruth. What I've got to do is fight to kill, fight for my life, to stop those bastards getting in. To do that, I've got to believe in Rhodesia and all that she stands for. If I don't do that I'm a gonna. And these terrs will stop at nothing.'

'Bruce. You've had too much whisky. Oughtn't you to go easy if you're going to get to the rugby match?' I said.

'Hang on, Ruth. Let the young man have his say. He is risking his life for his country,' said dad.

'You're dead right,' said Bruce.

'In my experience,' continued dad, 'In my experience there is a time for everything. There is a time for war and a time for peace. There is a time for staying and a time for leaving. We've come to a point in our lives when we need to set up a way for retirement. Dorothy and I are not getting any younger.'

'Speak for yourself,' said mum, coming across with the blue dish. She had heard only the bit about her not getting any younger, and not the rest of the conversation.

I looked at Bruce, thick-set, belligerent, and thought that the strain of so many call-ups must be telling. When he was in civvies he was an accountant in Mr Hall's construction firm. The job must be suffering. And our relationship was being damaged because I realized, more and more, that I considered the 'bush war' a civil war and a tragic mistake. I thought of Peter, and all that he had taught me about the life of Blacks in this country. I wondered if I were a little in love with Peter.

'Eat your food, Ruth. Stop gazing into space,' said Bruce.

'I was thinking about how much you can't say,' I quickly fabricated. 'About how much censorship there is of the press. About the numbers of people dying on the borders.'

'You just don't know, do you?' said Bruce. 'Like you just don't know how the petrol is getting in. But we're busting sanctions all the time. We're succeeding.'

'I wonder how long it can go on?' said dad.

'Forever,' said Bruce, emphatically.

There was a silence and I could hear the bees buzzing in the tree.

'They're back, Leslie. The bees are back. I thought you'd had them removed. Bruce, he's allergic to bee stings. One sting could kill him.'

'Perhaps they see this as their home,' suggested dad, seeming unperturbed.

'Just be careful, dear. I don't want to lose you. You've given us so many frights.'

We had ice-cream for pud and then I went inside. Bruce was still drinking whisky. There was one more thing I wanted to do. I wanted a last swim in our pool and I went to change in my old bedroom. It was empty although there were still curtains hanging. It had been stripped of my childhood possessions. The memories lay in the blank walls. There had been a bed, a chest of drawers, a desk, a lamp. I was re-furnishing it in my mind. There had been posters on the walls. They were down but I still had them. Mum had asked me to remove the loose stuff a few weeks before. There was so much of what others might call junk, to remind me of the years I had lived here. In particular, there was a drawer in my dressing table that I called a memory drawer. Old cinema and theatre tickets, a silver cardboard twenty-first birthday key with signatures of friends from the party, a sketch of myself drawn by a former boyfriend, a paper napkin with more signatures; my silver christening bracelet, a slender, engraved band; a nest of tangled, knotted, cheap jewellery… I had paused. In amongst the tangle I had caught sight of my gold cross. I had spent the next hour trying to extricate it, much to mum's annoyance. I kept it, along with most of the other souvenirs, and took it to my flat, which was now bulging with things of sentimental value.

'You've got to be ruthless,' said mum.

'Is that why you called me Ruth, without the 'less'?'

She was not amused.

I now gazed at the gutted room, the freshly painted walls, the windows with their burglar bars giving a sectioned view of one corner of the garden, with the giant cactus at its apex. I changed into my swimming costume and went outside.

'You shouldn't swim on a full stomach, Ruth,' said mum.

'Watch me.' I dropped my towel and dived in. Never had the pool felt so good, the soft water making me weightless. Swimming underwater, I felt like I was in a womb, timeless, airless and carefree. I shot up into the sunlight again and lay floating on my back, lazily watching the clouds. This was how life should be.

'You've got to get out now, Ruth.' Mum was hovering at the edge of the pool. She didn't swim but, if she had, I doubt if she would have then. She wouldn't have wanted to jeopardise her hairdo. Tomorrow would be an important day for her. Bless her. 'You've got to take Bruce to the rugby,' she said. 'He can't drive, in his state.'

'Bruce is not going to the match. Look at him. He's asleep.'

Bruce had lapsed back in his deck chair with his mouth open and his eyes closed. The whisky bottle was now only a quarter full. 'Let him be, Mum.'

'Well, in my opinion, he'll be very angry when he wakes up. You know how he loves the sport.'

'Maybe he needed to let himself go.'

'We'll leave him then. Dad is going to take Alfred to his new job.'

'Then wait for me. I've got to say goodbye to Alfred.' I leapt out of the pool, grabbed my towel and raced into the house to dress. When I got outside, Alfred, Elizabeth and young Jacko were waiting beside dad's car, having said goodbye to mum. Jacko was playing hopscotch in the sand, a game I had taught her, and I went to play with her. She laughed. Jacko was always laughing and getting up to mischief. I took her by the shoulders and drew her into a big hug. 'You be good, Jacko.'

'I'm always good.' She pulled away and began playing hopscotch again.

'That's what she say,' said her father. He was dressed in his pristine, starched cook's uniform, but with no cap. I noticed tufts of grey at his temples.

'Alfred, Dad tells me you've started to take driving lessons. So I thought I'd give you some money towards the cost of the lessons. As a farewell present.' I held out some dollar notes but he kept his hands to his side.

'Missie Ruth. I do not want money from you. The goodbye is enough.'

'Then I'll give it to Elizabeth. She can keep it for you.' I offered the money to Elizabeth who clapped her hands and took it with a smile.

Alfred seemed not to notice. He clasped his hands together and said, 'Goodbye, Missie Ruth. Goodbye. Goodbye forever.' Then he turned and opened back door of the car for his wife.

'But I might meet you in the street,' I stammered. There was a great lump in my throat. I spoke to deaf ears. It was as if he had decided on his last words to me and there would never be any more. He climbed into the car and Jacko got in to sit between her parents. The dignity of their farewell overwhelmed me. Dad came out and started the car. He backed it down the drive. They withdrew. I didn't wave. The occasion wasn't like that.

*   *   *

It was June 16 in that same year, 1976, and it was work as usual. I was busy writing a feature about a woman who had had her legs amputated below the knees after she was run over by a car when a child. She was now a woodcarver, working for Tonde Arts and Crafts. What was even more unusual about her was that it was mostly men who did woodcarving for the shop. Tonde's was a commercial enterprise that provided a shop front for disabled people who were artists and craftspeople. It was run by Tonde Sithole, a big, cheerful Black African man whose ease and cheeriness belied his skill at marketing. As a result of his hard work the business was thriving. He knew the boundaries of White and Black segregation but he pushed them to the limit. Although his employees were Black their clientele was mainly White. I had interviewed the woodcarver in the shop - we had got pics the day before - and I had transcribed the tape at home that night. I was now well into writing the feature.

There was a great clicking of typewriters – computers were to come later to 'The News' – and a buzz as reporters wrote and rewrote their copy, then delivered it to the news desk by hand. There must have been about fifteen reporters in the newsroom that day. Peter and Rashid looked as if they were collaborating on something because they kept reading each other's copy. The tea trolley came through and I had left my desk to get myself a cup of tea when the news editor stood up with a fax in his hand and said, 'We're starting to get news of a riot in Johannesburg. Some dead.' My immediate thought was for my parents. What if they were caught up in it? But I went back to my desk, drank my tea and waited. I couldn't concentrate on my work.

Peter, who had been one of a small group huddled around the news desk, came over to my desk. He looked at me as if for support and placed two hands on the edge of my desk. 'Eight dead, including three children. In Soweto. High school pupils were protesting against the use of Afrikaans in schools.'

'You said three children. They've started killing children.' My voice must have been very small.

'You heard me. Don't make me say it again.'

'It's just so awful.' My voice was cracking.

'That's Apartheid for you.'

'I tell you something, Peter. I am never, ever emigrating to South Africa.' 'They'll pay.'

'How can you be so sure? How much of this has to go on before there is change?'

'Sometimes you're like a child, Ruth. There'll be a bloodbath.'

'Don't say that. My parents are there.'

'Okay. I'm sorry, Ruth. I react with anger to these things.'

'But why kill children?' The tears were streaming down my face.

Peter straightened up. He looked at me sympathetically, and then went away to his own desk. I think he needed to contain his emotions. I went off to the women's toilet to try and control the flood of tears. I must have been in there a full half-hour. It took that long before I could present myself as a tough and hardened reporter again.

* * *

I had asked Bruce to come to the flat after work so that we could talk but he arrived early and I was just out of the bath when the doorbell rang. I answered the door wearing my summer gown and with a towel in a turban around my head.

'That's how I like you,' he smirked, reaching for my hands.

He looked into my eyes and said, 'You're a beautiful woman, especially in a state of undress.'

'Come in. I'll just get dressed.'

'Stay as you are.'

'No, Bruce. I've something to tell you, and I don't think you're going to like it.' I showed him into the living-room and then went into my bedroom, slamming the door shut. I hastily got into a cotton dress and rubbed my hair with a towel. He had the sense not to open the door.

The bedroom was almost as big as the living room and had a big double bed. The colour scheme was pink. The whole flat was sparsely furnished. I never had the feeling that it would be a permanent home. The living room had a small dining table and springy, plastic ribbed chairs in the sitting area, with a coffee table by the window. All the furniture was made of dark, African wood. The only particularly large piece of furniture in the entire flat, apart from the bed, was a sideboard that a friend had given me when she left for England. On top of that were a few drinks bottles and glasses on a tray. Next to them was the wood carving of a man and a woman holding hands that the Tonde woodcarver had given me. On the walls I'd stuck a couple of posters of wild animals, which I had brought from my bedroom in mum and dad's house. One was of the enlarged, fierce face of a lion, with dark mane and burning eyes. The other was of zebras and flamingos beside a pool of water.

Bruce had helped himself to a sherry and was sitting on one of the springy chairs when I went through.

'What's up? Time of the month?' He asked nonchalantly.

That annoyed me, the implication that women were temperamental, and had to be humoured; that my menstrual cycle could explain any deviation. However, I decided not to reply but went to the sideboard and poured myself a sherry. I was determined to control the pace of this discussion. I went over to the window with my glass and stood looking out at the grass and the line of jacaranda trees outside. I turned to face him.

'I can see straight through your dress you know. When you stand against the light. It's very provocative.'

I quickly sat down on one of the chairs. 'You don't think about much other than sex,' I said. 'And rugby.'

'Don't be like that, Ruth. I'm a hot-blooded male and what's wrong with liking sport? Playing rugby is better than collecting porn or doing drugs. Rugby is a great sport.'

'But, you're obsessed with it. Any wife you have will be a rugby widow.'

'Now, wait a minute, we've talked about getting married. You can't mean…?'

'What I mean is that I want a cooling off period.' This was the statement I had rehearsed in the bath, and I had tried to predict how he would respond. He might display hurt or, more likely, he would get angry and start to criticize me. I was ready to stand my ground.

Bruce responded by doing the thing I least expected. He laughed a laugh of disbelief. 'You can't be serious,' he said, putting down his glass on the coffee table.

'I'm completely serious. I've thought it through.'

'But, you and I have a history together. We've been going out for two years, for God's sake.' He left his mouth open and leaned back in his chair. 'Come here and sit on my lap and I'll show you what we mean to each other. The sex is good. Very good.'

I did not deny this. I hesitated, but said, 'A relationship is more than just good sex.' I stayed in my seat, taking a great gulp of sherry.

'It's about rugby then. You know I can't give that up.' He said this with his teeth clenched. He was starting to get angry.

'It's not even the rugby. I've changed Bruce. We've changed.'

'It's your job. You're always looking for excitement.'

'I've had the job ever since I've known you.'

'It's that kaffir you've been associating with.'

'Peter is not a kaffir,' I snapped. 'He's a Black African and, yes, he has made me see what the Whites are doing to the Blacks in this country. But, wait a minute; can't a relationship ever be anything but political in this country? Politics are all-invasive so that morals get left out in the cold.'

'What's moral about telling me you want a cooling off period?'

'I'm not sure…'

'You see, you don't really want this, Ruth. In any case, I'm going back to fight the terrs next week. You may not see me again.'

'That's one of the reasons I wanted to make myself clear.'

'When I'm in the bush, risking my life, I'm thinking of you.'

The worst possible thing was happening. I had started to feel sorry for him but he did not make the most of this opportunity. He continued, 'And you. You are all on your own without me. Your parents have left the country. You have no brothers and sisters.'

'I've got friends.'

'I know what this is about. You're thinking of taking the chicken run. You're thinking of leaving Rhodesia, and to do that you've got to extricate yourself from our relationship. Tell me if I'm wrong.'

'You're straying very far from the point. The point is that I don't want to see you again for a while.'

'I'll do one better than that. I don't want to see you again, ever.'

With that, he left. I couldn't help noticing again how short he was, a good two inches shorter than me.

* * *

Tonde's was having a private view. There was to be an exhibition of paintings in the shop with wine and cheese. And, to add spice, some witchdoctors would be there to tell people's fortunes. I had an invitation for two and I would have liked to have asked Peter if he would come with me, but that would have been socially unacceptable in the Rhodesia of that day. Nonetheless, I told him about it and he looked at me quizzically. 'Want to get your fortune told? I would have thought you'd know what direction to take, yourself.'

'I've never been to a witchdoctor before,' I said, a little embarrassed at being vulnerable enough to propose it.

'Good luck.'

The shop was its usual self, filled with soapstone and woodcarvings, prints and paintings. I was led into a room at the back by no less than the boss himself, Tonde Sithole. 'I'm glad you could make it,' he said, 'the press is always welcome here.'

Tonde led us towards a counter and gave me a glass of wine, and a list of paintings for sale. These were hung around all four walls and were exclusively paintings of nature, mainly done in oils. The artists were all disabled in some way. One of them painted with the brush in his mouth. I was attracted by a painting of a msasa tree that already had a red 'sold' sticker on its frame. The centre of the room was crowded with people, mainly White, talking and holding glasses of wine and I noted it was the same crowd who came to every art exhibition in Bulawayo. I moved among them, chatting. The artists, some in wheelchairs, the mouth-painter missing arms and legs, a blind man, were gathered at one end of the room and a few of the guests were speaking to them. Lined up along one wall, sitting on the floor beneath some of the paintings, were three witchdoctors, two men and one woman. The men were wearing tribal dress. The woman was all in white and wearing a large bone necklace and she had her hair braided. It was her eyes that drew me. They were burning with an awareness that mere mortals could only dream of. She was the one I wanted to see, so I joined the queue in front of her.

When it was my turn I felt a little churning in my stomach. I was afraid of what she might say. I got down on my knees, leaving floor space between us, as the others had done. I put my wine glass carefully to one side. She sat with her legs curled sideways on the floor. Her face, at close range, was mesmerising; at the very least the face of a person used to communing with spirits. I sat in a trance. Tonde, who was standing above me, prompted me. 'She's waiting for you to give her money.'

'Oh, sorry.' I rummaged in my bag and gave her payment.

She put that in an old treacle tin and picked up a leather pouch. She emptied this, throwing bones, seeds and stones onto the floor between us. I stayed very still, waiting for her to interpret the bones. She was also still, looking intently at the scattered pieces in front of her. Eventually, she said, 'Ah, ah, no madam.'

'What's the matter? Is it something bad?'

'I no say.'

'What's the problem, Tonde? Can you ask her in Ndebele?'

Tonde spoke to her. In fact, they had quite a long conversation, while I was feeling disoriented and nervous. Finally, Tonde said,

'She says you will go on a long journey. She refuses to say what else she thinks will happen to you.'

'Is it that awful?'

'I think you'd better give up, Miss Pearson. She is not going to say any more.'

'Long journey,' muttered the witchdoctor putting the bones away in the pouch.

I got up. 'That's unnerving,' I said to Tonde.

'She has her reasons,' he said.

'You had a good chat with her. What did she say?'

'The bones revealed something she did not want to tell you. That's what she kept repeating.'

I went back to the office to do a write-up of the exhibition's opening for the next day's paper. I had almost finished this when Peter came from nowhere and stood in front of my desk.

'How did it go?' he asked.

'Good exhibition. The witchdoctor didn't want to tell me what she saw in the bones, though.'

'What do you mean?'

'She suggested my future was too hair-raising. Oh, forget it.'

'Well, I want to talk to you.'

'I wanted to invite you to the exhibition. I would invite you to my flat. But it's not allowed in this society. It would cause a scandal.'

'Things will change, but not yet. You heard what the Prime Minister Smith said. Black majority rule in two years.'

'Ian Smith's *volte face*. But subject to conditions agreed with Henry Kissinger.'

'It doesn't matter, actually because the African Nationalists will never agree to those terms. Majority rule will happen despite Smith, his cronies and stooges.'

'It's such a pity conversation always turns to politics in this country. It was the same at the private view.'

'How can you not talk about a crisis? But, let's find a new subject. Although, even the personal is political,' he added with a mischievous grin.

I finished my piece and handed it in and then we took a lift to the second floor and sat down at a small table in the empty canteen. There, we could talk in private.

'Tell me how the other half lives? What's your flat like?' he asked.

'It's nothing grand. I haven't done much with it. I've never thought of it as anything very permanent.'

'What about Blacks? They are regarded as temporary residents in the towns. At least you can claim your own space. I live with my parents and I share a bedroom with my grandfather. He snores.'

'Do you have brothers and sisters?'

'Three sisters and two brothers, and umpteen nieces and nephews. They don't all live with us but the house is so crowded that I sometimes get up at two in the morning, for peace to write.'

'You write poetry, don't you?'

'Dead right, I do. Full of angst and fury.'

'Any published?'

'It will be. When the time is right.'

'You mean, when Black Nationalism becomes institutionalised.'

'Something like that.'

There was a silence. There was a little nervousness between us; the silence and emptiness of the canteen gave us privacy but it also suggested intimacy.

'How about that book you were writing? About the so-called pioneers.'

'I didn't think you'd want to talk about that. It was published by a small press. Just five hundred copies. Let's not talk about that, seeing as you disapprove.'

'You know, Ruth. I think I've been a bit hard on you.' He scraped his chair back and sat at a distance from the table, looking solemn.

'Don't be silly. You've opened my eyes to a lot of things. It's a legacy, being brought up as a White Rhodesian. As a child, you can't take it all in. Then, little by little, you see how much the political and social situation has been abusing you. You remember that woman in the car park after the bomb scare. Her calling you - a grown man - a boy was just as abusive towards me as it was towards you. I've had to watch incidents like that on a daily basis.'

'You showed her.'

'I showed her and I thought, through little gestures like that, I could earn a place separate from this racist society. But now, I'm not so sure.'

'You can keep up little acts of humanity or you can leave. Just imagine what it would be like to throw off the politics of a small society. You Whites, if you are not racist, have guilt written all over you. Imagine if you could go somewhere where you could wash off your guilt over time, where Southern Africa wouldn't torment you. Take Scotland, for instance. You're always talking about your granny's memories of Scotland. The hills and the heather. The lochs and the rain. The bagpipes and Scottish country dancing.'

'I didn't realise I'd talked so much about Scotland. It was my grandmother's dream to go back there one day. And she never did.'

'You can do it for her. You can break free, Ruth. I guess there'd still be racism in Scotland, but it might not be quite like it is here.'

'I love this country.'

'You love this country but does it love you? Look at what's going to happen. The best you can hope for is a moderate Black government. But even that will not dispel the hatred bred during years of White minority rule. The system has encouraged bitterness and a yearning for revenge. Take me, for example. I can never forget the insults Whites have levelled at me and my people. I am sitting here, talking to you but our friendship can never be unguarded. Forgiveness takes many years to achieve.'

'I'm sorry.'

'There you go. The guilt.' He raised an eyebrow.

'I do feel guilty. I can't get away from it.'

'Perhaps I'd better go.' He started to get up.

'No. Don't go.'

'Then listen to me. Look at what is going to happen. Already 'The News' is getting in another Black African reporter. It could happen that you become a minority in a mostly Black newsroom. Until it comes about that you are like me now, but a token White. And maybe they'll cut your women's' page which, as far as I'm concerned, is an anachronism anyway. And, depending who leads this country, the censorship could be just as extreme as it is now. And then, on the social side, your fellow Whites will still be calling us 'kaffirs' and 'munts', only, at that point, they'll do it behind closed doors. It will be just as pernicious. And you can repeat 'I never voted for Ian Smith' to your heart's content because it will no longer be relevant.'

'Stop,'

'I'm finished. It's my turn to apologize to you.'

'Your words were a bit hard-hitting.'

'As I said, I'm sorry. I care what happens to you, Ruth Pearson. And maybe I can come to Scotland and you can put me up in your terraced house with your two children and your husband who dotes on you. We can talk about old times and I can tell you what life is like in Bulawayo after Independence.'

The witchdoctor said I'd go on a long journey.'

'An adventure,' he replied.

*   *   *

The young African man sauntered out of the office and came to the only pump on the forecourt, to serve me petrol. Masvingo, which was then called Fort Victoria, was the meeting point for an armed convoy that was to take us to the border post at Beit Bridge and into South Africa. There was a queue of cars for petrol and now it was my turn. I searched in my bag for my precious ration coupons. I had been given holiday rations for this journey, and now I saw them go, and silently said goodbye to the rationing system we had lived with since UDI, when oil and other sanctions had been imposed on Rhodesia internationally. The man was in no hurry. I would remember that about Rhodesia. The pace was slow. In some ways, we lived in the nineteenth century, promoting old-fashioned virtues and a seldom-quickening pace, although we were relatively speedy in a busy newsroom. The petrol attendant filled up my tank.

That was one of the things I would have to get used to in Scotland – filling up my own petrol tank. It sounds silly but it took me months to really get the hang of it. This African man was employed to do this. He took his time, took the money and went into the office for change. I gave him a tip and started up my old Fiat car. I'd had it serviced so that everything was in working order. It was, the garage told me, in fine fettle. It had to be. I needed it to take me along a dangerous journey. I was about to move off when I realized the attendant was cleaning my windscreen of all the dust that had collected on the journey from Bulawayo to Fort Victoria. When he had finished, I got out my purse again and gave him another tip. He clapped his hands and smiled. I couldn't find it in myself to smile back. There was a deep pit in my stomach that was churning. My mouth was dry and my hands were shaking. And the journey hadn't even begun. I drove away from the pump and onto the tarred road, a road that led into the centre of Fort Victoria, a sleepy town with few people on its pavements. But that wasn't the way I was going. I turned left at the corner and drove to a vacant plot where the convoy was gathering. There I joined Tanya, who was the whole reason behind my taking this particular route. I rode over the bumpy ground and parked next to her maroon Renault. I was to have a vision of that car in my mind for years to come because I travelled behind her in the convoy.

'You all right?' she asked, coming over to my window.

'It's so hot,' I said, struggling with my dry mouth.

'Get out and walk about while you can. It's hotter in the car.'

'And we're going to have about three hours of driving,' I said, getting out and looking about. In front of us, parked, were three large army trucks. What looked like about fifteen soldiers were milling about the plot. For the life of me, I can't remember what uniform they were wearing. My memory has blotted out certain details of that journey. It must be a protection. Let's say they wore khaki. What I do remember for sure is that they were carrying automatic weapons. My attention was fixed on their guns.

'Looks like they're ready for trouble,' I remarked to Tanya, with a mixture of fear and doubt.

'I wouldn't like to get on the wrong side of them,' she said.

I had known Tanya, on and off, for years. Her mother was French and her father South African. They lived in Johannesburg. She had owned a clothes shop in Bulawayo and one in Salisbury where up until today, she had lived, and her clothes were good for pictures on the women's' page. I had met up with her when she was in Bulawayo at a party, about six months before, and we had confided in each other that we were both planning to leave the country. The friendship grew stronger, partly because we were encountering the stigma associated with 'taking the chicken run'. We decided to do the run together, to meet up in Fort Victoria. Although this added miles to my journey, I was glad to be making it with someone I knew.

I searched on the back seat for the food and drink I had packed. I had never been so thirsty. The car was brimming with all my belongings, in suitcases and cardboard boxes. They weighed down the small Fiat. I found a bottle of Coca Cola and was greedily drinking this, when I looked up and saw that Tanya was talking to one of the soldiers. He was standing legs astride, bronzed in his khaki shorts and shirt, in a boastful pose. She was standing with a hand on one hip, stroking her straight blonde hair. She was clearly flirting with him. I drank my 'coke'. Eventually, the soldier walked away and she came over to me again.

'No harm in getting to know them.' She giggled.

'They do this every day. It's their job.'

She tossed her head and her sleek hair fell back into place. 'I'm starving,' she said. 'Did you bring your sandwiches? I've got mine in the car.' She went to get them. At that point, the thought of food made me feel sick. I watched her chew through a cucumber sandwich.

'You had better eat now, while you've got the chance. I believe we only stop once.'

'I'm not hungry.'

'You're sad at leaving everyone behind. I am too. When I locked the shop door for the last time, I cried. I've been feeling like crying for weeks. And I'm nervous as hell. Just like you. What if we get ambushed? What if my car breaks down? What if I break down? The thing I have to do is treat this as an adventure and when I'm in Joburg I can put it all behind me.' She chewed a strand of her hair. 'If we make it, and we will, I've got a new life to go to, a new job and a boyfriend. And you… you've got an even bigger adventure ahead. You're going to Scotland. How long do you stay with your parents first?'

'Three weeks.'

'Well, you've got to keep up your strength. Now, eat.'

I did as she said, but struggled, although I felt marginally better for it. The pit of my stomach was still hurting. More cars had arrived and, in the end, there were thirteen cars in all. It was nearing the start time of two o'clock. Before we formed the convoy we were told to gather in a group beside one of the trucks. We were a sad, apprehensive collection of people, brought together under a relentless sun. There were couples, one of them very elderly, and singles, predominantly women. They were dressed in an assortment of light summer clothes and unfashionable hats. One girl in 'slip-slops' was told to put on some 'decent driving shoes'.

The man doing the telling seemed to be the person in charge. He spoke to the group in a manner which suggested he was used to giving orders. 'I'm Captain Frank Owen and I am the leader of this convoy. If you have any questions, you address them to me. Provided you play the game, the procedure is very simple. This is how we travel: one truck at the front then seven cars, one truck, six cars; then a military vehicle keeps up the rear. If there is any trouble at all, you obey the orders from myself and my soldiers. Do I make myself clear?'

He got a grim 'yes', in answer.

'What you've got to understand about a convoy is that we do everything in unison. I don't want any wise guys, or ladies, and I don't want anyone trying to speed things up. We travel at eighty kilometres an hour, no more, no less. No slowcoaches either. We stop once on the journey and when we do, you stay near your cars. You may like to stretch your legs but don't stray. The bush is dangerous. And if you do want to go into the bush to pee, one of my men must accompany you. He will be discreet. All right, so far?'

'Now, you probably know the reason why we travel in convoy is because armed insurgents have been known to frequent the area. A few weeks ago some motorcyclists, who chose to ignore the services of our convoy, were ambushed and killed on this road. So, don't take this too lightly.' He went on, 'Pretend you are in the army for the afternoon. What we need is unquestioning discipline. Do that for us, and we will get you to Beit Bridge safely. Happy driving, folks.' At last he smiled. 'Let's go.'

The group had come together so briefly but, there was instant bonding. We went around shaking hands and wishing each other luck until Captain Owen barked an order for us to get into our cars immediately. There was a little confusion as we assembled in the sequence outlined. Tanya tucked herself in behind the second truck and I, as I said, was behind her. I looked in my rear view mirror, and waved at the elderly couple behind me. I noticed that the wife was driving. She hooted in response to my wave. 'Start your engine,' said one of the soldiers who were monitoring the whole process. My hands were dripping as I turned the key in the ignition. This was it. We were about to embark on a long, tense journey. But the engine didn't take. My car would not start. I went into a blind panic, turning the key again and again. Still, it wouldn't start. 'You'll flood it, lady.' The soldier's face was right at my open window. His gun was slung over his shoulder. 'Give it a breather and then try again.' I was aware of all the other vehicles in front of me and behind me, their engines idling. My car couldn't let me down now. I'd had it serviced. I knew it was old but it must stand one long, last journey. Some of the soldiers were climbing into the back of the truck ahead, a sure signal that we were about to leave. I imagined having to drop out of the convoy and having to go through the whole horrible departure again. 'Try it, now,' said the soldier. My hands were now out of control, or so I thought. I managed to grasp the key with my thumb and forefinger. Somehow, it turned and the engine started. The soldier gave me a thumbs-up, turned and went off to leap into his truck. I put my quivering foot on the accelerator. We were moving.

It took a while for us all to get into the rhythm of driving in convoy. To begin with, Tanya kept going too fast, and then slamming on her brakes. The old lady behind did the opposite. She would go too slowly and I saw her receding in my rear view mirror. Then she'd come speeding up towards my bumper. It was almost like a dance. We had to keep in step with each other. Once the rhythm was established, the long journey had really begun. For the most part of it we were surrounded by bush; long grass, thorn trees and rocks. At first, I kept glancing sideways to see if

I could spot any stealthy figures in the long grass but I couldn't take the intensity of that. I let in my memories of what I was leaving behind.

I'd even gone to say goodbye to Bruce. I'd walked over to his office one afternoon and was shown in by a secretary. Wearing a suit and tie, he looked very different from the Bruce who wore rugby kit. I always thought he seemed slightly unhappy in formal clothing, like a young boy whose mother had made him dress up, his skin gleaming clean from scrubbing.

'I appreciate your coming, Ruth, but I must tell you I think you are making a mistake. Going to South Africa is one thing, but Scotland…well, you'll be a foreigner.'

'I can't live under Apartheid.'

'You've always had radical ideas. But, Scotland? Do you know anybody there?'

'I've got a few contacts and there is my father's distant relative, Adeline…'

'It's a big step. What about the job? You're leaving behind a good job.'

'Things are changing…' I replied, thinking of what Peter had said.

'They're not going to open their arms to a young reporter from a rebel country.'

'I'm willing to take the risk.'

'There's courage and there's foolhardiness. I'm not sure which category you fall into.'

'My mind is made up. I'm going next week. I just wanted to wish you well.' I hadn't sat down and now I turned to go.

'What's the bet we see you back here in a year's time. Can you close the door when you go?' I detected a little sadness in his voice, but when I tried to look at his face I saw it was already focused on the work in front of him. I remembered he had to work extra hard to make up for all the time he had to spend in the bush. His war became so much more real to me now that I was travelling through the bush, with armed guards, towards the border. It was always a secret where the men went on call-up. I knew there were insurgents coming across from the Zambian and Mozambique borders but they never told us where they'd been or what action they'd seen. They either came back alive, or not.

We must have been travelling for about three quarters of an hour when it happened. The first thing I noticed in my mirror was the elderly couple receding. Then I realized we were losing part of our convoy. The cars in front were oblivious until somehow the second truck got wind of this and alerted the lead truck. Brakes went on all the way down the row and soldiers sprang out to form a line along the verge of the road. They faced the bush, guns at the ready. Others positioned themselves in the middle of the road. Captain Owen walked to our end of the convoy to see what was up. The elderly couple had a puncture. Swiftly, two soldiers set about changing the tyre. We were told to wait in our cars. Tanya kept waving to me through her window. The atmosphere from the bush was ominous as we sat and waited. By now, the sweat was streaming down my legs and I had a nagging headache. I also wanted to go to the loo, but I didn't fancy an armed escort. Suddenly I saw a dark shadow move in the bush. The soldiers had seen it, too. They trained their guns in its direction. Then something made a dash for it, crashing through the bush and out into the open. A buck bounded across the road. The soldier's lowered their guns.

When the puncture was mended, we formed our unbroken

convoy again and drove towards our official roadside stop where we were allowed to get out of our cars after the soldiers had done a reconnaissance. By this time, I really had to go to the loo and I was escorted through the long grass and behind a rock. The soldier averted his eyes. It was pure heaven to stretch our legs and to have a drink of lukewarm water. 'I feel so foolish to have held up the whole works,' the old lady confided in me. She looked embarrassed or over-heated because her face was an unhealthy shade of red.

'It's all right. It could happen to anyone. Where are you going?'

'Natal. We have a house there. We were farmers, you know. Up, until recently.'

'It must be a great wrench.'

'Yes. Gordon's got a gammy leg. He can't drive.'

'So, you've got to drive all that way.'

'There's life in me, yet.' She laughed. 'If only it weren't so hot.'

'You're very brave.'

Our conversation was interrupted by the Captain, who wanted us all to get back into our cars.

'Let's get this show on the road,' he yelled.

There was a feeling of unity amongst us that allowed a little confidence. We had done more than half of the journey. We would manage the rest. With luck, we would reach our destination.

I wished that Peter could have been there to talk to, but then I thought that Peter could have been on the side of an unseen enemy in the bush. I always wondered why Peter never joined the nationalist fighters. He was such an outspoken critic of Whites yet he worked within the system, albeit waiting for it to crumble. Our friendship was an unlikely one, full of tensions and compromise. Yet that friendship was one of the good things I had experienced during my adulthood in Rhodesia. We'd had this farewell 'do' for me in the newsroom. The news editor had supplied some bottles of beer and we'd all gathered around his desk. The editor had spoken: 'Ruth came to us as a very young, very green junior reporter. I won't say that she's leaving as a hardened cynic, but I will say that she has matured in the job and has been an asset to this newspaper.' He went on some more after that but I didn't remember the content. I was dry-eyed but overwhelmed. I did recall him saying, 'We all wish her the very best on her journey. Here's hoping that bonnie Scotland will learn to appreciate her. Come over here, Ruth. We have something for you.' He presented me with a flame lily brooch.

'This will remind me of what a wonderful bunch of people you are. Thank you. I've been very happy here,' I said.

It was afterwards when I was clearing my desk that Peter came up to me.

'So,' he said. 'It's your last few days as a White madam.'

'Even my departure is political.'

'May you find freedom from African politics.' He took a pen and swivelled around my reporter's notebook to face him. He then drew two crosses and turned the notebook back again. 'See if you can work this out,' he said. 'There's one for each cheek.' It was the only legitimate way of kissing me goodbye.

'Goodbye, Peter, I'll miss you,' I said, but he was no longer there.

I took my left hand off the wheel and felt the curved outline of the brooch pinned to my bodice. It was a badge of achievement and a symbol of what I'd left behind, who I'd left. They clearly thought that I might be coming back. The editor had even said that he'd be holding a job for me, for a year. Yet I knew, as I drove those last miles to the South African/Rhodesian border, that I would never be going back.

You would think that, as we drew closer to Beit Bridge, I would feel a sense of triumph that we were about to make it. But I went into a different realm. My body tightened and my brain seized. Alone in the car, I watched dispassionately as the needle on my petrol gauge moved into red. I saw the bridge over the Limpopo River. I saw buildings and barriers. I saw Tanya leaping about with excitement. I heard the group cheer. But these things were at one remove from me. There was passport control. In a daze I showed my passport. The customs official looked at it, closed it and said, 'Welcome to South Africa, lady.' I backed away from him. I remember taking my overnight bag to the hotel where I was to share a room for the night with Tanya, before travelling in tandem to Johannesburg. I sat down abruptly on the bed and stared at a wall while she changed and applied fresh make-up.

'I'm going to have a drink with the boys.' She meant the soldiers. 'It's the least I can do. Are you coming?'

I shook my head, not wanting… not able to… open my mouth because, if I did, I was afraid I would scream.

*   *   *

Bernard and I went outside for a cigarette. He lit mine for me. 'You and Max have done very well to keep your quarrel under wraps.'

'You saw how he was all over Natasha. And the speech …'

'Nobody took any notice of the speech because most of them didn't know he was excusing his lie.'

'You did.'

'I took my lead from you and appeared to simply enjoy the joke.'

Just then Max came out.

'What? You two out for a fag? Disgusting habit. Ruth, you've left the tablecloths on the trestle tables. Can you unpin them so that we can dismantle the tables and take them into the garage?'

I felt a kind of nervous energy make me brittle. 'I'll do it later.' This was a compromise because what I actually wanted to do was ask why he didn't unpin the tablecloths himself.

'It's going to rain tonight,' he said and went back into the house.

'It's the little things that lead to fury in marriage,' I said to Bernard who told me to stay where I was, sitting on the bench, while he went to retrieve the tablecloths. I lit another cigarette.

I would go to stay with Adeline and then, maybe, I could sleep.

However, it wasn't quite so simple because a chain of events led to a tragedy that overwhelmed my needs. It started after nine o'clock when it was still light and when Sally came across from the cottage having put the children to bed. She wanted to know where Jack was. I said I thought he was in the conservatory with Henri and she went inside. I stayed sitting on the bench although I had long since put out my cigarette. Then Sal came out again. She still couldn't find Jack. I got up and went inside with her, to look for him. We searched the house from top to bottom, although there was little chance he'd be upstairs. Finally, we went into Max's study. No sign of Jack. I looked around and thought, at first glance, that everything was in order. The cheque I'd returned was still sitting, with the note, on his desk. Then something – I'll never know what – made me look at the gun display cabinet. I saw that Max's great-grandfather's pistol had gone and the ammunition drawer was slightly open, with the spare key in the lock.

'Sally, he has taken the pistol,' I said with panic in my voice. My mouth had gone dry.

She stood there, playing with her lips, mesmerised by the empty space in the cabinet. Then, as if there had been some invisible signal to act, we rushed through to tell the others.

'You don't know he has taken the pistol,' Max said.

'The pistol is not in the cabinet, and the ammunition drawer is open. Who else would have it?' I asked impatiently.

'How long has Jack been missing?' asked Bernard.

'It could be an hour. I've been reading to the children,' replied Sally.

Henri suggested we call the police, and George agreed with her.

'Not yet. We'll look for him first.' Max took command of the search. Sally was to stay behind, to be near the children and in case Jack returned. Henri and Bernard were to scour the lower slopes of the hill. Susannah and George would do the same. Susannah had come downstairs and, apparently, her headache was better. The pair of them were ready for action and surprisingly sympathetic towards Sally. Max said he would climb to the top of the hill.

'I'm coming with you.' I felt sure that Jack would have climbed to the beacon.

'If you're coming, you are going to go at my pace. Don't hold me back.'

'Right.' I was too anxious about Jack to be affected by the put-down. I was also convinced that I should be the one to talk to Jack.

'I'm coming with you, too,' said Henri.

'This is likely to be a delicate situation. We don't want your renowned tactlessness making difficulties. I'm quite sure Jack will be at the top of the hill, but you take your size nines and go with the others to see if you can find him on the lower slopes. If you do find him, try and be subtle.'

Thinking back, Max's snub compounded Henri's jealousy over Natasha. She looked stung and angry, but she didn't try to follow us.

Max strode out of the house and I had no time to change my flimsy sandals for more suitable footwear. He, on the other hand, was wearing brogues with their tough soles, and he pulled on a light, waterproof jacket. I raced after him and found myself ankle deep in mud. I dragged the sandals out of the murky paste. I looked up to see cows, chewing stolidly, staring with suspicion at me. I stumbled onto the heather. There was a gap opening up between Max and me. I struggled on, driven by the need to stop Jack. No-one had said it, but we all thought he was going to shoot himself. Never had I climbed the hill so quickly. It usually took me three-quarters of an hour. I scrambled past gorse bushes, over uneven clods of earth and grass. Give him his due; Max did wait for me by the drystane wall. He did not, however, attempt to help me over the stile.

'Get a move on, will you?' he grumbled.

This was the last lap, I told myself. Needless to say, Max got to the top before I did. I came around the curve of the hill, between chunky rocks, and saw Max standing a few yards away from Jack, who was by the beacon, holding the pistol to his head.

'Come on, old chap, we can work this thing out,' Max was saying.

'Don't move or I'll pull the trigger.'

'Jack, you've got to think of Sally and your children,' I said quietly, controlling my voice.

'They'd be better off without me.'

'They wouldn't. They love you.' I could not stop my voice from trembling slightly.

He was silent. I thought that, at any moment, I would hear a shot and my cousin would lie lifeless before me.

'Suicide is no solution. It only creates problems for those you leave behind,' said Max, with a hint of impatience. I thought that somehow he did not understand what or with whom he was dealing.

'You've come so far, Jack. You've been through so much. Just think, one day you can go back to Zimbabwe. It has changed but it's still there,' I said.

'Nothing is there for me now. Will you stop trying to talk me out of this. I've made up my mind.'

'You are a man of courage, Jack, a soldier. This is a coward's way out.' I was desperately searching for a way to persuade him to give up the gun. I thought that, if I could find the right words, I would succeed. My first suggestion had been Sally and the children and how much they meant to him. I returned to that, moving a little closer to him.

'Sal is very worried about you. She's with Pip and Robbie, waiting for you to come back. She has been reading them stories. And, tomorrow, you can read them stories. They'd like that. You don't need to go back to Devon tomorrow. You could stay longer, and we could talk about old times. I miss Zimbabwe too, you know.'

'You left it. Before the ceasefire. Took the gap, like all those others.'

'I did and I want to talk to you about that. Give you my reasons.' I thought I was getting somewhere. I had drawn him into conversation. Max must have thought so too, because he didn't say anything.

'Everybody betrayed Rhodesia. Britain, South Africa, everybody.'

'Then don't betray yourself and your family. People want to hear what you've got to say.'

'They do not. You should see the look of boredom on their faces. Or else, they're goddamned hostile.' As he was talking he lowered the gun, naturally, in order to gesticulate. He didn't raise it again as we talked.

He spoke of his longing for Rhodesia and his longing for Zimbabwe; the things he missed; the people he had left behind; the dogs he loved. He returned to his story about how the invaders had threatened them.

I was now very close to him. I put out my hand and took the gun. He did not resist.

Max stepped forward and put an arm around Jack's shoulders. They turned, facing the downward slope and, very slowly, stepped along the grass between the rocks. I was high on my success. I held the gun in one hand and stroked it with the other. I watched them stop and Jack seemed to want to turn back, but he changed his mind. I held the ruby-studded gun in both hands. It was cold to my touch. Then a feeling of elation and power overtook me. I held up the pistol, with my finger on the trigger, and pointed at Max's retreating back.

The shot rang out in the lingering light. Max crumpled up, his legs buckled under him and he fell backwards.

I stood, frozen. Jack's immediate reaction was to duck behind a rock. Then, when the shot was followed by silence, he crept out to Max's side. He looked at him, and he looked at me. I was still pointing the pistol. I could not make out what was in Jack's eyes. He stayed immobile while I lowered the pistol. Then he bent over Max, who was lying motionless on the grass. He felt for a pulse. Seeing him bending over Max, I stumbled down, holding the pistol loosely.

Jack felt for a pulse again. There was a pause during which the sky seemed to crowd in on me. 'It must have pierced his heart. He is dead,' said Jack without emotion, now in control, now torn away from his own pain. He said nothing more to me but attempted to lift the body of my husband so that he could start carrying it down the hill, towards the house, but Max dead was too heavy, even for a strong man like Jack.

'We can do it together,' I suggested.

'No. I'll get Bernard and George to help.'

*   *   *

As I careered down the hill it was starting to get dark. I could see the lights on in the house but I didn't go straight there. Instead I circled and danced on the rough grass, in my flimsy sandals. It was a mad dance of triumph, a peculiar reaction to the shock. Max was dead. No more to criticize me, betray me, verbally abuse me, strip me of my self esteem. For those moments, I was crazed through lack of sleep, and through the tension of talking Jack out of suicide. For those moments, I felt that I had held power in my hands. Now, I held the gun as if it were a familiar appendage. It was my agent. And it was my reminder of what I had done. He had scorned me, lied to me and belittled me. Now, that was over. And I had ended it. I shivered, flinging myself down on the heather. I gazed at the globe of the moon then looked down and saw that my legs were covered in mud. The cattle were silent shapes at the edge of my vision. The smears of brown oozing over my skin served to remind me of my culpability. What had I done? I had wanted to leave Max, not to kill him. I had not planned to leave

Auld Oak Hall for a prison cell. I had intended to free myself, not to be locked up for God knew how many years. Lying there in the heather, I was suddenly very afraid. How was I going to face my guests? But it was too late for appearances. And Nicky? He would never forgive me. Wherever he was, I needed my son to comfort me, although I feared it would never happen. He would revile me. Everyone would turn against me. Even Adeline. I thought of fleeing, getting into my car and driving. Somewhere. But I would be brought to justice in the end. No. I had to face my accusers. But I lingered on the hillside for what must have been a couple of hours, wallowing in my guilt, reluctant to go inside. I saw the men, led by George with a torch; the other two carrying the corpse. I watched them descend; I saw them in a detached way, shadows carrying a burden.

Perhaps Max was not dead? Perhaps Jack had been wrong? He could have been wounded by the single shot. It was beginning to rain. I got up to go back to the house. As I neared the dining-room door and the lights, I was aware that I must look like a wild woman - hair tangled, dress muddied and wet. Brindle came around the side of the house to greet me. She launched herself at me and licked my face as I bent down to her. I almost cried at this show of love, but I was beyond tears. It was almost unbearable to be loved in that way.

With heavy heart, I opened the dining-room door and went in. I dropped the pistol carelessly onto a small table by the door. Some of my guests were standing, with drawn faces, on the other side of the dining-table as if to put a barricade between themselves and Max's body. I knew immediately that Max was truly dead. He had been laid on the *chaise longue* by the window and Henri was kneeling beside him, talking to him, stroking his hair, crying in a wretched kind of way. Brindle went straight to Max and sat down beside him, whimpering.

'Will someone get that bloody dog out of here,' hissed Henri and she looked up and saw me. She heaved herself onto her feet and lunged at me. Bernard and Jack pulled her off me, and she went back to Max's side. Bernard took Brindle into the kitchen and shut her in. I looked at Max's body dispassionately. He was gone. Nothing could change that. He didn't seem peaceful. His face held an expression of shock. They hadn't closed his eyelids. Nothing had prepared him for the attack from behind. Nobody could have told me that I was to be a killer. It had been our last altercation.

'Ruth, the police are on their way,' said Bernard.

Things happened very quickly after that. I was conscious of Bernard putting a blanket around my shoulders and handing me a cup of tea to drink in the kitchen, with Brindle. By these tokens, I knew that he, at least, hadn't condemned me outright. Some time later, two policemen arrived; Detective Superintendent Clive Drummond from Edinburgh, and Detective Inspector Donald Main from Hawick. They came in through the kitchen. It felt like the concourse of a railway station. The house became public, just as my relationship with Max became public. I was very still, and answered their questions to the best of my ability, under the circumstances. I did not want to see Max's body any more. I shied away from the sight of his cold, pale corpse. However, DS Drummond didn't want Max's body taken away before he had examined some of the evidence.

'He wasn't killed in the dining-room,' I explained. 'It happened at the top of the hill. I did it. I shot him.'

'And what were you doing out there at night, with a gun?' asked the Superintendent.

'We were trying to stop Jack. He was threatening suicide.'

'So, there were three of you at the top of the hill. Any others?'

'Not as far as I know. The others were searching the lower slopes and I think they had come in by then.'

'How well do you know this Jack?'

'I would say, very well. He's a first cousin.'

'He was in a fragile state of mind?'

'Yes. Still is. At the time he was desperate. Things haven't been going too well for him.' I did not want to get involved in telling him about Jack's homesickness and depression.

'Would you consider him a reliable person?'

I hesitated. 'Usually. Yes. I don't know.'

'Let me tell *you*. I've had a word with your cousin, and he tells me that he shot your husband, Mrs Heriot-Ross, which doesn't match up with your story, does it?'

'Jack is just trying to protect me. I killed Max.'

'If, as you say, you killed your husband, where is the murder weapon?'

I saw him in a gingery haze. He had ginger hair, balding slightly; ginger eyebrows and forearms. He wore rectangular, gold-framed specs and he spoke with an authoritative air. I wanted there to be a humane character behind his cynicism. All the way through, I kept trying to reach the man behind the professional. I took him into the dining-room, and showed him the pistol and he picked it up, wearing thin rubber gloves; examined it carefully and handed it to his Sergeant, who bagged it.

'It will be examined by our firearms expert in Edinburgh. He will tell us whether or not it is, in fact, the murder weapon.

An antique, I see,' he said with an eyebrow raised. I made myself watch as he turned Max over and examined the wound. 'Judging by the entrance wound, the killer was a moderate distance away from the victim. Right now, I can't tell the exact distance. Note, DI Main, there is very little blood. He must have died instantly. We'll let the pathologist estimate time of death.'

'It was about ten fifteen, just before it started to get dark,' I said.

'We'll let Forensics decide that,' he said. He felt in the pockets of Max's waterproof jacket, and in his trouser pockets, and found nothing but a few scraps of paper and a handkerchief. 'Take these, DI Main. And call an ambulance to transport the body to the morgue.' To me, he said, 'Your husband will be certified dead by a doctor and the body will then be kept for forensic examination. Just so that you know the procedure.'

He wanted to know where the pistol had normally been kept, so I took him through to the cabinet in Max's study. He saw the space where it had rested on brackets.

He pulled an earlobe, a habit when he was concentrating it seemed. 'Do you notice?' he asked, 'that there's another gun missing. Those are the brackets for a larger gun. Does that tell you anything, Mrs. Heriot-Ross?'

'There was a rifle there earlier on. Max would use it for shooting foxes.'

'And now, it is missing. Why do you think that is? Did your cousin take that as well?'

'No. Jack had only the pistol.'

'That remains to be seen.' He was evaluating everything I said, taking nothing as fact until it was proved.

'Superintendent?'

'Yes.'

'Will you want to take fingerprints? You'll find my prints and Jack's prints on the pistol. So, either one of us could be telling the truth. In fact, there'll be other prints because Max showed the pistol to the guests, who passed it around.'

'A party piece? I *will* want fingerprints. I also want this ammunition store tested for fingerprints. Did you get that, Inspector?'

'Yes, Sir.' DI Main had moved quietly into the room and was standing behind us.

It was all so practical, so clinical. Meanwhile my mind was in turmoil. I had expected to be arrested immediately following my confession. But the Superintendent had just gone about his business, asking me endless questions. Jack's version of events had complicated matters. I was disturbed by Jack's claim to have shot Max, not because I didn't want someone else to take the blame but because it threatened my grasp of what had happened; the enormity of the reality that I thought I was facing. I had held up the pistol and, on impulse, had aimed it at Max. I had never used a gun before, but I knew where the trigger was and I had to acknowledge the truth as I saw it. I had fired the bullet that killed my husband, and I had to suffer the consequences.

The Superintendent told us all to gather in the sitting-room. We were all there, except Sally, who was still with the children. She had stayed behind with them when we went to look for Jack and had refused to leave their bedsides since Jack had told her what had happened. DS Drummond accepted her absence for the time being. He stood in front of the television, just as we had done when we were playing charades. Henri did not want to sit next to anyone else, so she made a great performance of bringing in a dining-room chair and sitting, as if on an island. I sat next to Bernard, cloaked in the blanket he had found for me. All the same, I felt shivery.

The Superintendent began: 'There has been a great tragedy here, tonight. A man has lost his life. A wife has lost her husband, and you have lost a friend. It's a sorry situation, and it's made worse by the fact that you all seem to be telling me stories. What I want is the truth. Mrs. Heriot-Ross and Jack are each claiming they murdered Max. As far as I'm concerned it could have been either of you, or neither. Time will tell. The antique pistol will be examined by our firearms expert. However, we must bear in mind that there is another gun missing from Max's collection and *it* could prove to be the murder weapon. As things stand, I'm not arresting anyone tonight.'

'It's probably time for you to go to your beds,' he continued, 'And *try* to get some sleep. Tomorrow, I will have my men searching the hillside for evidence that might throw fresh light on this sorry affair. I understand that most of you are weekend guests. May I ask you, please, not to leave until I say you can go. DI Main, would you take those other guns from the cabinet and put them in my car. That may give these people a better night's sleep.' This last remark was scathing.

I stood up to go and see the policemen to the door, and my blanket slid to the floor.

'We'll see ourselves out. Until tomorrow,' said the Superintendent.

I went over to Jack. 'You don't have to do this, you know,' I said, searching his eyes for some clue as to why he was trying to protect me.

'What does it matter?' he said tersely. It was hardly a question.

'You two are in collusion, aren't you?' Henri said accusingly, then she turned away so that I couldn't see her face. 'I'm going to bed and I'm going to barricade my door, seeing as you don't have any locks in this place.' She marched off.

Jack went back to the cottage, without another word.

Bernard came over to me. 'I don't believe you did it, Ruth. It would have to have been an excellent marksman who shot Max. Not that…'

'What makes you say that?' I interrupted.

'To aim for the heart like that. Henri, for example, is an excellent marksman, although it couldn't have been her.'

It was nearly four o'clock in the morning and when Bernard, too, had gone to bed I went into the dining-room. Max's body was gone. The ambulance had come while we were all in the sitting-room. There was just a vacant space on the *chaise longue* where Max had lain. I made myself believe that Max's murder had really happened.

Before I climbed into my absent son's bed, I had a shower. Then I went downstairs to dry my hair, so as not to disturb anyone. In the hollow of the early morning, my mind churned. Although I thought I had killed him, my earlier, crazy mood of triumph had gone, to be replaced by grief. Max's absence was tangible, enveloping me and swelling to the ceilings. The house was a stranger now, with no master. I stared, with anguish, at the void that Max's dying had left. I regretted the rejection of his gift that morning, the harsh words, the erosion of the love we once had. I wept quietly. I was so tired; I ached in every limb. Most of my tears were for myself, for what I had done.

*   *   *

At first I couldn't sleep but I finally let go of the shocking realization of it all. I awoke and found myself staring at posters of pop bands, and pictures of sexy women on black backgrounds. I turned over and pulled the pillows around my head. Nicky would 'phone and I would have to get him home so that I could tell him about his father. When he had come back, I would break the news; we would hold each other tight, and mourn. I would describe it as a terrible accident. I would not reveal that I had thought I had shot his father, as I could not take the inevitable rejection by him. He would have to give up the relationship between himself and Cherie, or at least to let it take a back seat for the time being. Both of them would have to come home and talk about their promises to one another. Zoe and Hank would welcome them both with open arms. There would be no accusations; only calm negotiation. Yet, I would argue against Nicky going to the States for, without Max and without Nicky, I would have no immediate family in this country apart from my in-laws. All the time I was thinking these thoughts I realised that it was not going to happen that way. I was fantasizing, grasping for comfort. My mind was letting me down. I couldn't really focus or see a stable future. I was trying to bring events under control, when all they did was taunt me.

I gave a thought to the guests. I reckoned they would be up and about by now, and I really ought to go and see to their needs. If the tragedy had not happened, they would have been going home that morning. But now I had to offer to do some washing for them, and to get in more groceries. I wondered if the Superintendent would object to our going to the supermarket. Surely not. We weren't prisoners.

I had been planning to leave Auld Oak Hall for good that day. Now there was no husband to leave. He had left me.

I got up, put on my dressing gown and went nervously into

Max's bedroom. I looked at the tidy bed, not slept in, and the book half-read on his bedside table. There was his alarm clock, ticking away no time for Max. My heart was sore. Did a part of me love him still? I didn't believe I could hate if I felt no love. Jack said he'd shot Max. How could Jack have done it? He was right next to Max in the last minutes of his life. They were in the well of the hill top when I aimed the gun. They were walking away. Jack insisted on his story, so just say it were true. Whatever else had happened, I had still aimed at Max's retreating back. That was real. In my confusion, I didn't remember clearly the seconds before he fell. One thing I was certain of was that at that time, on the hill, on my birthday, I had wanted him to die.

I gathered up clean jeans and a T-shirt from my room. Henri was not there. I found my trainers and went through to dress in Nicky's room, before going downstairs.

Bernard and Sally were in the kitchen with the children. George and Susannah were not yet up and Henri had chosen to have her breakfast alone in the conservatory. Sally was remote and abrupt and I was too worn-out and confused to attempt to have a private word with her. I could tell that she was not impressed by Jack's confession. I watched her go through the motions of housewifery and parenthood in a detached, even sullen, manner. For the first time, I looked on Pip and Robbie as a burden. They would not fully understand what had happened. They would want to be entertained by people who were light at heart. There would be more pretence to carry through.

As if she had read my thoughts, Sally made a lacklustre suggestion that we set up a badminton game on the lawn. We were putting up the net between the fruit trees when the police arrived. There were two cars, one police car and one red Ford.

Four Scene of Crime Officers got out of the police car, and DS Drummond and the Inspector got out of the Ford. The uniformed officers were to search the hill for evidence. We had to wake up Jack to go with them and show them the spot where the shooting took place. The Inspector went with them but Superintendent Drummond had a word with me before starting to interview us individually in the sitting-room. Henri went in first. She wasn't talking to any of us at that stage.

I had several 'phone calls to make. I had to phone Max's parents, my parents, Max's legal partner and his solicitor, the funeral director so that he could be on standby, and Zoe, among others. Each time I described the shooting as a tragic accident and said that the police were investigating. I evaded any probing questions and kept the conversations short. It felt as if I were talking on the edge of my nerves. I hadn't eaten breakfast. I hadn't felt hungry. I gathered up all the dirty washing and switched on the washing machine. Then I made a shopping list. I needed to keep busy. Sally had cleaned the worktops but I cleaned them again. I stood for a moment looking out of the window, wondering how this could be still such a charmed kitchen view. It had no right. Now, there were children playing on the lawn, just as Nicky used to do. I mentally resurrected the swing that had hung from the old apple tree and the sand pit that had long since been grassed over. The scene was so idyllic that it had to be lying.

The 'phone rang and I started, nervously. It could be Nicky. However, I was disappointed.

'Mrs. Heriot-Ross?'

'Yes.'

'This is Alasdair Hewitt from the Weekly Courant. I'm sorry

to disturb you. We've heard that your husband has been killed in a shooting accident. Is this so?'

'Yes.'

'If you don't mind my asking, how did it happen?'

'I do mind you asking. All I will tell you is that the police are dealing with the matter. Now, if you will excuse me...'

I put the 'phone down on Alasdair Hewitt, who would no doubt transfer his questions to the police. I was annoyed with myself for not having anticipated a call from the press. After all, I had been a newspaperwoman myself, at one time. Again, it shook me to think that the tragedy was going to be exposed to public view. The ripple of information went wider, to the community and to the press, beyond the police and the ambulance men who had taken Max away. It might have been a mortuary van that took him away. All I know for sure is that I did not see Max leave Auld Oak Hall for the last time, because the Superintendent was addressing us in the sitting room. Did I really want to see Max put in a body bag and lifted onto a stretcher? Seeing this would have made his departure so final, a confirmation of his death. Yet, not having seen this procedure meant there was a gap, a sudden absence, a nothingness where there had been somebody.

8

I took Brindle for a walk down by the river, near Zoe's house, and the dog waded into the water. It was hot and dry that day. Winter had finally decided to release its grip, or so it seemed. The sun shone on the sheep as they grazed in the fields. It shone through the trees, and the water was in dappled light. It shone on my back and the warmth was as soothing as a massage. My eyes watered in the glare as I waited for Brindle to come back to me.

Later, walking up the driveway, I had a sudden aversion to the house. It contained all the ghastly drama of the past twelve hours. It contained death and suspicion. Inside were guests who would make demands on me, when all I wanted was to be alone. I let Brindle in the back door and quickly shut it behind her. I turned on my heel and headed for the place I had always gone for silent retreat, the old walled garden. Looking around to check no-one had seen me, I turned off the road, not fifty yards from the house, onto the dirt track that led to the walled garden entrance. The peace of it under the sun welcomed me. Max had let it lie fallow for several years now, and the grass grew tall. It was terraced, with drystane walls covered with wild flowers. In the spring there were stabs of red from the poppies that grew in clumps between grasses. At the top of the slope, outside the greenhouse that was as big as half a bungalow, there was a lily pond. Lilies bloomed large yet delicate on their pads, afloat on murky water. They reminded me of Ted Hughes' poem, 'To Paint a Water Lily', which ends like this:

'...Now paint the long-necked lily-flower

Which, deep in both worlds, can be still

As a painting, trembling hardly at all

Though the dragonfly alight,

Whatever horror nudge her root.'

What horror nudged the roots of these serene lilies? They were a symbol of my life at Auld Oak Hall. On the surface, I lived in a captivating place, had everything I could need. We had a relationship that appeared functional to the outside world, but the roots... the roots of this living trailed in slimy depths.

The sun was unrepentant as I opened the glass door of the greenhouse. The glass walls and roof were covered with a thick and tangled old vine. We used to get black grapes from that vine although they were small and few in number. The place was still, with tools and pots left standing as though a gardener had been called away in the middle of his work, many years before. A tap dripped into a moss-covered drain. On the wooden worktops there were trowels and forks, dusty gardening gloves and a pair of hedge clippers with rotting wooden handles. Fern grew out of the crevices of the brick wall at the back. That day I didn't find peace, but I was able to tackle my confused mind. DS Drummond, when he had arrived that morning, had disclosed something that should have given me relief, but which I found highly disturbing. The firearms expert had reported that the pistol had not been fired recently. Its ammunition did not match the bullet that Forensics had extracted from Max's heart. The conclusion was, as far as I now felt sure of what had happened, that I could not have killed my husband. It was definitely the pistol that I had aimed at him. It was definitely the pistol that I had carried down the hill. My finger had been on the trigger but now I was being told by scientists that I did not pull that trigger. So, my guilt lay in my intention, in my thoughts and in my motivation for a crime I might have committed if someone else hadn't got in before me. With all the logic I could muster, I reasoned that I now felt guilt and fear. I felt afraid of my guests and for my guests. The chances were, there was a murderer amongst them and we had to carry on daily life until Superintendent Drummond found out who it was. What was the murderer's motive and was it possible that he or she would kill again? Was I at risk? Who else was at risk?

As I began to probe the possible motives my guests might have had, I looked across the grass and saw a figure entering the garden. It was Bernard. I tensed. I still couldn't fathom out Bernard. He was sauntering in, obviously unaware that I was there. I ducked under the work bench and waited for him to go, but it was futile. He was coming in the door. The tap dripped, but there was no other sound and I could almost hear Bernard breathing. I got up, pretending that I had been bending down to pick up something.

'You've been exploring?' I tried to put everyday normality into my voice.

He didn't reply to this, but said, 'My guess is that you came here to retreat. It's that kind of place. I'm sorry if I've disturbed you.'

'I was just going.' I started to move, but so did he. He went to pick up the hedge clippers and held them up in front of him. 'Fine implements. Must be as old as you or me.' He pulled them open and shut. 'Still sharp, mind you.'

In my imagination, this action had very quickly grown to be a threat. I fancied he was going to come at me with the clippers. 'Please put those down,' I said abruptly.

'Sorry. I guess I startled you.' He put down the clippers. 'There's no need to be afraid of me, Ruth. Far from it. I'm not the killer. I would not harm you.'

'Who should I trust? I've told you things about me, but I don't know much about you, Bernard. You come here as a friend of Henri's, and then you have very little to do with her.'

'I didn't come here with a hidden agenda, if that's what you mean. I am grateful to her but I don't always agree with her views.'

'And then you tell me you're attracted to me when you know I am married … was married. You kiss me …'

'I'm not sorry we did that. And I would do it again if you'd let me.'

'Not now. Can't you see I'm struggling to come to terms with my husband's death…with a crime committed here, of all places… in rural heartland where nothing like this ever happens?'

'I want to give you comfort, not to add to your distress. I can wait.'

*   *   *

When we got back to the house there were two strange cars in the driveway, outside the garages. They were not empty. Strangers spilled out of them as we got closer. With Bernard by my side, I found myself staring straight at the lens of a camera. It took me

234

a minute to understand what was going on and, in that time, the local newspaper had taken its picture of the grieving widow accompanied by a strange man. The media was determined to suggest that there was some relationship between Bernard and myself, and my husband not yet in his grave. Two reporters from two different, local papers were firing questions at me.

'Mrs. Heriot-Ross has been through a great ordeal. You should have the decency to leave her alone,' objected Bernard.

'Max Heriot-Ross was well known in the community. Our readers deserve to know what happened,' said one of the reporters, a man who wasn't Alasdair Hewitt.

'This was not just a tragic accident, was it?' asked Alasdair.

'What do you think the motive was for this killing?' That was the other reporter.

'Is it true that he was shot in cold blood on the hill during a house party?'

I felt bombarded.

'This is an invasion of privacy. Please leave,' said Bernard, putting an arm around my shoulders. They took this latter gesture the wrong way and used it to further their suggestion that I was a widow having a premature affair with another man. I didn't realize this at the time, but did when I later saw their stories in print.

I summoned up some energy. 'It's no good you asking all these questions. We do not know the truth yet, and nor do the police. You're right. My husband is dead. That's all I can tell you.'

'But who do they suspect? Who do *you* suspect?' asked Alasdair.

'Everyone and nobody,' I replied. 'Now, will you go away? I'm going inside. I have to speak to the Superintendent.

'Is it true they've got DS Drummond on the case?' asked the reporter.

'You seem to have got your story already,' I said.

'Then why won't you give us the facts. Make sure we get them right. Have you got something to hide, Mrs. Heriot-Ross?' asked Alasdair.

'Mrs. Heriot-Ross has given you enough of her time.' Bernard began to say but just then we heard another car draw up and a woman stepped out of it.

'I'm Kathy Mackay from 'Scotland's Express'', she said, pulling at her skirt and smoothing it down. She held a notebook and pen in her free hand. 'I'll take just a moment of your time,' she added.

'What does the 'Express' want with this story? You know what a backwater this is.' I must have sounded peeved.

'Precisely. Murder committed in idyllic rural setting. That's the story. I take it you are Mrs. Heriot-Ross?' She didn't wait for me to answer. 'Can you tell me who the police are questioning?'

'Everyone in our party who has been staying here this weekend.' She had a way of rooting me to the spot and demanding my attention. She must have been about thirty, with short, thick hair and slightly protuberant eyes.

'And do they have a prime suspect?'

Her photographer started taking pictures of me and Bernard.

'Not that I know of.' My voice was becoming hoarse. 'Bernard is just a friend,' I protested, seeing Kathy's eyes glinting at the thought of a romance blossoming and the husband not yet buried.

Yet another vehicle drew up outside the garages. This time, it was a van. Two men got out and huddled together, organizing equipment. Then they came for me with their camera and their microphone for me to speak into. The man holding the microphone tripped on a stone and nearly fell, but recovered enough to say, 'You must be Mrs. Heriot-Ross. We're from regional TV. I'm

Malcolm McCann. We hear that your birthday party turned into a tragedy and that your husband, sadly, died.'

I could not answer.

'Is it true that he was killed with one of his own guns? There seems to be some mystery surrounding the whole sorry affair,' said Malcolm McCann.

'He was shot on the hillside.' I was clinging to facts. I could not fathom why Max's death would be of interest to the whole of the Borders, and to the rest of Scotland if Kathy Mackay had her way. 'That's all we know at present. The police are investigating. They will tell you.'

'And how do you feel, Mrs. Heriot-Ross? Don't mind the camera, by the way. You're doing just fine.'

'I feel devastated, and exhausted, and I have to go inside to an interview with DS Drummond.' The only reason I was staying to talk to them was because I had memories of myself as a young reporter, investigating a murder. And I thought of how I considered my investigation, my questions, to be in the interests of the public's right to know. Now, I thought how intrusive the press was.

Malcolm was preparing to ask me many more questions. 'Can you think of anyone who would want your husband dead? I understand he was a wealthy man. Who stands to inherit his property?'

All of them were crowding around, waiting for my answers. At that point, I had had enough. I hesitated. 'I feel dazed. I can't answer any more questions…I'm sorry.'

'Speak to the police, if you need further information,' said Bernard, firmly pulling me away. We hurried into the house. Sally said later that she saw the press through a window, going up onto the hill.

Superintendent Drummond was waiting for me. I apologized and told him what I'd been doing. He muttered something about priorities. We went into the sitting-room and he shut the door.

'Please call me Ruth.' I sat on the sofa, still shaken by my brush with the press, while DS Drummond paced the floor.

'First of all, Ruth, I will confirm what I told you this morning. Our experts tell us that the pistol was not the murder weapon. Thus your claim that you shot your husband using the pistol is unsubstantiated. However, this doesn't, altogether, put you in the clear. There is the other weapon to consider. And I hope you're going to be a little more truthful from now on.'

'It was all so unreal.'

'That's as maybe. Now, Ruth, tell me what sort of relationship you had with the deceased?'

I hesitated. It seemed as if I had been answering so many questions already. I would have to answer the police's questions openly and truthfully.

He was impatient. 'Good, fair to middling, bad?' He didn't wait for me to answer. 'It must have been bad for you to aim a gun at his back.'

'I was planning to leave him. The relationship has, I mean *had been,* deteriorating for many years.'

'Did anything recent make you particularly angry with your husband?'

I told him about Florence's letter and about Grace.

'So he was unfaithful and that would give you motive.' He said this almost as an aside and then, turning to me, said, 'You certainly had motive. You're not beyond suspicion yet, Ruth. We still haven't found the second gun, as far as I'm aware. You could have taken that up on to the hill with you when you went looking for Jack. Pity your alibi has proved a bit economical with the truth, shall we say? He seems to have been trying to save you by claiming to have committed the murder himself. I wonder what his wife makes of that. Come to that, what is your relationship with your cousin?'

'We're usually very close but his depression has been getting in the way of the friendship.'

'Both Rhodesians. Blood relatives and immigrants.' He had a disconcerting way of saying out loud what for others would remain thoughts. Perhaps he lived alone and had become accustomed to talking to himself. I was curious to know what he was like, after all my future rested in his hands, but I was also annoyed by his remark.

'What has being Rhodesian got to do with it?'

'With your history, there will be an even stronger bond.'

'Just so long as you're not going to discriminate on those grounds.' He didn't seem to have heard me. 'Jack's wife is also Rhodesian,' I added. 'Our nationality has no bearing on the case.'

'I need to know who I'm dealing with. Don't worry; you won't be treated unfairly because of your origins. Let's get back to where we were. The question of the guns. The pistol and the rifle, these were your late husband's guns. Did he use them for sport?'

'He was a member of the gun club and he used the rifle to shoot foxes. But I've already told you that. The shotguns were for clay pigeon shooting, and for shooting pheasants.'

'Did you take part in any of this?'

'No.'

'Do you know how to fire a gun, Ruth?

'No. Just what I imagine you do, and what I've seen on TV and in movies.'

'And yet you claimed to have fired the pistol that you claimed had killed your husband? It strikes me that you have a vivid imagination.' He was probing for facts and unnerving me as he did so and I found some of his questions too penetrating.

'I was confused. When I aimed and there was a shot, I thought I had done it. I was very tired out by the stress of Jack's actions and by the day's celebrations. I hadn't slept well for days.'

'You had been drinking?'

'Not excessively, and not for some hours.'

'It was your birthday, I believe.'

I nodded.

'Your son wasn't here for it?' asked the Inspector.

'It's another story. It's complicated. He and his girlfriend have run away together because her parents want to take her back to America. I have no telephone number where I can contact Nicky and he doesn't yet know about his father.'

'Tell me, when was he last here in this house?'

'On Friday afternoon.'

'And today is Monday. He hasn't been here at all since then?'

'No.'

'Who has been here since Friday, apart from the people I know about?'

I told him about Niall. Then he asked if anyone bore a grudge against Max. I explained that George and Susannah had been having some difficulty over a loan from Max. I also said that Max had not been getting on very well with his work partner.

'Did he tell you this?'

'I read about it in his diary.'

'He wrote a diary?' His eyes brightened.

I went to fetch the diary from the study.

'Do you make a habit of reading other people's private scribbles, Ruth?'

'Only when I want to understand the person better.'

'So you think Max had some enemies, do you? Let's have a look.' He was already reading the diary. Then he raised his head and said, 'You can go now, for the time being.'

'I forgot to tell you that there were some other people here yesterday. Adeline was here. She's eighty something years. She brought her great-niece, Natasha, who is a student. And Zoe was here. That's Nicky's girlfriend's mother. An American.'

'Well, I won't hold that against her,' he said pointedly.

He continued to leaf through the diary.

'Max was very taken with Natasha, if that is of any interest.'

'Enough to inspire jealousy?'

'I was embarrassed for him. Henri was jealous.'

'By the way, Ruth, what do you stand to gain from your husband's will?'

'I don't know…yet.'

* * *

As I was coming out of the sitting-room, I found myself face to face with DI Main, who had come in from the hill, followed by two officers.

'Sorry, Madam.' I didn't know whether he was apologising for bumping into me or for what he said next. 'We have a warrant to search the property. To start with, I want to go through all the rooms in this house, with my officers.'

'If you're going to do a thorough search of the entire property, it's a big task,' I said, thinking that I'd rather they didn't invade our privacy.

'My men are used to doing a search, and they know what they're looking for.'

'The rifle?'

'Aye. We want to look for any clues as to what might have put your husband at risk.'

I could tell that DI Main was making an effort to talk English to me, when he would naturally talk in broad Scots. He dropped a Scots word here and there. He struck me as being very polite and, for a policeman, sensitive. All the same, what he was proposing to do was overturn the whole property. Inside, I rebelled against this, but I reasoned that if I could be part of the search I could keep an eye on what DI Main was doing, so I said, 'You can start upstairs. I will come with you.'

We went upstairs and I showed him Max's bedroom and dressing-room, while the officers searched the other bedrooms. There was not much for him to see in Max's bedroom, but he took in with sharp eyes the bed; the two bedside cabinets, each with a lamp on top; the alarm clock, the book. He lifted the duvet to see underneath, and then crouched down to look under the bed. He was a professional doing a job. I tried to emulate his attitude, but the sight of Max's black leather slippers, ready and waiting for him, made the back of my throat ache.

DI Main had soon finished his search of the bedroom and we went into the dressing-room. This was a small room looking out across the field with the chestnut tree. It housed a wardrobe stuffed full with Max's clothes, and a chest of drawers. DI Main felt his way through the wardrobe, checking its base and feeling with his hand around the top where we could not see. He then moved to the chest of drawers, made of mahogany, with its standing mirror on top of a glass surface. On this lay several items including Max's wallet which was thick with twenty pound notes and credit cards.

'I'd say your husband wisnae very careful about where he left his money. Anyone could have taken this. Would you say, Madam, that all the credit cards are here?'

'I don't know. We kept our financial affairs separate. I suppose I'd better cancel those cards.'

'You do that.' He fingered through a few invoices lying on top of the chest of drawers and then his hand came to rest on a gold fob watch and chain. He picked this up and examined it. It had engraving on the inside of the case that read: '*With all my love H.H.*'

'Who is H.H?' asked DI Main.

'I presumed the watch was something he inherited from his uncle. It's an old-fashioned thing to keep, but he always wound it. To my knowledge, he never carried it on him.'

He put the watch down and picked up a photograph, in a red leather frame. I explained that the photograph was of Monica and Walter, Max's parents. The Detective Inspector examined it for a while. He seemed to find everything of interest. Next, he went through the drawers, careful not to cause too much disturbance. Then he said, 'It seems to me that you and your husband didnae share the bedroom or this dressing-room. Can ye show me your bedroom?'

I took him into my room, which was a combination of a bedroom and a study. I explained to him that Henri was using the room at present. He worked his way around it, taking in everything. The bed. He searched under it and lifted the duvet, pushing Henri's nightgown back under the pillows. The dressing table on which Henri had put an assortment of make-up and toiletries. The bookshelves. The antique desk. The computer on its table, the filing cabinets, the kettle. 'I am a freelance writer,' I said, trying to explain the combination of bedroom furnishing and office equipment.

'Looks like ye practically live in here,' he remarked candidly.

I did not reply. However sensitive he was, I couldn't help feeling that I was seeing my world being horribly exposed.

*　*　*

The house that the police were searching in such an invasive kind of way held so much history, not just of Max, Nicky and myself, but of Max's uncle, his grandparents and great-grandparents who had lived here. Dead, but their lives informed Auld Oak Hall. The very furniture they had sat on, eaten at, dusted and cleaned. It had come down to new caretakers and Max's generation. I took refuge in the study and sat at the great desk that Max had used and that Nicky would use. And Nicky's future children. I found some paper and a pen. I wanted to make a list, to remember the good things about Max, the things that made him human. I wanted somehow to forgive Max for what he had done to me. As it turned out I wasn't giving myself enough time, but then it seemed urgent that I do it before the funeral, so that I could lay him to rest without malice in my heart, so that I could try to be the loving wife at his graveside. There seemed nothing worse than acting out the part of the distraught widow. I wanted to have done with pretence.

The first item on my list was easy. I wrote it down and then let myself drift into the memory of it.

*　*　*

A half moon shone over the great house and before us a vast stretch of grass to 'float' across. The night air was alive with the sound of Scottish music coming from the grand marquee. Fiddles whipped up the wish to dance among couples, and groups still arriving at the ball. I had borrowed a green satin dress from Adeline and wore the gold shoes I had bought with money my mother sent me. Max looked fantastic in his kilt and jabot. Black shoes, black jacket, black hair. And a sporran. There is something very sexy about a sporran swaying strategically over tartan. His eyes were the eyes I saw when I first met him: ingenuous, blue, before they became calculating. But I was trying to forgive… suffice it to say, that night his eyes were alight, dancing, happy when he looked at me. Arm in arm, we entered the marquee and there was a scene of splendour. A series of round tables with white, starched cloths and flowers on them. People milling around in their finery. Other men with other tartans. In those days I didn't know that different clans wore different tartans. I saw only colour and variety. Inside, I was still a young girl from Bulawayo, who was caught up in the wonder of this scene. The women wafted around wearing satin, sashes and bows, many of them in Princess Di style dresses. Blue was a favourite. With diamonds. But the attitude of dominance belonged to the men. Even Wilf's large Australian form was clothed in kilt and jacket. He and Henri were keeping us a table, and we went and sat down.

'Angela is with Lord D______,' Henri whispered loudly to me, oblivious to the fact that her whisper was akin to my normal voice, although she probably wasn't heard amongst so many loud voices and the music of the band. Nor did she take into account that I did not know who Angela was, let alone Lord D______. I looked across in the direction she was rudely pointing and saw a man in his fifties with thick silver grey hair and a carefully trimmed beard. He had broad shoulders that were emphasized by his neatly fitting jacket. The frill of his jabot was pristine white, matching the almost embalmed quality of his lightly wrinkled skin. He had presence, and so did Angela. She was dressed in white with a tartan sash. She slid a manicured hand down from one broad shoulder and onto his chest, fingers splayed to show off a couple of diamond rings. To reassure myself, I stroked the brooch, pinned to my dress, which 'The News' had given me.

'His wife died not so long ago,' Henri was continuing. She shuffled in her chair, her red dress plumping out around her.

'Where's your partner?' I asked her.

'Ken? Somewhere around. He's just a friend. I've known him a long time. He is my nanny's son. I mean, I don't have a nanny now. He was… he is her son. We used to play together. He helps me out on occasions like this. He's in the printing trade. You should talk to him. He has a job vacancy.'

'I didn't expect to find a job at a ball.'

'It's not what you know. It's who you know. Look, over there, at the couple sitting down. That's the Earl of A________. No. Not the one with black hair. The one next to Lord D________. He's English but he comes from Scottish ancestors. A touch effete, wouldn't you say? And his wife, the Countess, looks like Alice in Wonderland. I don't know why we're graced with their presence. Probably because of Angela. Most of the titles are at those tables over there.' She pointed, and then seemed to lose interest. She took out a lipstick and mirror and applied bright red to her lips.

I turned to Max, who was on the other side of me, but he was engaged in talking to the Lord. Across the table, Wilf was in close conversation with his partner, a petite woman with curly brown hair and glasses. I wondered what they would look like as a couple standing up together. He was so tall and she was so small. Soon, Ken came up and sat down next to Henri. She introduced us and suggested that she and I swap places, so that Ken and I could talk. I thought afterwards that it was a convenient ploy to enable her to sit closer to Max, but that was only part of her intention.

Ken, I was to discover, was one of those clean-cut people who always look well, as if they've just showered after stepping off the squash court. He was always measured in his responses and was very egalitarian. He gave the impression, even right at the start, that he valued my input; that he would consider carefully what I had to say. I was to work for him for a couple of years. Now, at the ball, I was somewhat in awe of him.

'We do leaflets, brochures, newsletters, magazines, short books. That sort of thing. I rely on my receptionist to keep the office ticking over.'

'I can work to deadlines. I worked for a newspaper for nearly ten years.'

'The vacancy has arisen because Megan, who has been with us for seven years, has stopped work to have her first child. She wants to be a full-time mum. It's sad to see her go. It's a close-knit unit. She has been a godsend. You'll need to answer 'phones and type.'

'I touch type and I have shorthand.'

'That would be handy. You have quite a strong accent. Is it South African?'

'No. Rhodesian.' I became aware of my flattened vowels, like a bit of food stuck between my teeth.

'Have you left Rhodesia for good?'

'Yes. I've emigrated. I'm here to stay, if Scotland will have me.'

We had a long talk about Southern Africa. He said he had

visited a cousin in Cape Town, a couple of years before. 'You'll find the Scottish weather very trying,' he said.

'I'm getting used to it. It's a beautiful night, tonight.'

'You've noticed we always talk about the weather. It's because it's so unpredictable. You're here with Max Heriot-Ross, are you not?'

'I am, when he is about.' Max was dancing with Henri.

'How did you meet him?'

'I met him playing bridge. A distant relative who lives in Edinburgh got me to join a set.' I didn't tell him my opinions on bridge because I guessed that he liked a team player. We went on to talk about sport, squash and football in particular. I was at a disadvantage because I had never, at that point, watched a football game in my life. I could have told him plenty about rugby. I had a vision of Bruce, strangled by his tie, sitting behind his accountant's desk in the office, when I had gone to say goodbye. Ken and he would get on, though I judged that Ken was more balanced. We made an appointment for me to go to his printing works the following week.

Max and Henri were back from the dance floor and she nudged me to swap seats with her again. Max put an arm around my shoulders and said, 'The next dance is with you.'

The compère announced the Eightsome Reel and Max pulled me to my feet. I was hastily trying to remember what Adeline had told me about this reel. She and I had been practising reels in her sitting-room. I thought the Eightsome was one of those we'd paced out to music from an old, crackling gramophone record but I couldn't, at that moment, recall how it went. 'Just follow what the other lasses do,' said Max. I rehearsed the Pas de Bas in my head as I followed him onto the floor. We found a set and waited for the dance to begin. Henri and Ken were in our set. Max quickly told me the sequence of the reel. 'Remember, don't bounce when doing the Pas de Bas,' I heard Adeline's voice saying. None of that mattered because, the moment the music began, I was sucked into the group's exuberance. I learned that Scottish reels were not necessarily genteel affairs. That Eightsome was a wild whirl that was reckless and addictive. The men were the controlling force, whooping and flinging their arms in the air. And when they came to take my hands I had to pull to keep my balance.

'I think it would help if I knew what I was doing,' I told Max, breathlessly, as we left the floor. His eyes were even brighter, and he had a heightened colour.

'Some people know exactly how it should be done and they get very annoyed with ditherers,' he warned.

'I had Henri pushing me in the right direction. I haven't told you yet, she might have got me a job. With Ken, the printer.'

'Well done. Nothing beats networking.'

Dinner was served at the tables, and we ate a three-course meal of smoked salmon, beef stroganoff and trifle. I was happy, happier than I had been since I left Rhodesia. Never had I dreamed that, not many months after leaving, I would be dining and dancing with a man I was falling in love with; dining with lords and ladies in a marquee full of men in kilts and women dressed as princesses. How little this had to do with a braaivleis in the Matopos or a rugby dance at the club. How would Peter interpret this occasion, these people? There wasn't a Black face there. I missed seeing African faces. They were so much part of my life. I did pass Black people sometimes in Edinburgh streets and that was comforting.

'Hey, Max, cobber, where's the haggis?' Wilf called across the table.

'You'll have to wait for Burns Night,' said Max, smiling.

'I want to see them stab it,' said Wilf.

'You mustn't be too taken in by Scotland Ltd.,' Max replied, lifting his wine glass to his lips. 'The tartans and the thistles and the haggis are not all that Scotland's about.'

'I like it,' said Wilf. 'I like all this fanfare. Beats Wimbledon and tea on the lawn. I've even got my kilt on. Did you see?'

'I noticed.'

'Nothing underneath, ye ken. That's the tradition.' His girlfriend put a restraining hand on his arm, and he gave her a sloppy kiss on the cheek.

After dinner, we danced more reels. I couldn't get enough of them. I gained in confidence as the night went on and I had more wine. Adeline had taught me well. I was provoked by the reel, I don't know what it is called, where the man dances towards one woman and then suddenly shifts to dance with another woman. This was teasing *par excellence*. I got caught out every time. Still, the men pulled and whirled us around so that my grip was becoming stronger. Henri, of all people, landed up in a flounce of red on the floor at one point. 'What a hoot,' she cried and clumsily got back onto her feet. However, when we landed up in a set with the lords and ladies of the evening the dancing was a little more genteel.

Max and I walked off the floor, hand in hand, panting with the exertion. 'To the great outdoors?' he asked, wiping his face and neck with a large white handkerchief, which he got from his sporran. I remember wondering what else Scotsmen kept in their sporrans. And then there was the little dagger some of them slid into a long sock. It was called a Sgiandubh. That whole evening, before I had become used to Scottish ways, was like being in a pageant. History was woven into the age-old activity of partying. While we were dancing, we were flirting with an invisible background of stag- and fox-hunting, pheasant- and grouse-shooting, brooding dark mountains, salmon fishing, haggis and the Loch Ness Monster. All this informed the stately home by the sea that was our setting. 'Culture shocked?' Max asked. He did notice things in those days.

'You might say so.'

He took the glass of wine from my hands and led me towards the marquee exit. The night air was chilly, but invigorating. He let go of my hand and lifted up two light chairs, expecting me to follow him to the centre of the lawn, where we sat under the moon and stars in splendid isolation. We did not look at each other but took in the noise and the light thrown out by the marquee. We weren't even touching. I sensed his mood becoming sombre. 'Are you sure you want to stay in Scotland, Ruth?'

'I can't go back.'

'That isn't an answer. The question is whether or not you want to go back.'

'I've told you how I left Rhodesia. I can't see myself ever taking that journey again.'

'You could go to South Africa to be with your parents.'

'No.'

'You've told me about your father, and your grandmother, being born in Scotland. But wasn't your coming here a little bit like sticking a pin, at random, in a map?'

'We were always taught that Britain was the motherland.'

'It seems to me that you've jumped from the nineteenth century to the twentieth century. You've told me about the slower pace. Scotland is not just this sort of thing.' He gestured towards the marquee. 'Scotland means competition and hard work and harsh weather. I wasn't joking when I told Wilf not to be fooled by Scotland Ltd., that being the way this country is marketed abroad.'

'I'm Rhodesian-born. That means I'm strong.'

'You see, it matters to me because I find myself becoming serious about you.'

'I'm glad I met you, Max. I'm not fickle or a traveller passing through, if that's what you think. If Ken will give me a job I can start to put down roots.'

'I have an uncle living in the Scottish Borders. He's very old and frail. He has told me he is going to leave me his property in his will. When that happens I will need a wife.' That night he didn't go so far as to ask me to marry him. It was too early on in our relationship. Yet he kept hinting at it. I had to express my doubts.

'What worries me about my relationship with you is that you are in a different league. You're at home with lords and ladies. I'm at home with people who wear sun hats and flip-flops and drink beer.'

'I'm sure that the lords and ladies, as you put it, would do the same given a different climate.'

'I don't have a public school background and...'

'But you have wide horizons...'

'And I haven't any money.'

'Money is not important,' he said, and I think he meant it at the time. 'If those are all your objections, the next thing for you to do is to meet Mummy.'

He didn't say that he loved me then, but we were already in love that night of the ball.

*   *   *

I was trying to think of an occasion when Max did say he

loved me. He was always more practical in demonstrating what he felt for me, but one time he actually used those three words was when he took me to see Auld Oak Hall for the first time. Strangely it hurt me to think of it.

'Where are we going?' I asked him. We were driving in his Porsche along a road I now know is the A68.

'I told you. The countryside. This is Soutra Hill. Can be blocked by snow in the winter.'

I sensed with a little quickening of emotions that this was meant to tell me I would be using this road in the future. Why the secrecy? What was he about to show me? My anticipation was increased by the mystery of our destination. We passed farms and hotels and a scattering of houses. 'There's where we will be having dinner.' He pointed out a stone-built hotel with a painted stagecoach outside, and children's play things. He was driving fast so I didn't catch the name. We sped past trees, whose leaves had turned to autumn red and gold. Some way along, he turned off the A68.

'It says this way to Hawick.' I pronounced it as I saw the spelling.

'You say 'Hoyick', and we're not going there. Close your eyes, and keep them closed until I tell you to open them.'

I did as he said, sliding back in the seat, feeling the lurching as we went around corners. Then the motion of the car stopped. 'Keep them closed. I'm going to open the gate.' When he got back in, he said, 'Okay. You can open your eyes.'

I saw before me a long, gravel drive dominated by a massive oak tree at the entrance, by the gate. I remember thinking, 'We must be going to visit somebody.' As we drove up the drive a large, stone house came into view. Max parked the car by the back door and we got out. He took some keys out of his pocket. Although I was beginning to realize that this was Auld Oak Hall - the oak tree at the entrance to the drive had given it away - I was still playing the game that he had instigated. I asked, 'Aren't you going to knock?'

'Why would I knock to be let in my own door? This is what my uncle left me in his Will. This is mine, Ruth, and you can live here too, if you will consent to be my wife.'

'Max...'

'Wait. Don't give me your answer yet. Let me show you around.' He unlocked the door and we entered a large kitchen. Max almost danced around it, opening units and drawers. The smell of cleaning agents hung in the air.

'It's very clean and neat,' I said, feeling something of an intruder.

'Home help has been.' He dismissed my remark and went on to open the doors of a large, pine dresser.

'The old boy has kept the family silver.'

I saw, sparkling in front of me, an array of silverware; platters, bowls, trays, candlesticks, and items I didn't know the names of. I'd never owned any silver and had used only the few pieces my mother treasured. I felt slightly in awe of this collection. I had this same feeling as Max ushered me through the rest of the house. Everything in this house was of good quality, from the grandfather clock to the French silk curtains in the dining room, to the mahogany tables and cabinets, to the brass loo-roll holders.

I took in the house with half of my mind, the other half daring to believe I had received a marriage proposal. I had thought it might come and I had tried to decide what I might say. I might have been more positive but for what Jack had said. 'Max doesn't know where you're coming from,' was what he had said. Did Max understand me? Would he see me as just a decorative addition to his own happiness in this gift of a house? Even at that time, I could see that he thought the house was small whereas, with its five bedrooms, I thought it was big. I had told Max that people thought I was a gold-digger in a relationship with a rich man. He replied to the effect that he was not a rich man. Lord D______ was rich. The Earl of A_____ was rich. Whereas, to me it seemed that Max owned treasure. Even then, we were coming at things from different angles - but that's with hindsight.

'Needs a dishwasher,' Max said, leaving the kitchen behind. He pulled me up the stairs and into what appeared to be the master bedroom, which was furnished in blues. He went to the window. 'Come here,' he said. We looked out onto a field with a large chestnut tree standing some way into it. 'Mine,' he said. 'Acres of it.' He drew me to him and kissed me lightly on the forehead. But that was all, because he couldn't stay still. 'Definitely, a new bed. A king-size bed,' he said as he left the room. I followed.

The other bedrooms had clearly been used for guests. They had single beds, with linen pillow-slips and silky eiderdowns. Beside each bed was a carafe, and a glass for water. They all had views of the garden, or of the fields, or of the driveway.

Max had opened the linen cupboard at the end of the passage. He was frantically pulling out lace and linen and soft blankets. He came across some old-fashioned, pottery bed warmers. 'We won't need these,' he said. 'Come on. Let's do the rest of downstairs.'

'Aren't you going to put those back?'

'Home help has got to have something to do.'

In the hallway was a coat stand, which was groaning with coats and hats. Beside it was an ornate wooden tub filled with walking sticks, umbrellas and, oddly enough, a carpet beater. Max tried on a bowler hat and wore it when we went through to the study.

'Desk. Books. Guns. Ideal, apart from these wretched pipes. I'll bin those. No. I might get a good price for them. We don't want smoke in the house, do we, Ruth?'

'You're aware that I've tried to give up.'

'Well, try harder. Talking about smoke, let's light a fire. I see there's one laid.' He tossed the hat onto the desk. 'All these papers will have to be sorted through. Job for the winter evenings. Now, that fire…'

I sensed that, once we were sitting beside the fire, I would need to have my answer ready. He had been acting as if he expected me to say yes to his proposal. Now, I had to commit my life to him, or not. I became nervous and self-conscious as we sat together on the hearth in front of the fire. However, my indecision evaporated as he reached for me, and subtly aroused me. I'll never forget the way we made love on the hearth that afternoon in our new house.

'Will you marry me, Ruth?'

'Yes.' My decision came on the wings of instinct.

'I love you.'

'I love you, too.'

*   *   *

When I was pregnant with Nicky, I used to watch the lambs playing in the field. I would get a chair; sit out on the lawn and watch, fascinated. They frisked and gambolled, tumbling over bales of hay. They didn't need to be taught how to play. I felt the child kick inside me. Max had felt it, too. I had taken his hand, and I held it to my burgeoning belly…

No. Remembering the good times was too painful. It reminded me of what I had lost. I might have persevered with my list, but Sally came to the door, saying there was a phone call for me.

When I knew who it was at the other end of the line, I found myself stumbling over my words: 'Something has happened, Nicky... I don't want to give you the news over the 'phone. You must come...'

'You won't get us to come back that easily. Why is it imperative?'

'Don't ask me questions now. I will tell you...'

'We have decided to stay away until we get a promise from you and Dad, Hank and Zoe, that you agree to us getting married.'

'It's all right. We are willing to talk to you and Cherie. But you're forcing my hand, Nicky. I'll have to tell you.'

'What's happened? Is it serious?'

'It's about your father...'

'Tell me, Mum.' I could hear from his tone of voice that he had begun to realize that I was not just trying to trick him into coming home. 'I can take it,' he said.

'I don't know if you can, but I will tell you all the same. There's been a terrible accident.'

'And it involves Dad...'

'Come back, Nicky, please. So that I can tell you in person. I just can't...'

'If it's that serious I'll come, but I'm not bringing Cherie.'

'You'll need Cherie, son. Both of you come and we'll sort things out. Get here as soon as you can.'

'We'll come today.'

Nicky wouldn't commit himself to a specific time, which was going to make the waiting more anxious for me. I needed to do something. For instance, I had to feed everybody. This might include the Superintendent and the Inspector, and I didn't know how many police officers. DS Drummond was busy interviewing Jack, who had come back into the house having shown the police the spot where Max was shot. Sally was now openly furious with Jack, refusing to believe that he could have killed Max. She was convinced that his confession was a foolish attempt to protect me. On top of this, she was exasperated that Jack had gone back to his old lethargic state; putting this down to feelings of remorse. As she put it, he blamed himself because his suicide bid had led to Max's death. We all gave her a wide berth, for the time being. The children had tired of badminton and were again painting pictures at the kitchen table. Bernard was giving them some tips. I looked at him, and he seemed too good to be true. I had a nagging feeling about Bernard. He was a painter. He was divorced from his wife, and he had grown-up children. He could have come here as a conspirator with Henri. Yet that wouldn't have included falling for the victim's wife. Or, was that a ruse?

Sally. Behind her rage, could there be concealed guilt? Together, she and Jack could have been driven by jealousy; envious of Max owning a farm. As Jack admitted, if he hadn't set out to commit suicide none of this would have happened. We would not have been out on the hillside at night. There would have been no gun. If I let my imagination lead me, I could think that the suicide attempt was just a ploy. They were used to guns.

George and Susannah had an obvious motive. Max seemed out to ruin them. The question was - would that be enough to lead them to kill him? Max's lawyer could still act on his behalf. It would have been a bit naïve to think they could escape the problem by killing Max. And yet, Max may not have had time to instruct his lawyer about foreclosing on the loan. In such a case, Susannah and George would get a reprieve.

'Are you with us, Ruth? You've been daydreaming again. We have to make lunch,' said Sally.

I had some mince and there was lots of pasta, so we made spaghetti bolognese. It turned out that the policemen weren't going to stop for lunch, and DS Drummond was going into town. Before he went, he informed us that the police had not found the gun in the house, the outhouses, the garages or the cottage. They'd finished their search of the buildings, for the time being. We asked him if it was all right for us to go to the supermarket. He said that he had no objection. There were now too many associations in the dining-room, so we ate in the conservatory, some at the small table and others eating on laps. Henri grudgingly joined us.

*   *   *

George had interrupted his meal to take another call from his assistant in Edinburgh on his mobile.

'You could use the landline,' I told him when he had finished the conversation. 'It would be less expensive for you.'

'I don't want to block the 'phone. You'll have important, incoming calls.'

He looked haggard. The wrinkles on his brow were more obvious than they had been before. He was restless, going outside to take the calls, coming in to pick at his food. 'I've got my assistant manning the shop, but he can't leave it to make deliveries. There's an expensive bureau that should have been delivered to a new customer today. What do I tell my customer? That I've stayed on in the countryside because of a murder? But, really, the dashed thing is I don't know when I can get back to my business.'

'You must understand that George lives for his business,' Susannah informed us. She had risen from her sick bed mid-morning and was looking fresh and headache-free, dressed in white.

George ignored her remark, and told her that it was a good

259

thing that she had come downstairs. Otherwise we might think she was being laid low with guilt. 'Dashed awful this being on the suspect list. It feels like we're all guilty until proved innocent,' he said.

'If you're not guilty, you've got nothing to worry about,' said Henri. It was as if she had spoken despite a resolve to keep silent.

'And this Drummond fellow. Seems a decent enough chap,' said George. 'A bit arrogant.'

'I think he knows his job,' said Bernard. 'I wonder how often the police have to deal with murder in this rural area.'

'Not often, is my guess,' said Susannah. 'The general impression I get of our Super is that he likes to be top dog. Once I'd understood that, I got on with him very well. Mind you, my poor head was throbbing.' She was obviously very hungry because she wolfed down her spaghetti bolognese and asked for more.

Henri left the room as soon as she had finished her meal. We saw her go outside and disappear around the corner of the house.

'She's probably gone for a walk. I must say it's a relief because she is not making matters easier,' complained Sally.

'Perhaps she is just being honest,' Bernard defended her.

'That's what I mean. It's like we're all guilty. I, for one, would never have laid a finger on my poor, dear friend,' said George.

'Darling. Whoever could think such a thing?' Susannah was well on her way through her second helping.

Jack, who had been silent, also left the room. He appeared to be going back to the cottage where the children were. Sally had fed them earlier.

'When something big happens, people usually stick together. But we can't, under the circumstances, so we just have to muddle along,' I said, and then abruptly changed the subject. 'Sally and I are going to the supermarket. Does anyone need anything?'

I took a few requests, and then Bernard asked if they could use the scrabble game that he'd spotted in the sitting-room. When we left, he and Susannah and George were settling down to a game of scrabble, George with his mobile handy.

*   *   *

Sally was now putting on a good face. She and I, and the children went to the supermarket and, fortunately, I did not meet anyone I knew, or the press. Unfortunately, I was not to be so lucky when we returned home. Alasdair Hewitt had turned up again, this time without his photographer. He raced up to me as I was getting out of the car.

'Mrs. Heriot-Ross. Sorry to bother you again. Is there any more news?'

'You are bothering me,' I said. Sally carried on unloading the shopping from the car.

'But you, yourself, must want to know who did this terrible thing to your husband. Did he have any enemies? Is there anyone you suspect?'

'You've asked all these questions before. You and the rest of them.'

'Is it true that your son is missing?'

'Don't try that one. Nicky has been away with his girlfriend but he'll be back soon. He doesn't know about his father, and I want to be the one to tell him.'

'My story will be out tomorrow.' He worked for a weekly paper. 'That's why I'm asking you for the latest facts.' He seemed to be trying to move the conversation on, to a personal level. 'I thought you might want to give priority to your own, local paper.'

Perhaps he thought this was winsome but I replied curtly, 'I'm sure you've got good intentions, but at the moment I'm busy.' I turned and hurried into the house. Give him his due. He did not try to follow me.

We unpacked the food and I was going through to the sitting-room with some tea and biscuits for the Superintendent when I heard DI Main talking to him. The door was slightly ajar. I hovered outside with my tray, and listened.

'I have now interviewed all the guests individually,' said the Superintendent, and I imagined him pacing the room, both men standing. 'And each of them has a different view of the events before and after Max's untimely death. I have also read the deceased's diary, and it shows that he had a fair number of enemies outside of this circle. I will be interviewing his legal partner and his computer consultant. The guests and Ruth must not think, however, that that lets them off the hook. All of them have motives for wanting Max dead.'

'Just so, Sir,' said DI Main. He coughed.

I hoped they hadn't heard me at the door but I kept my post, nervously.

The Superintendent continued: 'There is little forensic evidence forthcoming at present. There was nothing of note on the body, apart from one, long, blonde hair from which we can extract DNA, but my guess is that it belongs to the young lady who came to the barbecue. At the site of the murder, there is little to be seen. There are no footprints in the grassed area where Max fell. In any case, the coming and going of the party would make it difficult to isolate the footprints of the culprit. It seems that the bullet entered the back of the deceased and lodged in his heart. The pathologist has taken a single bullet from the heart of the deceased and the serrations on this will, most likely, match the serrations on the gun, when we find it. It is most likely that the single, fatal shot was fired from the missing rifle. A lot depends on us finding this rifle which, you are aware, we haven't done, as yet.'

'We will find it, Sir. The SOCO's are still combing the hill.'

'Mm. It's my guess that's where it is. Now, Inspector, if you haven't done so already, I want you to take fingerprints from all of them tomorrow. Oh, and take fingerprints from the ammunition drawer.'

'Right, Sir. Have you any idea yet how the crime was committed?'

'In my opinion…'

He seemed to have turned and his voice became fainter. Although I strained, I could not hear. I desperately wanted to know what he was saying, but I had to be satisfied with a gap in his reply. Then his voice became louder again. '…this theory seems to vindicate Ruth and Jack, but it is only one scenario. For instance, even though this looks like a deadly accurate shot, how do we know that Max was, in fact, the intended victim? I'll leave you with that thought, Inspector. I'm for going home now.'

Thinking I might be discovered any minute, I hastily knocked on the door and took the tray in. Fortunately, they seemed to have no inkling that I'd been eavesdropping on their conversation. They welcomed the tea but drank it rather quickly and DI Main left with the other policemen. DS Drummond was taking his leave of us in the kitchen when Monica burst through the door, followed by Walter. 'Where is my son? What have you done with him?' she demanded. How old she looked and Walter, as ever in her wake, appeared drained and aged. They were then in their eighties.

I rose to greet Monica, but she would never be touched. I kissed Walter on both cheeks.

'Well, where is he?' she repeated.

'Monica.' I wanted to phrase the stark facts sensitively but it was almost impossible. 'He's in the mortuary. We can't bury him until the investigation has been completed, and there is to be an inquest,' I blurted out.

The Superintendent stepped forward. 'I'm very sorry for your loss, Madam. I should explain that we need to establish just how your son died.'

'And who might you be?'

'I am in charge of the murder enquiry. Name's DS Drummond.'

'Murder? You said it was an accident, Ruth.'

'I didn't want to upset you. I couldn't bring myself to tell you.' I was facing Walter as I said this, pleading with him to understand.

'I'd rather know the truth. If someone has murdered Max, they will pay,' said Monica.

'We haven't caught the murderer yet, Madam, but I assure you, when we do, that person will be brought to justice.'

Just then, Nicky walked in the door. I rushed over to him and hugged him. Suddenly all the sadness, the shock and bewilderment encircled me. My legs had become weak and I anticipated the horror of having to tell him the facts, as we knew them. Nicky helped me into a chair and he himself stood stiff and pale. Fortunately, DS Drummond took it upon himself to explain the situation to him. While he listened, Nicky's eyes were swimming with tears and his lower lip trembled.

'...This is just an outline. Until we know the facts, everyone who has been in the house during the last twenty four hours is under suspicion, along with any others who might have a grudge against the deceased.' He paused. 'I'll want to question you tomorrow. Meanwhile, your grandmother needs to pay her respects in the mortuary. If you'd like to come too, I can lead you there, now.'

Monica, Walter and Nicky went to the mortuary, while I stayed behind to do something more mundane. I was going to cook a large fish pie for supper. It focused my mind and, as ever, I had Sally and Bernard assisting me. Zoe telephoned to say she had Cherie back, and they were just sitting down to talk to their daughter. She was curious to know what stage the investigation had reached, but I put her off, saying I didn't want to talk about it. She told me that the gossips were saying I had something to do with it. I told her to ignore what they said, but I felt vulnerable. This on top of Monica's attitude made me feel I could not cope. I went over to Brindle in her basket and stroked her.

They came back from the mortuary, looking very sombre. We had opened up the dining-room because it was practical to eat in there, but the memory of Max's body lying on the *chaise longue* was an indelible part of the atmosphere. We sat down to eat.

Monica broke the silence. 'Today I learned that my son is dead, and you give me fish pie to eat. I ask you, Walter? Fish pie?' She swirled her fork around in the mashed potato.

'Ruth is just doing her best,' said Walter.

'And all you others just sitting, eating this wretched meal. No doubt choked by guilt.'

'Come dear, you're overwrought.' Walter tried a smile at the group but was faced by a wall of silence. 'We're all desperately sad about Max but harsh words won't bring him back.'

'I have no children left in this world.'

'That reminds me,' I said, partially aware that I was about to be rash. 'We must let Lawrence know what has happened.'

'How dare you mention his name, Ruth? Have you no sympathy?'

'Granny, will you stop criticizing my Mum?' Nicky was upset by the way the conversation was going.

'And now my only grandson is siding with her.'

'What do you expect, dear?' said Walter.

'Well, at least somebody has a son left in this world.'

After supper, Monica and Walter went back home and Nicky asked if I minded him going over to see Cherie. The others sat about, not saying very much. The children went to bed, and Henri also. I could have gone to sleep early too but, with Nicky in residence, I could not use his room and I was going back to the sofa again.

I was considering climbing onto it when the doorbell rang. It was the local church minister, the Reverend William Wetherspoon. He was a man of medium height, with a chubby face and a compassionate air. He came in, apologizing for disturbing us in our time of sadness. He had heard about the tragedy and wondered if he could be of assistance. I was in two minds about his visit. Max and I hadn't been to church since Christmas, and I couldn't say I was anything more than a believer who didn't support organised religion. At the same time, I felt a glimmering curiosity about how God could help me, and an even deeper need to know where Max had gone. I took the Reverend through to the sitting-room.

'You might need help with the funeral arrangements,' he suggested.

I explained that the funeral could not take place before the inquest.

'You'll need to bury him at some point.'

I was to discover that he was a very practical man, who did not thrust religion at me. Instead, we discussed an order of service for the funeral, and I got out an old hymn book so that we could choose hymns. I cautioned him that Monica would want to have a say, and suggested that Nicky might want to give a tribute to his father. I said I would arrange for him to speak to the two of them, and to Walter.

'The Lord knows your needs, Ruth. You can rest in that knowledge. You can't go through this terrible ordeal trusting in your own strength alone. Believing in Jesus Christ will take some of the pain and worry from you. Think about that.' That was the closest he got to evangelizing.

He asked if he could say a prayer for me, my family and guests; asked if we could pray together. I agreed and afterwards I did feel a lifting of some of the weight on me.

When he had gone, I found the downstairs of the house empty, except for Todd and Brindle. Everyone, it seemed, had decided on an early night. I set up my bed on the sofa. I slept for a few hours and then was woken by a terrifying dream. I was in a boat in the middle of the ocean, a small fishing boat, and I remember thinking that no-one could get me. However, the sea changed from calm to turbulence. I was in the middle of a wild storm; a high wind blew, rain was pelting down and the waves were crashing around me. Suddenly, everything stilled and there was someone walking on the water towards me. At a distance, he looked glorious, someone who could help me back to shore but, as he came closer, I recognized him. It was Max, with anger in his eyes, a bloody torso and carrying a rifle. He came right up to the boat and raised the gun, pointing it at my head. His eyes were mesmerising, mad even. He wanted revenge and I was going to die. I woke up, bathed in sweat, trying to drag myself out of the aftermath of the dream.

I lay there, half asleep on the sofa, which was too short for my legs. Uncomfortable. Then I got up to try and ease my brain, and quietly went through to the kitchen where I had a cup of tea and a cigarette. My hands were shaking. It was guilt. No-one but I knew the suppressed anger in my heart towards the man I had been living with for twenty-four years. It had been gnawing away gradually at my soul for the past fourteen years. As well as his infidelities, it was the constant haranguing. Why was I so slow? Why didn't I serve a starter with dinner? Why did I wear yellow when it didn't suit my hair colour? Why did I spend so much time in the garden? Why were my nights so restless? I was to make sure I didn't wake him. Why was I cutting down on alcohol? It should not be allowed to affect his intake. Why didn't I earn more money? It went on, so that I couldn't relax. He would not let me be myself. I remember thinking that I should have left him a long time ago. Then all this might not have happened. He had died on my birthday so that whenever I had a birthday in the future I would remember his death. I would never get away from it.

Who was responsible for the death of my husband? DS Drummond had said he thought there was a fourth person up on the hill. He would flush out the killer. He was canny, and had experience. I switched from thinking about the Superintendent to imagining that someone had been trying to kill me. There was no reason why not. If the murderer had aimed from behind, he or she could have missed their target. The shot could have been meant for me. Or Jack, for that matter. The killer could have hit Max by mistake. With my slim hold on reality, anything seemed possible.

All was quiet in the house, but were they all sleeping? Were any of them having nightmares like me? Were any of them plotting a second act of violence? I went to the kitchen drawer and got out a knife for protection, then put it under my pillow.

I must have slept for about half an hour when I woke again, this time convinced that there was someone in the room. It was dark. I lay very still, scarcely breathing, not sure if I were awake or dreaming still. The grandfather clock in the hall ticked loudly. I dared not move. Then, little by little, I inched my head around, trying to see in the darkness. I slowly worked one hand up and under the pillow until I had a grip on the knife handle. I couldn't see anyone in the gloom, but that did not mean there was nobody there.

I lay clutching the knife for some minutes, my heart competing with the tick of the clock. Nothing stirred. Nobody moved in the room as far as I could see or hear. I thought I must have been imagining a presence. I let my hand rest lightly on the knife, and tried to make myself more comfortable on the sofa. Then I was startled by a scraping sound, like a drawer being opened. It came from the direction of Max's study. I tried to remember if I'd left the door open or closed. I could not. I peered up over the side of the sofa, now drawing the knife out from under the pillow. The door must have been open because I saw a beam of light, as from a torch, shine in the study.

I no longer hesitated. I crept out from under the duvet and made a dash for the hall. I felt my way up the stairs and quietly opened the door to Nicky's bedroom. I went over to his sleeping form and shook him. He eventually gazed at me with half-seeing eyes.

'What are you doing with that knife?'

I hadn't thought that I would appear threatening. 'I'm just trying to protect us. There is someone downstairs.'

'Are you sure?'

'Positive. He's in your Dad's study.'

'How would he have got in and why didn't Brindle wake us all up with barking?' He was wide awake now.

'Nicky. Stop asking questions. We've got to do something.'

'If he is in the study he can use the guns.'

'The police took them away.'

'That's a relief. Put that knife away, Mum. There's going to be no more violence in this house.' He got out of bed and put on his dressing gown. Contrary to his advice, I took the knife when I followed him. At the bottom of the stairs, he stopped and whispered, 'Don't say a word.'

I nodded, although he could scarcely see me. I was trembling in my thin nightgown. We crept into the sitting-room and felt our way silently past the sofa until we were outside the study door, one on either side. Peering into the study we could see a dark figure holding a torch beamed on a stack of papers. Nicky's hand was sliding up the door frame and around onto the wall. Without warning, he switched on the central light. George's head shot up from the papers he had been reading and he blinked. He stood there, looking abashed. He did not appear to have a weapon.

'What do you think you're doing?' demanded Nicky.

'It's not what it looks like.' George tried to excuse himself.

'I know what he's doing,' I said, putting the knife down on the desk. 'He's looking for the loan agreement so that he can destroy it.'

'I'm ashamed to say, you've got me all figured out.'

'You haven't bargained for Max's cautious ways. He'll have given his lawyer a copy,' I said scornfully. I was relieved that

George had not threatened violence, but angry that he had given us such a fright.

'I hope you don't mind. I borrowed your torch.' He held it out, clearly having given up his search for the time being.

Nicky and I laughed wryly at the impertinence in his apology.

*   *   *

I was glad to see the police return in the morning. This time I looked on them as protectors, although Superintendent Drummond was away interviewing Graham Thomson.

Henri was difficult at breakfast. She still wouldn't eat with us. I gave her a glass of fresh orange to take through to the conservatory, with the toast she had made. 'How do I know you haven't put something in this?' she asked.

'What do you mean?'

'Cyanide or something.'

'I can assure you it came straight out of the carton and nothing else went into the glass. You have to trust me.'

'I can't trust anybody. I'll get another glass, and pour my own this time.'

'It's up to you.' A part of me sympathized with her, as I didn't trust anybody either.

'I'll drink it,' said Bernard. 'Watch me, Henri.' He drank deeply from the original glass. 'Nobody is trying to poison you.'

'Some weekend in the country you've given us, Ruth,' said Henri.

'We're all on edge,' said Bernard. 'Don't make it worse, Henri.'

'We should all be in mourning for my beloved Max. The way some of you are behaving, you'd think nothing had happened.' Henri was looking at me.

271

'I'm just trying to cope in my own way,' I protested.

'Don't feel the need to excuse yourself, Ruth,' said Bernard. 'It's sympathy you need, not criticism.'

Henri walked off haughtily to eat her breakfast, alone. Sally came in to say that Pip had a cough and was running a temperature. She took away milk and cereals for their breakfast, which they would have in the cottage. Jack was still in bed and she wanted to keep an eye on him, as well. Nicky, George and Susannah were also apparently asleep, so that left Bernard and myself in the kitchen. 'Did you ever play the game, Murder in the Dark, as a child?' I asked him. 'We were all given slips of paper, and one person was the murderer. The lights were switched off and, with great shrieks, the murder was committed. When the lights were switched on again, we had to guess who the murderer was. Something like that. And that's what this feels like now.'

'Only, it's not a game,' he said. 'This is the first time in my life I've come so close to being accused of murder. Of murdering a man I hardly knew.'

'You must tell me more about yourself, Bernard.'

'Suspicious still? Well, I'll tell you if it satisfies you. I was born in Glasgow of working-class parents. My father was a baker, and my mother took on cleaning jobs. I had three sisters and one brother. Two of my sisters are still alive. When I was old enough to leave school, I got a scholarship to study at the Glasgow School of Art, but my parents did not think studying art was a secure enough career direction for me to take. I ended up going to university and studying biology. I became a teacher, and taught for many years in Glasgow and in Edinburgh. It was only after I took early retirement that I could devote my life to painting. That's me, in a nutshell. Pretty innocuous stuff?'

'That sounds more like a curriculum vitae. What about your marriage?'

'That doesn't bear talking about. Fiona and I married in the full flush of love and soon had a daughter and a son. The marriage became stale, and we decided to part company. You know the rest.'

As he talked, I couldn't help but admire what seemed like simple honesty. He certainly came across as someone I'd like to see more of, when this ghastly business was over. As he opened up to me, I decided that Bernard would rather lift a paintbrush than a gun, but you never knew…

Nicky, arriving downstairs for breakfast, interrupted our conversation. This was convenient, in a way, because I didn't want to get any closer to Bernard as yet.

'Why didn't you wake me?'

'We only have to see Hamish McGuire at noon.' We were going into Hawick to see Max's solicitor.

'What about my interview with the Superintendent?'

'That will be this afternoon. He's seeing Graham and Niall this morning.'

'The sooner they find the culprit the better. Although it will not bring Dad back. It's so unbelievable. One day I see him and the next day I don't. I didn't even have a chance to say goodbye.'

'Think of all the years you did see him,' I said.

'That's just it. I can't think. All I can see is his dead body, lying in the mortuary. He looked grim. Oh God, I don't want this to have happened.' Tears were running down his cheeks. 'My Dad,' he said. 'My Dad.'

His show of grief was infectious and I felt tears welling up. Bernard diplomatically left the room.

9

McGuire & Sons Solicitors, in Hawick, was an estate agent as well as a legal firm. Its front window was decked with advertisements for properties on the market, but inside was a very different picture. We entered a plain, wood-panelled corridor. On one side was a door to the waiting room and, before that a sliding glass window, behind which sat the secretaries. Every time I went in there, they appeared to be sitting chatting but I'm sure they had some very long documents to type. Hamish's secretary took a while to open the window after I had pressed the buzzer. She was a young woman, with painted nails and heavy make-up. She had the longest hair I have ever seen, hanging way down her back and almost to her thighs. She informed us that Mr. McGuire would see us shortly and, in the meantime, we should go into the waiting room. This was a small room and it was possible to think of being slowly deprived of air in there. Nicky grimaced. The only distraction in this all-wood tomb was a few pictures of Hawick in the old days, and business magazines on a small table in the corner. Nicky and I sat down on two of the chairs lining the walls. They were hard and uncomfortable.

Hamish, himself, came down to greet us, and led us up a creaking staircase with a sharp bend halfway up. We reached his spacious office. Suddenly, we were in light and I looked around at bookshelves and cabinets. On the floor were thick white documents tied with pink ribbon, and piled one on top of the other. Hamish had a full head of grey hair, a high forehead and an intensely wrinkled face and he wore round spectacles, which he used like props in a drama. He had a pleasant, deep voice.

'Tragedy. Utterly tragic,' he said, as we all sat down. 'I didn't expect to outlast my young friend, Max. You'll be better off when the police enquiry is over. These things can be traumatic and confusing. Yes, it will be helpful if they can clear up this business. Establish the facts.'

'Everyone in the house is under suspicion, and the police ask so many questions,' I said. 'Nicky got back only last night and he is to be interviewed by DS Drummond today.'

'Drummond. I know the fellow. Good chap. Now, let's attend to the Will. I must warn you, first of all, that, as there is an ongoing murder enquiry, Max's assets are temporarily frozen, pending the outcome. I called you here today to disclose details of Max's Will, which he asked me to alter a couple of years ago. We don't usually read a Will before the funeral of the person concerned, but as you are old family friends, I'm bending the rules.You'll have to forgive the legal jargon.'

Nicky and I didn't look at each other. Instead, we had our gazes fixed on Hamish, who began reading from the thick document in front of him.

'I Maximilian Walter Heriot-Ross residing at Auld Oak Hall, Hawick, in order to settle the succession to my estate after my death, provide as follows …'

It was long and complicated and we were there for an hour and a half. The upshot was that I was to inherit nothing, while Nicky inherited all Max's properties as well as the rest of his stocks and shares, and his capital. What was to happen to Max's business interests, I wasn't quite certain? I was dazed by the legal jargon and surprised that Max hadn't even left me a few stocks and shares. I was, you could say, shocked but philosophical from the start and not deeply envious. I was pleased for Nicky that he was to have such a good start in life while, at the same time, wondering if this wouldn't be a burden, in a way. Nicky wasn't giving away his feelings. He was trying to look mature, sitting there in a straight-backed, antique chair. Yet, his attempt to be reserved crumpled as he blurted out, 'I'd still rather have Dad back.'

'Of course you would. I'm sure your mother would, too.' Hamish got up and shook our hands. 'Once the culprit is found, I, and the other executors, can get on and process the Will. So much depends…' His voice trailed off. Then he seemed to recover his authoritative air, saying, 'I'll keep you informed.'

Going home in the car, Nicky was quiet. Then he said, 'I'm sorry Dad didn't leave you a penny.'

'That's just the way it is. And, that's the last time you'll mention it.' I hoped to put an end to the subject, which was hurtful and something I had to think through for myself. To distract him I commented. 'So, you've become the laird.'

'If it means I can marry Cherie, it is good.'

'You love her, more than anything?'

He nodded.

'I didn't hear a clause saying you can't sell the property.'

'Mum, I have a duty to keep it in the family.'

'Of course, you mustn't disrupt your studies, and you could employ a caretaker while you go to the States, during your holidays. Anything is possible.' I was playing the devil's advocate here with my reference to the US because I hadn't changed my mind about not wanting him to go, especially for any length of time. There were occasions when I was still locked in his teenage phase, when I had learned to suggest the opposite of what I wanted, expecting him to react. In retrospect, perhaps he wasn't as locked in it as I was?

'No. I will marry her and we will live at Auld Oak Hall. I'll get a job. I won't forget you, don't worry. You can live in the cottage, or in one of the houses.'

'Nicky, I have a confession to make. When all this is over, I'll be leaving Auld Oak Hall. I need to start afresh, even at my age. I've been planning it for a while.'

'You were going to leave Dad?' He turned to look at me, in horror.

'If we are to be truthful, yes.'

'Did you dislike him enough to kill him?'

'I did not kill him.'

*   *   *

When we got back, Nicky went in to be interviewed by DS Drummond while I walked across to the cottage to see how Pip was. As I neared the door, that was slightly ajar, I heard shouting. It was Sally... 'I can't bear it. You're just like a dead weight. Never doing anything. Never motivating anything. Refusing to see a doctor. I'm carrying the whole family. Can't you see what an effect this is having on the children? You go on moping. You see Pip is sick, yet you go on in your own world, like a zombie. The most active thing you've done recently is threaten suicide. Lord knows, I don't want you to harm yourself, but I can't monitor your every move. And then there was that ridiculous business of you claiming to have murdered Max. Did you think of us when you did that? Or, were you just thinking of your cousin? A lot of good you would be to us if you landed up in prison. Really, sometimes I could murder you.'

'You are right,' replied Jack. 'I've told you, I'll go to the doctor when we get back.'

'You had better, because I don't know how much more of this I can take.' Her voice was high and shrill. His was a mutter.

I stepped back, not knowing whether to knock or to slip away. I chose to do the latter. I felt I had intruded on their privacy, heard Sally in a mood she would not normally show. I wondered that she could use the word 'murder' so lightly after all that had happened. Again, I let myself think that the usually kind and capable Sally was involved in Max's death. Her claim to have been with the children, at the time of the murder, was very convenient. It was not impossible that she could have left them sleeping, taken the gun and crept up behind us, near the summit of the hill, meaning to shoot Jack but, instead, hitting Max. Yet, did she have time? When I limped in after the murder, she was not amongst the guests hovering by the dining-table. The story was that she had insisted on staying with Pip and Robbie, shielding them from danger. Could there have been a very different tale?

When I got near the house I saw a black BMW in the driveway. It was Monica's. I found her sitting impatiently over a cup of tea, talking to Henri, George and Bernard. Once again, she was intent on demonstrating that, while she looked old, she was disinclined to act frail. As she had proved, she still had the energy for fierce words or sharp criticism. 'I came to see my grandson, and now that wretched little man is interviewing him. What for? Nicky wasn't even here when it happened.'

'Superintendent Drummond has been very reasonable so far,' I said.

'I can't agree with you there,' retorted Henri. 'He twists the facts.'

'What would he want with Nicky?' asked Monica. 'He is so young. Poor Nicky would never lay a finger on my dear Max, God rest his soul.' When no-one replied, she carried on. 'I want to have a word with the funeral directors, and your minister. I will be organizing the funeral. I want it done properly.'

'I'd like to choose the hymns, if that's all right by you. I've already started discussing this with Reverend Wetherspoon.' I did not want to be cast to one side by Monica, yet again. I looked at her, and thought she was remarkably composed that day. I knew there was one question she was eager to ask and that was about the contents of the Will. She would not ask me while guests were present.

'There will be no flowers. Letting them rot on the graveside is such a waste. Or else they are distributed to people who don't even know the family.'

'I rather like flowers …' I faltered.

'We'll have one bouquet, from Walter and me, on the coffin.'

'No. We will invite people to send flowers,' I insisted. 'I am Max's wife and I want a say.'

'Well, if such a trivial thing is important to you, let there be flowers.' She looked at me with small, penetrating eyes and a slight smile of amusement on her lips.

I had started to stand up to her. I couldn't continue to demean myself. If it weren't Max dictating to me, it was his mother. Yet, I could draw comfort from the fact that my plan to leave was settled in my mind. Nicky wouldn't have to worry about looking after me. As I sat, with Monica and Henri talking, I started thinking that someone needed to tell Florence that Max had died. I almost interrupted their conversation to ask Henri if she could contact Florence, but I decided against raising the whole subject in front of Monica.

Henri and Bernard went for a walk, with Brindle. It was the first time I'd noticed them doing anything together since Max's death. George went up to check on Susannah who had again succumbed to a headache, and had retired to her bed. Nicky came through, the interview having finished, and Monica made a great fuss of him. 'Poor Nicky, having to answer all those questions.' She moved into the conservatory and clearly expected us to follow. 'Come and sit near me. Get your son something to drink, Ruth.'

'I can get it myself.' Nicky took a fizzy drink from the fridge.

'Well then, tell me all about it, Ruth,' Monica said in a conspiratorial tone. This was what she had come for.

'You mean the Will?' I was deliberately trying to make her spell out her curiosity.

'What else would I mean?'

I told her what we had learned during the reading of the Will.

She had a shrewd look on her face. 'He has always been very generous to you, especially as you brought nothing into the marriage, but he has kept the property in the family. Max was wise.'

'Yes. It's very sensible.' This was all I could think of to say.

'Grandma, we haven't even buried Dad yet.'

'I realize that, but you must be aware that you have a duty to your poor father to uphold his standards, the family's standards.'

I don't know what Nicky would have replied for DS Drummond entered the room. He told us that a rifle, thought to be the murder weapon, had been found and it was being examined for fingerprints. I knew that any prints found would be compared with our fingerprints, which had been taken by DI Main. He would have the results later on in the afternoon and we were all to gather in the sitting-room at four-thirty.

'Will you want me there, Superintendent?' Monica wanted to keep her eye on the suspects.

'No, Madam. Just those who were here on the evening of the murder.'

'Does that rule me out?' asked Nicky.

'You can come.'

*   *   *

It was nearly four o'clock, half an hour before we were due to meet DS Drummond, when Henri came into the kitchen, where I was having a cup of tea with Bernard and a revitalized Susannah, and told us she was leaving. She was dressed all in black and seemed to have discarded her short-lived image of an overgrown schoolgirl who enjoys playing with children.

'I've been too long away from work,' she said determinedly.

'But the Superintendent has asked all guests to stay,' I objected. 'In any case, what about Bernard? He needs a lift back.'

'He can go with George and Susannah. His cottage is *en route* to Edinburgh,' Henri said.

'I'm sorry but we can't give you a lift. It's a two-seater,' said Susannah.

'Bernard will just have to come with me now. Come on, Bernard.'

'I will not risk being had up for perverting the course of justice. I'll get home somehow.'

'Suit yourself.' Henri went upstairs to pack her bags, while the three of us considered how to stop her going. However, as we could not force her to stay, there seemed to be nothing we could do.

'The only person who has the authority to stop her is Superintendent Drummond and he isn't here,' I said.

'Even he might not have the power. She's not under arrest,' said Susannah.

Henri came down with her bags and went to the back door. 'Goodbye. I can't say it has been a pleasure. Don't see me out.'

We wished her goodbye and soon heard her car start up.

*　*　*

About a quarter of an hour later I went through to the sitting-room to tidy it before the meeting. I began by removing a couple of used mugs and then went back to plump up the cushions. As I did this, I heard a noise coming from Max's study. Something like the noise I had heard before we discovered George in there. My immediate thought was that it was George again, still looking for the loan document. Determined to stop him in his tracks, I made for the study. 'George,' I said as I went through the open doorway, 'You can stop now.' But it wasn't George I discovered in there. It was Henri. As I entered the room and went over to the desk, she stepped out behind me and shut the door, blocking my exit. 'Henri. But you left. We heard your car go down the driveway.'

'I went as far as the walled garden, parked my car and walked back in. Your security isn't very good. If someone enters through the dining-room door and you are in the kitchen with the door shut, you don't hear.' She appeared sly.

At that stage, I could not work out Henri's motive for sneaking back, but I was a little uneasy about being shut in the study with her. I couldn't see why she would want to detain me. 'What are you doing in here? What are you looking for?' I asked.

'I have no keepsake to remind me of Max. You've got it all. I'm looking for the fob watch I gave him all those years ago.'

I saw that she was becoming increasingly angry. It suddenly became clear to me that the *H.H.* engraved on the watch in the dressing-room, stood for Henri Houston. 'Of course you can have the watch. If you'd asked I would have given it to you.' I suppose I must have sounded patronising because I unwittingly provoked her.

'You mean *back* to me,' she snarled. 'I gave it to him, so it should rightfully come back to me.'

'It's in the dressing-room. I'll go and get it.' I started to move towards the door but she was blocking my way.

'Get back, and sit down,' she ordered and, because of the harsh tone in her voice, I did as she said.

She picked up the kitchen knife that I had carelessly left on the desk the night before. 'You, Ruth, have become used to having what I want. Max was yours for all those years and, even then, you weren't always very nice to him. Now that he has gone, you can't have him any more. No-one can have him. You were born to have a beautiful body, a woman's body; whereas, I was born to be fat and clumsy. Well, now we're equal. Neither of us has a man. Max has gone beyond the grave, and he never knew how much I loved him.' Her face was puce, angry and tormented. She had the knife in a tight grip and was pointing the blade in my direction.

'Max thought a great deal of you.' I tried flattery, thinking it might get me out of this situation.

'What do you know about Max's thoughts?' she snapped. 'You didn't give him enough of what he needed. That's why he had to be unfaithful. You couldn't satisfy him.'

'You can't speak to me like this.' I was annoyed but, then, looking at her torn and twisted face, I knew, with absolute clarity, what this was all about.

There was a silence between us. I broke it by saying, 'You killed Max, didn't you, Henri? It was you. You sent a bullet through his back and into his heart. Bernard told me you are a good marksman. And, all because you couldn't bear for any other woman to have him, couldn't bear it any longer.'

She did not confirm this, but the look in her eyes was proof enough. I stared at the knife. She was now holding it aggressively in one hand, with the blade pointing upwards. Fear had been rising within me and now I started to panic. If she had killed once, she could kill again. I began to scream. My cries rang in my ears as though they were from someone else. What happened next did so very quickly. George and Bernard flung open the door and were in the doorway looking in, tensed, ready for action. However, in the time it took them to appear Henri had come across to me and had pulled me to my feet. She grabbed, great handfuls of my hair and pulled my head back. With her other hand she held the knife to my throat, the blade cold and hard against my skin. I tried to strain away from the knife. I could not see it but I could feel it.

'Come any closer and she's gone,' said Henri to the two men in a tight, hard voice.

'You can't do this, Henri,' said Bernard. Neither he nor George moved from the doorway.

'Oh, can't I? Watch me,' said Henri. 'If you do exactly as I say, she won't get hurt.'

The knife dug into my skin and I couldn't speak.

'Move away from the door, back into the sitting-room,' she told the two men. 'Go on,' she ordered them. 'You, Ruth, are going to come with me, out of the house.'

Henri tugged harder on my hair and pulled me backwards, so that I was shielding her; past the silent, serious men in the sitting-room, through the dining-room and out into the garden. Her grip was so tight that I could feel her chest rising and falling. She was breathing heavily as if she, too, were afraid. She smelled of sweat.

Through the open dining-room door I saw Bernard and George joined by two other men. They were DS Drummond and DI Main. Seeing them in the house gave me a little confidence but I didn't understand what they could do and I was unable even to blink in acknowledgement. Henri continued to haul me backwards until I could no longer see them. All of a sudden I felt her remove the knife. Releasing my hair, she gripped one of my arms, a vice-like grip, for she was strong. The blade of the knife now dug into my back. 'Run,' she commanded. She forced me to run with her down the driveway and across the road to the track by the walled garden, where her car was parked. I could not tell if anyone was following us.

When we reached her car, she seemed to decide she had no more use for me. She gave me a brutal shove off the edge of the track, next to where it formed a bridge over the burn, and sent me down the bank. I went staggering down but still on my feet, over grass and stones, until I came to a stop on my knees at the water's edge. I stayed there briefly, my knees aching from my fall on the hard stones. I heard her car start up. She couldn't drive forward because, beyond the walled garden, the track petered out and became a path through some woods. She had no choice but to reverse out onto the road. I stood up, straightening out, and saw that a red Ford had driven up and was blocking her exit. In the car was DI Main. I saw Henri jump out of her car and run towards the walled garden. DI Main ran after her, followed by DS Drummond. Then four hands were reaching out to pull me up the bank. 'Are you all right?' Bernard and George asked in unison. They would have comforted me but, although I was shocked and aching from my fall, I had one aim in mind and that was to see Henri caught. I led them on, towards the walled garden.

When we got there, DI Main was in the greenhouse, some paces away from Henri, and DS Drummond was outside, covering the entrance. We moved towards the Superintendent and he motioned to us to stay back. We heard the sound of the voices in the greenhouse but we could not make out what they were saying. DI Main had his hands out, presumably in an attempt to quieten her, and he was edging towards her. She still had the knife and she was stabbing the air, threateningly. She was moving backwards, step by step.

'There's a back exit,' I whispered to DS Drummond. He merely put a finger over his mouth, advising me to be silent. I recalled afterward that birds were singing innocently.

The gap between DI Main and Henri was growing smaller. She seemed to be saying something that meant a lot to her, and to have lost her concentration. The knife now hung loosely by her side. The Inspector seized his chance. He leapt across the space between them, grabbing her wrist and shaking the weapon out of her hand. He pulled her arms roughly behind her back and handcuffed her. As they came to the door, DS Drummond stepped out to meet them. 'Henrietta Houston, I'm arresting you for the murder of Maximilian Heriot-Ross. Anything you say may be used in evidence...'

Henri stared into the lily pond, down into the murky water. 'I loved him more than anyone ever did,' she said, as if to herself. Then she lifted her head, tossing it in the air. 'Now, no-one else will have him ever again. He is mine. I've made sure of that.'

* * *

Bernard, George and I watched as the two policemen took Henri away in their car. I felt cold towards her, and what she'd put me through. Yet, the days of tense suspicion were over. I was aching from my tumble down the bank of the burn, and I could still feel the steely touch of the knife at my throat and in my back. Bernard took my hand as we walked to the house to tell the others what had happened, and that there would be no meeting, because Henri had been arrested. If they felt surprise, they did not show it. There was an atmosphere of immense weariness and sadness.

'We'll go then, Ruth,' said Sally. 'Pip is a lot better and we should get her home.'

'You are welcome to stay another night, and leave in the morning.'

'I have to get back to work as soon as possible. I've been away too long already.' It took them about half an hour to pack and load up the car and they drove off, apologizing for not being able to attend the funeral. 'I'm so sorry about Max,' said Sally as they were about to leave. 'You have been very strong, but now you can give in to your grief.'

Susannah and George loaded up their Morgan. 'Goodbye darling. Thank you so much for putting up with us.' Susannah went through the formalities, as if it had been just an ordinary stay. George's farewells were a little more appropriate. 'Well be at the funeral. Let us know when it's going to be. You'll have more peace without us. Look after yourself, dear girl.'

I did not feel strong. I had been weakened by the incident with Henri. While it was happening, adrenalin had been pumping through me. However, after it was over and the Superintendent had arrested her, I was shaken.

Bernard seemed to understand. We re-parked Henri's car, so that he was ready to drive it to his home. However, he chose to stay another night. Nicky had gone to see Cherie. Bernard cooked us a mushroom omelette and we sat and ate it at the kitchen table. The 'phone kept ringing, as it had done over the past few days, but now I ignored the grief-stricken, sympathetic or simply polite calls.

'I wish that I could leave with you, tomorrow,' I said to Bernard.

'Why don't you? Come to the cottage and nobody will find out where you are.'

'I can't. There's the inquest and then we've got the funeral to organize. After that, I'll go to Edinburgh.'

'Do you want to prevent your mother-in-law from taking over the organization of the funeral?'

'I am determined to stay and have my say.'

I must have left my hands just where he could reach them, because he leaned over and clasped one of them in his own. I longed to nestle into his body. I put my other hand on top of his. We sat like this for some time, and then he came over to me and drew me up out of my chair. We kissed. It wasn't the same as the first kiss. It was more passionate. He pushed the chair away with a foot and held me tight, saying nothing. Then, after a moment, he released me.

'It's a surprise that we can trust each other, after all the suspicion there has been in this house,' I said.

'This is more than trust.'

'Don't forget I'm a widow in mourning.'

'You'll be running out of excuses, soon. Or, perhaps you'll find that you don't need them?'

'Bernard, I owe it to myself to follow my own path.'

'As long as it leads to my front door.'

'You seem so sure …'

'Shush, woman.' His hands began to move over my body. They reached parts that had been untouched for so long. I re-awakened to sex. We went upstairs to his bedroom and made love on the single bed. Afterwards, we lay, side by side, and I put my head on his naked chest. At last, I felt that I could sleep. I would have lain by his side all night but for Nicky possibly coming home. For Nicky to find me in another man's arms so soon after his father's death would have completely destroyed my credibility, in his eyes. Not to mention the press. They would be jubilant, but they'd never know. This left me again wondering where to sleep. Henri had vacated my room for a prison cell but did I really want to sleep where a killer had lain? I would have to clean the room thoroughly and disinfect it before I could return to it, even for a short length of time. Max's room would, no doubt, bring me endless dreams. Nicky's room would be taken, if he returned that night. George and Susannah's beds had to be re-made and I didn't relish the scent of Susannah's potpourri. Perhaps, the truth was that I'd outgrown Auld Oak Hall? So, I went reluctantly back to the sofa. Yet, I slept better than I had done for months, with only a vague recollection of Nicky coming home.

In the morning Bernard prepared to leave. We had a secret knowledge of one another that was warm and comforting. Bernard said he would keep away during preparations for the funeral, but that he would come and see me in Edinburgh. We went outside to take his bags to the car.

'Will you pick up Henri's table from Trees Unlimited?' I asked.

'Yes. She might be able to use it a good long time from now.'

'Henri certainly put on a good act of suspecting all of us when, all along, she was the guilty party,' I said.

'She is pathetic in a way, but I can't condone what she has done.'

'I wonder if she'll try to get out on bail.'

'I doubt they'll grant it, despite her father's influence.'

'Strangely, I think she loved her victim more than anyone ever has.'

'It was a desperate act. Nobody should go that far.'

Before he got into the car, he kissed me and held me tight. 'I'll 'phone,' he said.

When he had gone, the silence in the kitchen was overwhelming. So many voices filled with so many different emotions had occupied this space. I sat down and Brindle leapt onto my lap. Nicky had gone out early so I was finally alone. I talked to Brindle quietly and stroked her. Todd came and fawned around my legs. I ran my free hand over his back. Being married to Max, the way the marriage was, made me no stranger to loneliness yet I wasn't lonely then. I was just quietly being, with my animals. All the same, there were echoes ringing in my ears. What people had said. How they had said it. I thought of DS Drummond's search for facts; Henri's cold commands when she held me at knife-point;

Bernard's praise of me; Max's denials when I showed him the letter; Max's silence when he was shot. He did not cry out. He just crumpled and fell. Henri murdered my husband. I stared at the kitchen dresser, seeing nothing of it contents. I began to cry. This so disturbed Brindle that she put her paws on my chest and began to lick my face. Todd left the room. Still, I cried, with great heaving sobs, seemingly endless tears.

*   *   *

I was standing, staring into the past, face blotchy, when Nicky, Cherie and Zoe came in. Far from looking startled by my appearance, it seemed to be what they expected. They apologized for coming in at a time like that. I shrugged, and made them some tea.

'Are you able to talk about our future, Mum?' Nicky asked.

I nodded.

Zoe started up, 'We've had a long, hard talk with these two young people, and we must let you in on this.'
'I will tell her,' said Nicky with authority.

'Yes.You explain,' said Zoe.

Cherie was quiet but not retiring. She looked blooming, happy, hopeful whereas Nicky looked tense and Zoe, strained.

'You know that Cherie and I love each other and want to be together. You also know that Hank and Zoe are planning to go back to the States. Now, the two plans don't seem to match up because Cherie and I want to be married, and I will inherit Dad's property. So, Cherie, as my wife, will want to come and live here, at Auld Oak Hall.'

'I have no problem with that,' I said. 'Although you are both very young for such responsibility.'

'We may be young, but we are certain this is what we want to do. We are positive,' said Cherie.

'What do you think, Zoe?' I asked.

'If you want the truth, it's not, shall I say, convenient for Hank and me. We don't want to be across the ocean from our only daughter. On the other hand, Hank says he might try and delay our departure, for a limited period, because we realize how serious Nicky and Cherie are. We'll certainly be here for the wedding.'

'I'm not pregnant, if that's what you think,' cut in Cherie, looking at me.

I did not respond immediately. It would be a wedding coming so close after a funeral.

'Aren't you going to say something?' asked Nicky.

'Congratulations.' It was as if the news had finally come to rest. I got up and kissed them both, searching Zoe's face for her reaction. Then I realized she was smiling.

*   *   *

For the journalists of this world who subject people to trial by media; and for those, including myself, who were determined to implicate me in this crime, I want to get a few facts straight. Over the following weeks - during the inquest, the funeral and Henri's trial – I learned again how to confront reality; I latched onto the facts as they were, in as far as the law and religion assert and reveal facts. If I didn't know them already, I was told of Henri's powerful motives for killing Max. It was a fatal mix of love and jealousy. She had experienced unrequited love for so long. What led her jealousy to become lethal that day was the way Max responded to Natasha, the young blonde student, against whom Henri could not compete.

On the night in question… that's how the court referred to the evening of my birthday. On the night in question, she became more jealous and determined than ever. She was in a mood that drove her to try to control and command Max's affections. Snubbed by Max, she snapped. She went out on the search for Jack along the lower slopes of the hill with Bernard, but she managed to lose Bernard, also evading Susannah and George. She then doubled back and picked up the rifle, loaded it and went out again, up the hill, in search, not of Jack but of Max. The murder was opportunistic, if not premeditated. There was no-one in the house to see her take the rifle. The others were on the hill and Sally was protecting her children in the cottage nearby.

For a big woman, Henri could move swiftly. That's what the prosecution lawyer said. I think that she was so feverishly motivated that she could have done anything. She raced up the hill, propelled by the need to find Max and bring an end to his life and loves, using a different route from the one we had taken. She crept up, unseen by Max, Jack and me. Being a seasoned marksman, she knew how to position herself to fire the gun. She aimed at Max's retreating back, coincidentally, at the same time as I aimed the pistol, ignorant of how to use it. Henri fired the fatal shot. Her aim was perfect. Max died instantly. She then hurried down the hill using a small wood as cover and burying the rifle under leaves and twigs. Then, she lost no time in getting back to the house. She was there in the dining-room when the men brought in Max's lifeless body. Henri then put on a great display of wailing and grief which, ironically, was genuine. Lunging at me the way she did - as if she thought me guilty - helped convince me that I had shot Max.

Not so.

10

It is Bernard, more than anyone else, who has helped me, finally, to forgive Max. Bernard and I are living together now. His advice has been non-religious whereas Adeline has kept sending me little texts from the Bible that she thinks will help and support me in my widowhood. These texts have comforted me a little and perhaps, at some later date, you'll find me entering the portals of a church, as Adeline did in her old age. There is one in particular that I carry with me in my purse, printed on a little card. It goes like this: 'Peace I leave with you. My peace I give you. I do not give to you as the world gives. Do not let your hearts be troubled and do not be afraid.' This passage comes from John, chapter 14. Yet, this does not stop me being afraid. I fear being murdered as my husband was. This is not rational, but is fear always rational? I have come to know how close death is and how treacherous people can be. One moment Max was alive and then, in less than a minute, Henri had shot him. The space between life and death closed and he lay lifeless on the ground. Henri could not undo what she had done. I fear that there are other murderers around; in society, in the community and, given the motive, they could take control of my being. Someone, other than myself, could be the arbiter of whether I live or die.

Why does God allow people to commit murder? In my opinion, people don't have to be mentally ill to become murderers, unless the very act of killing is a sign of illness. Henri's emotions were twisted by jealousy but hers was 'a moment of madness' and not a symptom of a certifiable condition. Mentally ill people are just as afraid of themselves as other people fear them. Look at Jack. He is a trained soldier and was suffering from a mental illness and yet, contrary to his claim, he did not kill Max. His intention had been to kill himself.

The chances of going out in the street in the Scottish Borders and being gunned down are remote, Bernard tells me. And I see that in places like Iraq, in Israel or Palestine, death is much closer. But I could surprise a burglar or bump into a gang in the dark. I lock all the doors, stay in at night, yet still there is that tiny element of fear. I know first-hand that people, even 'normal' people who I invite for a weekend in the country, can be killers. By one change of attitude or mood, a familiar kitchen knife used to chop vegetables could become a weapon, used to maim or kill. Yet, to live with fear, and to face it, is what I strive for. If life experience has prompted fear, it is a greater thing just to live. One of the symptoms of my fear of being murdered is that I read countless crime novels, watch endless detective dramas on TV.

When I am sitting on the bench in the sun in Bernard's garden I begin to worry that I have an obsession. Do crime novels and TV dramas relieve the fear, or feed the fear? It depends on how awful is the crime. Some of the fictional characters have mutilated bodies; some have been decapitated, some tortured. So the crime depicted is serious and sadistic. Here again we hit my weak spot – my sense of reality. These are just stories; just as *the news media bombards us with a holocaust of stories, filtered through the reporters' personalities and need to sell their wares. The world seems a more menacing place because of professional imagination. In the Scottish Borders, the police don't find cold, treacherous death at every turn. In reality, murder is very rare here; low-level crime being dominant. Perhaps I am taking television crime too much to heart? Perhaps what gives me my fix is the combination of a dead body and a puzzle? Is it true that the law usually triumphs? I need to know what is real. The fact is that Florence did not die in a car accident as Max had told me. She was alive then, and probably is still alive. Max presented me with a story and I believed it to be true. Why would I imagine my then husband-to-be was lying about his former fiancée? Why would I think my husband would nurse an untruth until so late in our marriage? Discovering Florence's letter meant that I lost confidence in my ability to differentiate between the real and the unreal.*

Max not only deceived me, he humiliated me and nagged, and my response was to become passive, taking it all, never reacting until I drove the anger deep into my being. I never want to be possessed by such latent, festering emotions again. That's why I trust Bernard when he encourages me to remember what Max did. He cautions me about pardoning Max for his actions and attitudes. He never forbids. He always suggests. What he wants me to do is isolate and highlight the hurt. I am meant to remember Grace, to remember Florence and all the demeaning, domineering behaviour. However, these memories and thoughts must not be allowed to poison my soul. It's only after I've acknowledged these memories and thoughts that I allow myself to think of Max as a human being. What made him vulnerable were the expectations delivered to him as a birthright. Even at birth, a naked dependent baby, he was somebody. The ring with the family crest engraved on it was ready for his finger. He was, automatically, a son in a superior line that had titles safely and comfortably settled in its ancestry and on its peripheries. Even in the name, Maximilian, the expectations could be found. It was not for want of trying on Monica's part that the name Maximilian gave way to Max. In her view, this degeneration was a trial to be borne.

Brought up by Monica and nannies, Max had to see himself and Lawrence as special. Perhaps this was why he married a penniless Rhodesian, because my status was no threat to this view of himself? Max had to be somebody. He had to own property, be a successful lawyer, to be in command. Like so many people, he had a mask and when he dropped it I saw emotions that no-one else viewed. He was confused and isolated, even angry. This was when 'perfection' eluded him, when others challenged his position. I saw him cry only a few times during our twenty-four years together, and that was mainly out of frustration, when discipline alone could not bring the world to order. One of those times was before our marriage. He cried over Lawrence. He was, after all, a twin and this was the really special thing about Max. He was used to the intimacy of having a brother only minutes older than himself, and when Lawrence went to Paris, cutting off most communication, Max had to do without it. He cried from the pain of the loss and, ashamed, he dried his tears and seldom spoke of Lawrence after that. He was human.

Was he happy when he died? No. I don't think so. He did get a great deal of pleasure out of his son, but Nicky was not taking the path that Max had mapped out for him. He was studying philosophy, when Max would have preferred him to study law and join the family business. It became obvious to us after the reading of the Will, that he wanted Nicky to inherit the property. It was always obvious that Max wanted his son to be like him. I think he was convinced that Nicky would eventually come around to his way of doing things. Given time and responsibility. He did love Nicky. And yet it was the same as with me – he loved him as an extension of himself. It seemed that Max could not love in any other way. At his centre he was always master, even when it came to heartfelt feelings.

He wasn't happy during my birthday celebrations because of our talk about the letter, and because of what he saw as the preponderance of Zimbabweans. He looked for comfort to this new, young, charming creature, Natasha. His susceptibility to women had led him into trouble before, but now this fleeting infatuation was lethal. It embarrassed me. It incensed Henri. Natasha couldn't be blamed for the effect she had on the party. She was just young and beautiful. Still is.

This is one of the occasions when my resolve to find the human being in Max breaks down. What I really think is that Max made a fool of himself, salivating over a girl young enough to be his daughter. His admiration of her was so transparent. He was so unfaithful in intent. Grace, Florence, Natasha. Why? Are all men disloyal? Was I not enough? I'm not going down the road of self-recrimination. I have told Bernard that if ever he is unfaithful to me, that would be the end of the relationship. No discussions. No explanations. If it happened, and I have faith that it won't, I will move out and never see him again. The fact is that I do not condone Max's actions, whatever his excuses.

Stop, Ruth I admonish myself. If I am to forgive Max I have to find compassion for him, but I am struggling. The only way in which I can try to empathize with Max is to criticize myself and that is harmful. I would be dishonest, or mad, if I claimed that these things don't matter. It was not just the shock of the truth of his affair with Grace that counted. It was not just the blow of finding them in bed together, with my young son in the next room. It was the humiliation and the rejection, the deception, and the suspicion that all my friends knew about the affair. I was made to look a fool and my response was to try and change myself to suit a husband who had chosen another, rather than me. I tried to become less immersed in motherhood and adopted what I now see as pathetic, self-denying ways; I tried to please Max. I even imagined that buying some sexy nightgowns or changing the way I did my hair would help, but by that time we were too far gone along a cold and stony road. The time to appeal to the sexual attraction we had once felt was long gone and I found myself on my own, making gestures of appeasement, while Max turned and walked the other way. Guilt did not seem to bother him. If we had made the decision to separate then, who knows whether it would have been better for Nicky? I suspect it might have, depending on how we worked out custody. There is no doubt that things would have been less aggravating and there is a chance that Max would still be alive today. There would have been no birthday party for me at Auld Oak Hall.

I not only have to forgive myself and Max, I have to forgive Grace and Florence. Natasha was just a passing flirtation, whatever Henry thought. I ask myself why there are always women, waiting in the wings, to tempt, and to destroy the bond of the marriage vows. Yet, if I can't forgive them I can't forgive myself, and I can't be free of Max and the past. If I had never done anything wrong in my life, I could keep levelling accusations and these could destroy me. Apart from that, my bitterness could spoil the relationship I have with Bernard.

I am sitting on the bench in his garden. My eyes are shut. Using a trick that Adeline taught me, I have called up images in my mind of Max, Grace, Florence, Henri, one at a time. I hold each vision there before me, calmly, and mentally surround each face with the outline of a balloon Then, I imagine a pair of golden scissors and I cut slowly beneath each image, as if cutting the string on the balloon. One by one, they float and fade into the distance. I open my eyes and see that they have floated into the air, into the clouds. They have gone. They are nothing. I have released them. Bernard is standing before me. He is a little puzzled that I am gazing into the sky so calmly. I don't enlighten him. I take what he is offering me. It's an envelope containing air tickets for a holiday in Zimbabwe. We are going to stay with Peter and his family in Bulawayo.